TURN KILLER

a novel by
Brian Lecomber

a Simon and Schuster
novel of suspense

**SIMON AND SCHUSTER
NEW YORK**

Designed by Elizabeth Woll
Manufactured in the United States of America

1 2 3 4 5 6 7 8 9 10

Library of Congress Cataloging in Publication Data

Lecomber, Brian.
    Turn killer.

    I. Title.
PZ4.L4538Tu3   [PR6062.E34]   823'.9'14   74-34338
ISBN 0-671-21994-4

ACKNOWLEDGMENTS

Thanks are due to Mr. Maurice Williams, the London stamp expert, who painstakingly invented a near-authentic set of valuable stamps for me, and also to Mrs. Neville Browning, who allowed me to use her late husband's name. Thanks are due also to Tony Cheshire, who always held it steady when I was out on the wing, and to Wing Commander Charles James Chabot, who kept telling me I'd never fall off.

TO JACKIE
who never stopped believing

BOOK ONE

CHAPTER 1

The old Gypsy Major coughed, snarled asthmatically for a second, then picked up its even bellow as gravity resumed pushing fuel in the direction of the carburetor. Earth and sky rotated back to their proper positions as I trod energetically on the rudder to keep the nose up. Slow rolls are not a Tiger Moth's favorite maneuver.

I pushed the nose down until we had 90 knots, then hauled the stick back and looked past the wing tip to hold her vertical. At 50 knots I poured on full power and kicked full right rudder. We pinwheeled in the early-morning sky, the new sun dappling shadows of struts across my face as the nose scythed down through the horizon. As we hung vertically downwards off the stall turn, the Tiger's nose pointed straight at the wreckage of Bill's Stampe. I could see white upturned faces around the pathetic, rumpled remains. As the noise of our airspeed rose from a sigh to a rushing roar, I twisted the scene in the frame of the Tiger's center section by doing a half aileron roll, then pulled back for a final loop.

I wasn't going to be popular with those white faces down there. They were probably in the middle of picking bits of Bill out of bits of aircraft when I arrived, and this wouldn't make them receptive to a display of low-level aerobatics. Well, the hell with them. For once, I didn't give a damn what the spectators thought. The horizon appeared under the top wing and I heaved the Tiger round a roll-off-the-top, changed my mind, continued the roll until I was upside down again, then pulled back hard on the stick to finish the loop. As we swung past the vertical, I relaxed the back pressure so that we passed over the disaster on the ground at about 100 feet.

More upturned white faces, and a vision of a tarpaulin over the cockpit of the crashed Stampe. So they hadn't got the body out yet.

Or maybe they had, and the tarp was just to cover the blood and guts in the remains of the cockpit. Show the people the nice broken spars and jolly crumpled fabric and the engine stuck a few feet into the ground—but be sure to cover up the cockpit, or they might get a glimpse of what they really came to see.

Picture of Holland being bloody morbid.

Still, I felt morbid. The people on the ground would never understand, but I was saying good-bye to Bill. It was a lovely summer morning, just like the ones when Bill and I had crawled out of our tents, disentangled ourselves from the muzzy shroud of sleep, and hauled our early-morning aches into a couple of biplanes for a prebreakfast workout over some resort town to attract the holidaymakers to the show. Eight A.M. is too early for any flier not equipped with feathers, but there's nothing like the wagging of landladies' tongues over the breakfast table, as they prattle about the two aeroplanes that were flying ever so low just off the breakwater this morning, for getting people thinking *flying circus* before they'd got round to planning their day. Bill and I used to do it because we didn't drink much and therefore didn't suffer too badly from hangovers: and anyway, we both liked the early mornings.

So good-bye, Bill. Up here, twisting and tumbling in the sky, I can talk to you and you'll understand and there's nobody else around to see me crying like a baby.

I slid along the side of the Isle of Wight hills at a few hundred feet and headed for the grass field that is Sandown Aerodrome. Now that the aerobatic adrenaline pump had wound down, I felt leadenly weary and very alone. I'd been flying since first light to get down from Blackpool, after a sleepless night following the phone call that told us Bill had crashed. I hadn't washed or shaved or eaten, and a dull tension headache, aggravated by the tightness of my goggle strap and the cold roaring wind of flight, throbbed away behind my gritty eyeballs. From my own choice I was the first of the gang to arrive at the Isle of Wight, and now I was going to have to be civil to the busybodies who were going to descend on me when I landed. Damn them all.

I turned finals and went almost subconsciously over the prelanding catechism of slats—fuel—harness—hatches.

Why couldn't it have been me in the Stampe? I wouldn't have crashed, because I'm Ken Holland and I've got nine lives. Everybody says so. And even if I had crashed I'd have walked away from it, because at the last count I've still got at least one life left. And anyway, I don't care one way or the other.

I touched down in a silky three-pointer of the kind you only ever pull off when you're not trying, then spoiled the effect by opening the throttle and rolling cowboy fashion tail-up into the parking area beside the green-painted hangar.

I parked untidily beside a crash wagon, undid my harness, and stowed away maps and things while the engine performed its customary imitation of a dying tractor and supposedly "cooled down evenly," like the book says, then switched off and climbed stiffly out of the cockpit.

After letting the post-Tiger buzz in my ears drop to a civilized decibel rating and making the usual vain attempts to unravel the post-Tiger kinks in my spine, I moved towards the clubhouse in a brisk lurch. My left thigh was hurting fiercely, the way it always does when I'm tired.

The controller-cum-manager said he guessed I was a friend of the man who'd hit the hill last night—which wasn't exactly a masterpiece of deduction, since my Tiger had THE OLD TIME FLYING CIRCUS painted in big letters along the side.

I grunted at his perspicacity, and grunted again with slightly better grace when he said not to worry about the landing fee and refueling because he'd look after it, since he imagined I'd be a bit tied up as soon as the coppers and that arrived.

The only other occupants of the clubhouse were two lads and their lasses who appeared by their number of maps to be planning a trip to the Antipodes or at least to Portsmouth in the Cessna 172 that was keeping my Tiger company outside. They had the air of a group who had stopped talking about the accident two seconds before I walked in and were now searching for some harmless alternative.

Scarface spreads happiness wherever he goes. Crawling in out of a colorful but obviously hard-used Tiger Moth, limping like Long John Silver and wearing scruffy boots, jeans, and a leather flying jacket, I must have made a bit of a dent in the executive-aviator image they were putting across to the feminine attraction. Peeling off my helmet revealed the total length and grubby glory of the livid scar down the side of my face. Dumping my flying jacket on the floor, followed by the tattered roll-neck sweater that was beginning to give me prickly heat round the neck, left me standing in a once-white tee shirt which hung smartly round my kinked-up right collarbone and also exposed the whitened skin of an eight-inch line of stitch marks along my right forearm.

Throw in the facial puffiness of lack of sleep, the empty eyes of someone deeply hurt, and the tear and goggle marks competing to make drawings in the dirt on my face and you had a sight calculated to perk up anybody's Sunday morning. I'm a bit on the short side and was never any oil painting before flying-circus stunts started to leave their trademarks on me. But when I fly and work on aeroplanes all through the day, get the news that my best friend is dead in the middle of the night, and charge off on a 300-mile flight to get there as soon as it's light enough to aviate without nav lights, I am liable to arrive at the end of it looking like a multiple road accident.

Holland spreads happiness *whenever* he goes.

I was wondering whether it was worth settling intò a chair for a catnap before the coppers and that arrived, when a police Austin drew up outside with its blue light flashing.

It disgorged an inspector, a constable and a brace of men in plain clothes, all of whom marched into the clubhouse wearing their best This-is-your-nemesis expressions. I got the distinct impression that I was meeting part of the audience from the scene of the crash—a part, moreover, that had used blue light and siren pretty industriously in order to get their fangs into me with the least possible delay.

"Are you Kenneth Holland?" asked the inspector.

I nodded wearily.

"Were you flying that aircraft over the accident a few minutes ago?"

I nodded again. They had me bang to rights if they wanted to do a bit of book-throwing, and at that moment I just didn't care a damn. So they did me for coming within 500 feet of a person, vehicle, or building. So they did me for reckless flying. So the Department of Trade and Industry took my licenses away. So I got sick of living and went for a walk under a bus. So what?

There was a loaded pause while the inspector contemplated having me dragged out and shot; then he contented himself with a welding-torch glare and said, "Come with me."

Maybe he'd seen people in shock before. Or maybe he simply didn't know enough aviation law to know just what to threaten me with.

I scraped up my flying jacket; kicked sweater, gloves, and helmet into an orderly heap; and limped out to the police car. One of the plain-clothesmen held open a rear door, and I got in. The door-holder followed, and the other plainclothesman got in the other side, which left me sand-wiched in the middle with my feet on the transmission tunnel and my hip hurting like hell because of the cramped position. The pincer technique.

The inspector got into the front passenger seat, the constable slid behind the wheel, and we whirled off down the bumpy track to the airfield gate. My hip jarred at every pothole.

The breeze drifting in through the open windows as we turned out into the road had a salt tang to it, the way seaside air always has until the heat of the day sets in. It reminded me of all the other holiday towns filled with happy holiday people. It reminded me of Bill, and for a bitter moment it reminded me of Janie. I closed my eyes over my headache and thought it might be nice to be an African native or something. Anything.

CHAPTER 2

The crash looked every bit as nasty on the ground as it had from the air. It was still only 8:45A.M. when the car pulled through the farm gateway and dragged up the steeply sloping field to the wreckage—but already the rubberneckers were out in force. Realizing they couldn't stop up all the holes in the hedge, the cops were contenting themselves with standing around the pieces looking officious. This is a well-proved formula for keeping the public at barge-pole distance from a disaster.

The car pulled up close to the shattered fuselage, and Tweedles Dum and Dee poured themselves out of the back seat. I climbed stiffly out after them and leaned against the car.

The Stampe had gone in at high speed and a fairly shallow angle. The first ten feet of the fuselage, including both cockpits, was telescoped into a ghastly buckled mass about four feet long. The Stampe has an all-wood airframe, and the fuselage had snapped clean in two just aft of the rear cockpit on impact. The back end, including the tail assembly, had jack-knifed over the rest of the fuselage and crumpled itself up where the center section of the top wing used to be. The top wings themselves had shot forward and broken up, while the bottom wings had practically disintegrated. The biggest remaining piece of the right lower was a four-foot length of trailing edge which pointed accusingly up and back from the remains of the forward fuselage. The gay red and yellow of the crumpled fabric made a macabre shroud: a corpse in Pierrot's costume.

The scene smelled of oil and petrol and newly turned graveyard earth.

I pushed myself off the car and stumped slowly round to where the nose should have been.

I couldn't see the motor at all, but previous experience told me that the prop boss would be about three feet underground. The front of the rear cockpit was somewhere round the back of the engine, and the remains of the cockpit were liberally smeared with brown, drying blood.

Bill's blood.

At least they'd had the decency to move the body. The tarpaulin I'd seen from the air was spread out on the ground now, covering a sinister-looking shape that shouldn't have reminded anyone of a man at all. A sort of humped-up bundle that was very final. The crash must literally have broken every bone in his body.

I don't know how long I stood there, staring at the crash and the tarpaulin. This was what I'd flown down from Blackpool to see, and now I was here I was surprised to find I hardly felt a thing. Just drained and very alone. Eventually the inspector's voice penetrated through.

". . . very sorry," he was saying, "but I'll have to ask you to identify the body. Just a formality, but it will have to be done sometime. We can wait until it—he's—been, er, cleaned up, if you like . . .?"

"If he's dead, he's dead," I snarled. "I don't want to see him stuffed like a bloody hunting trophy."

The inspector's face went rigid. I was sorry I'd said that, but it didn't seem important enough to dredge up words of apology.

I lurched over to the tarpaulin and pulled it back.

Bill was practically unrecognizable. His head had slammed into the instrument panel, which had been going in the same direction but about 50 knots slower. His neck was broken and the crown of his skull was horribly smashed, the shattered bone all mangled up with the cloth flying helmet. His limbs were at odd angles, and the whole body was covered in blood. It soaked his trousers and matted the fur collar of his flying jacket. Both arms and legs were obviously broken, and his chest was probably stoved in under the leather jacket. There was vomit down his front, and his face was a black and bloody mass under the remains of his goggles.

I dropped the tarp, feeling sick. I'd seen dead men before, but never anything so brutally battered as this. Distantly, I was aware of the nearest rubbernecks backing away with chalk-white faces. This wasn't the pretty crash they'd come to see: this was the unexpurgated result of the ground stepping out in front of you at over 100 knots. It was anything but pretty.

I stood there for a while watching myself come out from under the shock, then spoke without turning round. My voice sounded tired and old.

"That's the man who was known to me as William Charlton. He lived at Twenty-three Ickenham Gardens, Slough, and the only relative I know of is his wife, who left him a year ago. He was flying down here last night from Redhill for a show we're putting on this week. Is there anything else you need?"

The inspector coughed. He still regarded me as one of the less desirable elements of society, but the Mark One Tactful Cough seemed to be deeply ingrained.

"We've had a doctor to look at the—at Mr. Charlton," he said. "But with the body in that state he couldn't tell very much. There'll be a postmortem examination later on, of course."

Oh, yes, of course. We must have a postmortem. He was only doing about two miles a minute when he slammed into the side of the hill and

17

broke every bone in his body. We'd better have a postmortem to make sure he didn't die of bloody hiccups.

The inspector hurried on. "The thing is that we'd like to try and get some idea of the cause of the accident as soon as possible. I expect the formal crash investigation will take some time. That's why we brought you up here. You may have noticed traces of vomit on Mr. Charlton's jacket. The obvious conclusion is that he was taken ill in the air. But since you're a pilot, and knew Mr. Charlton as well, I'd appreciate it if you might just have a look round."

"Any eyewitnesses?" I asked.

You never know your luck: two 707 pilots and a Crash Investigator *might* just have been watching. Or if a few hundred laymen had seen it, you might even get them to agree about the number of wings the aircraft had. All you'd learn beyond that would be that bits fell off it, it blew up in the air, and it fell down out of control. Nonflying witnesses to an air crash always feel cheated if the kite doesn't do one or all of these things.

"We've got one. He's the farmer, who said he saw the plane dive into the ground. He said the engine was still running and there didn't seem to be any attempt to pull out of the dive. It happened just before dark last night. No one else saw it—or no one that we've found, anyway."

I stared over at the wreckage again.

"That sounds about right," I said. "It looks as though he hit the ground at an angle of about twenty degrees, going pretty fast. If he'd spun in or anything, the back end would have gone in a different direction."

I'd had enough of this wreck, but the man had asked nicely, so I kicked through the remains and leaned into what was once the rear cockpit.

The death smell hit me.

If you fly aeroplanes a lot, particularly old fabric ones, you get sensitive to the smell of them. Not only to the usual aircraft-dope, oil, and glue smell, but actually to the *mood* of the machine. You can smell fear, for instance. I'm an authority on the smell of fear. Sometimes I've smelled my own fear in an aeroplane twenty-four hours after the event.

Death is a different smell altogether. I'd only smelled it in an aeroplane a couple of times before; but it's not something you forget. It's a mixture of torn earth and freshly broken wood, ripped fabric, oil, petrol—and blood.

Especially blood.

And there was no lack of blood in the telescoped wreckage of that cockpit. The brown stains on the outside were only a small part of it. Inside the splintered remains, it was everywhere. If anyone ever tells you that a corpse doesn't bleed, you can say from me that he doesn't know what he's talking about. It'll bleed, all right, if there's enough holes in it.

There was blood all over the shattered instrument panel, down the sides and on the floor. All going that nasty brown as it dried. The seat was the only thing more or less free of blood, and on it lay the shoulder-harness straps. They were clean.

I'd been right about the speed: the ASI needle was mashed firmly into the 110-knot figure on the dial. I looked at the throttle, but the impact coming back through the linkage had whipped the lever fully open, then buckled the rod. The trim lever was just forward of halfway in its gate, and the magneto switches were still on. Futilely and automatically, I snapped them to Off and pulled my head out of the cockpit. My headache was running like a single-cylinder compressor, and I felt the taste of bile in my throat.

I lurched back to the police car, where the inspector was looking expectant.

"I think you're right about Bill being ill. The magneto switches were still on, and the trim was set for level flight under power. If he'd had engine trouble and was trying to make a forced landing, the switches would have been off and the trim farther back for the glide. And he'd have been going a lot slower." I thought of something else. "Did your men undo his harness getting the body out, or was it already undone?"

"It was already undone."

"That proves it, then. He'd never normally undo it in flight. He must have wanted to double up with pain or something before he passed out."

The inspector nodded: he'd worked that much out for himself, I expect. "We'll have to wait for the postmortem to see what made him ill," he said. "I take it he didn't suffer from anything you knew of?"

I shook my head. The powers that be aren't keen on handing out commercial licenses and instructor's ratings to epileptics. I'd never known Bill to have more than a cold.

I had a sudden terrible vision of him writhing in agony in the cockpit of the Stampe. Clutching his stomach and frantically unclipping his harness so his long body could bend round the pain. It must have happened quite near here, and he'd probably had Sandown in sight when the final screaming wave hit him and he passed out.

I saw him clawing at the last shred of consciousness, desperately trying to hold out long enough to get down. And then, nothing. The attack must have been very quick.

Dully, and without much interest, I wondered what the pathologist's knife would find.

CHAPTER 3

Lunchtime found me in the bar of the clubhouse at Sandown, drinking lunch alone. I don't normally drink much, especially by myself, but right now there wasn't anything else to do but club myself over the head with the bottle of Black and White provided by the manager.

It had not been a jolly morning. From the crash, the police had driven me through the holiday crowds to the cop shop in Sandown town. Through the lobster mothers and fathers and the ugly kids, and past red-and-black posters advertising THE GREATEST AERIAL SHOW IN THE WORLD—THE OLD TIME FLYING CIRCUS. What with pirate posters and crowd problems and now the crash, the Isle of Wight law were treating me like an outbreak of the Black Plague. One squeak from an irate resident about low flying in the next week, and they'd tie a stone round all our necks and heave us off the end of Sandown Pier.

At the police station I'd had a prickly session with a superintendent. I told him Bill had been flying to Sandown from Redhill yesterday evening, after flying down from Blackpool in the morning to pick up some things from our base at Denham and a few spare plugs and exhaust gaskets from Redhill. I told him we were due to put on a circus performance to tie up with a Chamber of Trade fête at the airfield on Friday. Which he knew perfectly well already, since he'd probably been listening to complaints about the posters for the last two days.

In spite of the questions and the regulation scowl, the super obviously knew as much about air-crash procedures as I know about flower arranging. He'd managed to have the Accidents Investigation Branch of the Department of Trade and Industry informed, but towards the end of our interview he began fishing for clues from me on what he should do next. I told him bluntly that he ought to keep his men's big feet off the bits, order an autopsy and inform the local coroner, and have the inquest opened and adjourned *sine die* pending the conclusions of the investigation lads. This was received with the sort of look you normally get when you threaten to report an inspector to his chief constable, and Holland was ushered out with what the old-time writers called scant ceremony.

I'd wandered the town for a while after that, letting my depression feed on the sight of so many happy people, and when both hip and spirit couldn't stand it anymore, I got a taxi back to the airfield. The controller told me Ted had phoned and was expecting to arrive about three o'clock, so that left me with a couple of hours to wait in the deserted bar letting my tonsils practice the breaststroke.

Conscience told me that tragedy or no tragedy, I shouldn't be sitting around at the start of what promised to be a busy week. I ought at least to be walking round the airfield getting a general idea of what areas we were going to have to talk the organizers out of putting marquees on. In a small outfit like ours, everyone has to work like hell all the time or the whole thing falls flat. My main jobs are stunt man and spare pilot, but I also fill in taking engines to pieces when the D.o.T.I. isn't looking, writing handout stories for newspapers when our "road manager" is otherwise engaged, and cooking over butane-fueled Gaz rings while those with sound hip joints get on with the manual labor.

So I dutifully plunked down in a barroom easy chair and prepared to let the brain cell chew on a few constructive thoughts. But after the morning I'd just had, the Constructive Thought department seemed to have gone on strike. So I had another drink, and then another, and ended up half-dozing with the stale taste of Scotch in my mouth and the ever-nagging memories of Janie wandering through my mind. Which was about as constructive as sitting in a flat spin at 1,000 feet and thinking about the parachute you left in the hangar.

My stupid treacherous brain kicked around in the ashes of the might-have-beens, dredging up for the ten-thousandth time that morning four months before when my world had ended.

I still remembered every detail. The way we'd lain in bed in the morning in a cold, terrible silence while I prayed desperately for a miracle to join us again before one of us moved or spoke and finished it forever.

Watching the hands of the clock creeping until it was eight A.M. Giving it five minutes and really praying: Dear God, if she reaches out and touches me before five past, everything will be all right. We won't have to part. I'll stop flying and we'll get married. I'll do anything—only let her reach out and touch me. Please, God, *make* her reach out. . . .

Five past.

She hadn't touched me. I got up.

We moved like automatons, still in sullen silence, getting dressed. Janie made coffee and we sat on the bed drinking it. The clock ticked on. Our separate suitcases stood by the door. End of the winter. Start of the circus season. Today was the day I gave up my winter flat and started living in sleeping bags for the summer. A beautiful spring day.

The day we were due to walk out of each other's lives.

At that moment, I'd have promised her anything. The bitterness, the rows which had come more and more often as this day drew steadily nearer, meant nothing. The hours and weeks and months had suddenly come down to this last few minutes.

"Janie . . ." my voice hoarse. Just minutes. "Janie, look, suppose I

23

get a caravan? One of those beautiful big ones. Just for this season. Then I'll give it up. Go back to journalism.''

She looked away. Shook her head. Her brown hair rippled. There were tears in her voice.

"No. Don't say that. You know you wouldn't give it up. You want your planes more than you want me.''

Not at that moment, I didn't.

"No, please . . . darling. Listen. It's just for five months. I could go out and get one of those big holiday caravans tomorrow. We could get married. It'd be like a long holiday. Then in September I'll sell it, get a house and a newspaper job. It's bloody silly us parting like this. . . .''

She turned to me, eyes wide and tearful. Her voice was high and near to breaking.

"No, you wouldn't. You'd bumble through the winter doing odd free-lance jobs, then you'd be off again in the spring. If you really wanted a newspaper job you'd get one today instead of going to the airfield.''

The bitter ring of truth.

"You know I can't do that. We're committed. Those film people are coming down today. Ted couldn't get anyone else for this season now.''

She looked away again. I rushed on, grasping desperately at anything.

"We could in a couple of weeks, though. Look, darling, I'll tell Ted this morning he's got to get someone else; then I'll just stay till he's got someone settled down; then . . .''

"*No!* Don't say that. You know you don't mean it. We've been through this so many times. If you really wanted me, you wouldn't go to the airfield today. You'd have got a job a month ago. But you're going. And you'll keep on going. In a few weeks you'll say they haven't found anybody, and you've got to do the season. Then the next season, and the next. Because you're the great Ken Holland. They couldn't replace you in a couple of weeks. Not with anyone they could afford, anyway. If you'd trained someone over the winter, you could have—but no, you haven't got any intention of giving it up.''

I tried to butt in, but she rounded on me, tears rolling down her face.

24

"Don't try and change it now; it's too late. You won't change and I can't share it with you."

"But *why* not? If . . ."

"Oh, God, you *know* why not!" The tears started coming now. "What wife could stand watching the crazy risks you take twice, three times a day? Who could be married to a man called 'Nine Lives' and not be counting them off as they went? But worse than that, who'd have her children in a caravan year after year while her husband went out twice a day with another lover? God, I've *seen* you when you're flying. I've watched you take risks and half-kill yourself. You love it. You love flying and your aeroplanes. You *need* to take risks. There's some quirk in you, something no woman could ever share. A wife'd only be married to half of you. Look at you: you want me, but whatever happens you're going off to that airfield today. I know it and you know it."

Her voice ended with a sob. She sat there staring at me, tears coursing down her cheeks. I tried to put my arm round her, but she pulled away. I knew she was waiting for me to say the words. To say I wasn't going to the airfield today. To change everything.

I looked away. She was right. I *was* going to the airfield.

We left a few minutes later. Just picked up our suitcases and walked away in different directions. I nearly killed myself that day doing a triple slow roll at low level.

It was only later I found that the price I'd paid was too high. The pain, instead of getting better, got worse. I used to love flying, but now I hated it as well. Hated it because it had lost me Janie, and loved it at the same time because it was all I had left.

That and the might-have-beens and the cold deep-down loneliness that friends can never begin to reach.

I had another drink and drifted into a hot, haunted doze.

I woke up to the blaring crackle of a Gypsy Major passing over the runway at twenty feet. By the time I'd scraped myself up out of the chair and diluted the old army blanket in my mouth with a gulp of Scotch it had gone, but I knew what it was. Ted Reeves arriving in our other Tiger.

I even knew what he'd just done: a slow, low run down the right-hand side of the runway with stick and rudder crossed and the Tiger flying nearly sideways, just holding its height on full power. For the last three years I'd seen him do it before landing on dubious grass fields all over the country. It was his method of having a look, studying the surface before committing his wheels and his neck to it.

To see him picking up a handkerchief from the ground with a two-foot fishing rod on his wing tip you'd think he was the craziest airman since Lincoln Beachey—but when he's not performing in the show, he's the most cautious pilot I've ever met. And the best. Maybe he feels that by being supercareful ninety-five percent of the time, he's building up a reserve of good luck to see him through the other five.

My headache was still ticking over lumpily as I stepped outside the clubhouse into the hot sun. Ted motored slowly over the boundary fence, kept it flying just above the stall until he was about 50 yards from the hangar, then eased back on the power and three-pointed neatly. As he cleared left and taxied towards my Tiger, Mark glided across the fence in our remaining Stampe, the Renault engine pobbling happily to itself. The two biplanes parked side by side, and after the usual head-scratching and eye-rubbing the intrepid aviators got out and walked towards me.

The three of us now represented the entire aircrew section of the Old Time Flying Circus. I guessed it was likely to stay that way for the rest of the '71 season now, too. The chances of finding a replacement for Bill at this time of year were pretty remote. There are plenty of pilots who want circus jobs but aren't good enough, while most of those who *are* good enough think it's too dangerous and badly paid. The latter school of thought has things weighed up pretty well, too: it's a great life until the glamour wears off, which it does after about three days, and then it's just an endless grind of flying, maintaining aircraft, staking out fields, and living in perpetual dirty exhaustion with most of your meals snatched out of a frying pan on top of a Gaz stove. The performances are represented by an aching buildup of tension over the twenty-four hours beforehand, punctuated by a never-ending series of contretemps over sequence details and minor items of equipment. Like someone can't find the toy rabbit for the poacher sequence; then someone else suddenly realizes we're fresh out of 9mm blanks for the Sten guns; and at the same time I discover that the box of ground maroons for the crash sequence is still sitting in my bedroom at Denham. So I make a quick command decision to solve all our problems by whipping up there in the Tiger we aren't using for joy-riding at the moment. I'm all ready to go before I find out *why* we aren't using it—there was a big magneto drop, and Johnny Hawkin currently has the port mag spread out all over the field. And so it goes on. The tension reaches a climax at the final briefing, an hour before the show begins. After that it's nervous smoking, unfunny jokes, and stretched nerves jangling like piano wire until we get into action.

The only person who seems to be immune from the tension is Ted himself. Fifteen years and eight thousand hours of flying have left him with a fatalistic calm which I alternately hate and envy. I suppose he must feel his nerves sometimes, but when the going gets tough his only reaction is to become more polite than usual. Which admittedly isn't difficult.

He's about six feet four and well built, running slightly to a beer gut, and perpetually to be found in roll-neck sweaters and ancient flying boots. His wavy black hair and untidy beard combine with the shoe-leather face and crinkled-up blue eyes to give him the rakish air of Your Friendly Hometown Pirate. Although gruff and blunt, he has a happy knack for making everybody feel they're his long-lost buddy whom he loves like a brother. It often takes months for the effect to wear off and the victims to slowly realize that ten minutes after meeting him for the first time they'd been performing some service for him that they wouldn't normally have undertaken for their next-door neighbor of ten years' standing.

Mark Grandis, the other pilot, gives the first impression of being an economy-sized version of Ted. His hair and beard are also black, though usually a little better trimmed, but he has the same piercing eye and the same knack for getting on with people. However, like me, he is about half Ted's age. He's often taken for Ted's son, and when you tell people they aren't related you can almost hear them thinking it's a case of the apprentice imitating the master. This isn't fair, since the resemblance in both appearance and manner is pure coincidence. The similarity doesn't run right through, anyway. Mark doesn't hide his emotions the way Ted does. Before a show he's jumpy as a cat, the same as the rest of us. Right now he was sad because of Bill. So he looked sad.

Ted, on the other hand, merely looked irritable.

Mourning makes him bad-tempered. In his devious way he probably figures that when he's sorrowing the best thing to do is show any other kind of emotion except sorrow.

"Seen the police?" he asked shortly as he reached me.

"Yes."

"How'd it happen?"

I told him what I'd found and what the police found and what the farmer said, and the current theory that Bill had been taken ill in the air. I added that we were waiting for the result of the postmortem.

"Christ," said Ted. "What a way to go. He was a good bloke, old Bill. Good pilot."

That last ultimate accolade, something Ted would never have said of any of us so long as we were alive, was evidently his way of closing the subject. I respected that: coming from Ted it was a compliment suitable for an epitaph.

"Is the Stampe a write-off?" he asked.

"Absolutely. Engine as well. I've never seen such a mess. Leave it to the insurance people. It's a bit . . . messy."

Ted looked at me sharply, taking in my unwashed state, deadened eyes, and total weariness. With sudden gentleness he put an arm around my good shoulder and said "We're going to get you drunk tonight, Ken, mate." Reeves the psychiatrist.

He turned to Mark. "Ken here's had enough for the moment," he said. "I want you to get a train back to London tonight and fetch the Auster down here first thing in the morning. I'll drop you in Portsmouth later on. Ken and I'll do a turn round the towns first thing, and you should be here before too many of them start coming in."

This meant that I'd be up at sparrow-burp the next morning trying to give everyone heart failure. This would get the joyride crowds rolling in after breakfast, by which time we would have a third pilot and the four-seat Auster which we use for the bulk of the joyriding.

This program didn't exactly promise to be a rest cure, but it sounded better than me having a three-hour train journey tonight followed by a dreary sleepless night at Denham and an early-morning flog back again in that echo chamber of an Auster. I stumped off with Mark to see to the refueling while Ted went to turn some charm on the airfield manager.

Three hours later the whole troupe was assembled at Sandown.

Lyn Mallet, our road manager-cum-publicity-manager-cum-illicit-poster-sticker, arrived in a shower of dust and small stones in my Jaguar XK 120. He was shocked by Bill's disaster, but he was wearing it better than the rest of us. Being the most nonflying man among us, he hadn't been so close to Bill. I had to go through the explanations again with him, but after he'd made the right noises of horror and shock his natural ebullience started showing through again as he explained a new idea he had for me to grab a petrol can from Mark in the car while I was dangling from the rope ladder underneath the Tiger.

I asked him how the hell he thought I was going to climb back up the ladder with my hands full of petrol can, and he said he was sure I'd think of something. My headache-and-Scotch-inspired temper was not improved by the realization that he was probably right, I *would* think of something. My perverse brain has a habit of chewing on these crazy ideas until it comes up with a way of trying it that doesn't *have* to prove fatal. One day I am going to think of something once too often. And then I'll be a little red memory smeared along some grass runway.

The next and last arrivals were John Hawkin and Rick Hale in the circus truck. I was glad to see that red-and-yellow 30-cwt because it meant that for once it hadn't digested some major part on the way. It does this about one trip in three on average, which strands not only sixty-six percent of the ground crew, but also all the apparatus from fences to firearms, cooking stove to comedy car lashed on the trailer behind.

I had to go through the same explanations yet again to John and Rick, and they both looked shocked by the futility of Bill's death until Ted came over and told them to stop moping and get on with erecting tents and fencing off our bit of runway.

Lyn went off in the XK again on a lightning tour of the island to see whether we needed another poster session. The authorities would undoubtedly have been busy since his nocturnal visit with John and a pastepot a week ago. He carted off a couple of invitations for free rides, to be dumped through the letter boxes of the local papers so that they might take full advantage of our munificence and furnish us with a goodly blurb in their Friday editions. After the crash I considered this to be somewhat superfluous: the place would be knee-deep in reporters and photographers tomorrow whether we wanted it or not.

Anyway, if he drove that car round the island long enough, we wouldn't need the posters or the stories. The XK was my personal baby, the only decent thing I owned apart from shares in a couple of aeroplanes, and I had vowed that one day it was going to look like an XK again—but for the moment it was a perambulating advert and a ground-support vehicle rolled into one. In garish red and yellow with THE OLD TIME FLYING CIRCUS painted on the sides, it boasted a pair of parallel bars on the bonnet for the attachment of loudspeakers when we wanted to use it for barking, a bit of curved and padded metal on the nearside front fender for John Hawkin's right knee when the script called for him to kneel there firing a Sten at the Tiger as the car bounced across the grass at 50 mph, and U bolts sprouting out all over the place for the clipping of harnesses. On the rear cowl were a couple of narrow metal trays for Rick's feet when he stood there holding the balloon which I, climbing down a rope ladder beneath the Tiger, had to burst with my foot as we flew over the car.

The windscreen was gone, and in its place was a tiny aeroscreen for the driver, plus a very tough tubular edifice resembling a rollover bar across the rear cowl. This was for me to grab hold of as I let go of the rope ladder and dropped into the car for our dodgiest stunt to date.

With Lyn gone and everybody else working, I found myself at a loose end. Ted had said I was due to get drunk, but I knew perfectly well that if I was flying the dawn patrol I'd already had my quota, whether I felt drunk or not. I wanted to go and help somebody do something as a temporary therapy against the cold, dark slug of loneliness. But John and Rick were fencing, which my hip wasn't up to at that moment, and Ted and Mark were starting up Ted's Tiger to drop Mark off at Portsmouth.

I sighed and started looking for the bean tins and the Gaz ring. The cold, dark slug hitched itself up a couple more sizes.

CHAPTER 4

Eight o'clock the next morning found me tensed up against the cold in the cockpit of the Stampe at 50 feet over Sandown's beach.

Fifty feet to my right and slightly behind me was Ted in a Tiger. Two hundred yards to the right of him, on the dry sand above the high-water mark, were the two-legged sharks getting their joyride boats into the water before the crowds arrived. The boat-hauling operations came to a stop as they watched our gaily colored biplanes snarling across the sand.

Level with the end of the beach I waved my left hand and hauled round in a tight climbing turn. With the beach on my left wing I rolled the Stampe on its back and thumped the inverted fuel lever forward. For half a minute I hung upside down in the straps, looking up at the crinkled blue sea. Then the oil-pressure gauge flickered, indicating that the lubricant was fed up with trying to fall upwards, and I half-rolled the right way up again. At the far end of the beach I stall-turned and kept the Stampe's nose down, pulling out with the wheels three feet above the water.

In front of me, Sandown Pier grew hugely until it filled the horizon between the wings. I held down until I could see the cracks in the wooden supports, then hauled the stick back into my stomach. The nose leaped skywards, I had an instant's vision of metal hand railings ten feet below me—and then the Tiger shot past in the opposite direction with a blattering roar that cracked across the blare of my own engine.

I caught a camera-frame glimpse of Ted's head in the cockpit as we crossed—and then he was gone and I closed my eyes for a second and breathed out.

That one always worries me. In spite of knowing that Ted's going over the *end* of the pier while you're going over 100 feet *in* from the end, it's always a heart-stopping moment as you head straight for a structure knowing there's another aeroplane doing exactly the same thing on the other side. However many times you do it, you always have the same terrifying thought that maybe this time you've got your wires crossed and you're *both* tracking in 100 feet from the end. . . .

Anyway, the stunt would undoubtedly achieve its purpose: the story of the near-disaster would be all over town before the breakfast cups had been washed up. We might get an angry visit from the fuzz, but the local vested interests in our presence should be able to chill any serious beefs about low flying. You can get away with almost anything at resort towns providing you don't actually kill anybody. Or stop them spending money.

I did one more pass over the beach rolling all the way, pulled a final vertical flick-roll to prove to myself I could still do it, and ambled back to the airfield.

The sky was a canopy of washy blue from horizon to horizon. From where I sat I could see the neat lines of parked aircraft at Bembridge, the island's other, busier airfield, and beyond it across the Solent the buildings and cranes of Portsmouth. The Renault engine was running sweetly, the wind was cold on my face below the goggles, and the Stampe felt live and taut through my body the way only a Stampe can feel. For the moment I was happy. No loneliness, no depression, no aching hip. But only birds can fly all the time, and they don't cost £5 an hour to run. I landed at Sandown.

An hour later I was sitting in the shade of the Stampe's port wings giving a press conference to a pair of slightly sick reporters, and wondering which of them would throw up first as their glassy eyes followed the demise of my breakfast toast and beans. Ted had insisted that I deal with the press this time, taking the view that since they'd want to talk to me anyway because I'd seen Mike's crash, I might as well do the whole PR job while I was at it. To start them off on the right foot, Lyn Mallet had strapped them into the front seat of the Stampe in turn and I'd thrown them round the sky for ten minutes each to soften them up.

Now, suitably softened, they'd run out of questions about the crash and were starting on the more usual stuff about the circus and the show we were putting on. I was thoroughly sick of them because they'd made me think about Bill again, and I hoped to Christ they'd hurry up and puke if they were going to and then push off. Their photographers had already left after taking pictures of a low pass, more pictures of the heroic reporters grinning weakly as they got into the Stampe, and a few final shots of Holland sitting in the cockpit with the undamaged side of his face towards the camera.

They were still prattling when the first joyride customers rolled up in a twelve-year-old Consul. Ted spotted them and swooped, and a few minutes later one of the Tigers clattered into life and hauled itself busily into the air. A second car arrived and a young man and a girl got out, looked around, and headed for the Stampe.

Holland's cue to start earning money.

I hauled myself upright, disposed of the last mouthful of breakfast, and told the reporters I'd be available for further statements in a little while, but in the meantime would they excuse me while I earned lunch? They evaporated in the direction of their offices and the free beer that would be forthcoming for the rest of the day on the strength of their death-defying experience.

The boy and girl were examining the six-foot hoarding that advertised

SPECIAL ACROBATIC FLIGHTS FOR ONLY £2.50. AT LEAST 15 MINUTES IN THE AIR AND THREE DIFFERENT MANOEUVRES! Beneath the wording were drawings of a Noddy aeroplane with its path traced through a loop, a stall turn, and a roll. Mere mortals contented themselves with a conventional whizz-round in an Auster or Tiger for £1.50, while the really intrepid paid another pound for the privilege of being chucked about at the same time.

These two were going to be really intrepid.

I took the boy first, and he actually seemed to enjoy it. The girl obviously didn't trust the six-strap harness an inch, since she held on to the center-section struts with white knuckles all the time we were in the air. I did the loop and the stall turn and then landed.

As we taxied in I shouted above the engine: "I forgot the roll. Do you want to go up again and do it?"

She shook her head, and I came in for a grateful look out of the corner of her eye. The negative G of a roll would probably have finished her off. Holland the Gallant Knight lurched smartly out of the cockpit as soon as the prop stopped, to help unstrap her, but when the boyfriend hove into sight she forgot all about me and started telling him how wonderful it all was.

The next customer was a portly gent who said he'd flown in the RAF twenty years ago and it was grand to get back into a Tiger Moth again, and could he have a go at the flying? I pointed out tactfully that it was a Stampe, not a Tiger, and that the front stick wasn't in because we didn't have time on the joyrides to mess about with passengers who wanted to try flying themselves. He looked a bit huffy at that, so I added that the stick was in the lorry over the other side of the field, and that while I naturally wouldn't have any objection to *him* flying it for a bit, I simply couldn't spare the time to go and get it. The stick was actually in the locker just aft of my cockpit, and there it was going to stay.

The Air Commode had his flight, looked a little queasy at the end of it, told me I reminded him of the pilots in his squadron twenty years ago, ho ho, and left.

So far, a normal morning.

The normality ceased with the arrival of Mr. Anthony Haydon. I didn't know his name then, of course: he was just a dark-haired, medium-tall man who got out of the Auster that Mark had finally condescended to fly down to the sunny Isle.

My first thought was that Mark had managed to get tangled up with a man from the Department of Trade and Industry, and had been obliged to fly him down here to view the crash. This was quite ridiculous, since Mark had only been at our home base at Denham last night and early this morning, and would hardly have found a D.o.T.I. man lying in wait for him in the cabin of the Auster. But I couldn't help the impression, because Haydon looked more like a typical government man than the average typical government man. He was wearing a dark blue pinstripe suit, waistcoat and all, and his conservatively cut black hair was carefully combed and had just the right amount of gray in it. He was about 40, smooth-faced, freshly shaven, and he moved with the purposeful deliberation of a taxpayers' salary. As Mark ushered him over to me I cast my mind back over the last few days and prepared to lie like a trooper over the heights I'd been flying.

"This is Anthony Haydon," said Mark when the two of them reached me. "He caught me at Denham just as I was leaving. He's interested in buying that Auster you and Bill had in France. He wanted to see you as soon as possible, so I gave him a lift down."

I ceased working out the case for the defense and regarded Mr. Haydon with a little more brotherly love. To tell the truth, I'd been vaguely worried about that Auster in what few spare moments I'd had since yesterday morning. Bill and I had been in the habit of pooling our slender resources and buying cheap aircraft from France, doing enough work on them to get a British Certificate of Airworthiness and then selling them at an average one-hundred-percent profit. That was how we'd come by the Stampe I was using this morning.

Our latest venture was a tatty old Auster which Bill had found at some airfield down near the Alpes Maritimes. I'd turned over my £ 90—half the purchase price—to Bill, and he'd paid for it and arranged with the current owners to try and get it an export permit in time for when we were in France for a circus job next week. I hadn't even seen the machine myself, but Bill had said we might just be able to fool the French authorities into giving us a temporary C of A to fly it back to England if we worked on the kite every spare second while we were over there. Now, without Bill, who had a bagful of fitter's licenses, I didn't have the least idea what I was going to do about it.

Maybe the problem was about to be solved. Haydon started talking. He had a smooth British voice with no accent.

"I must offer you my condolences over Mr. Charlton's accident," he said. "I'm sorry if I've arrived at an awkward time, but I didn't know about the accident until I met Mr. Grandis at Denham Airfield this morning."

"Mr. Haydon jolly nearly missed me altogether," chipped in Mark. "He came running out on to the airfield just as I was taxiing out. He thought I was you."

"The people in the control place told me you were just leaving," Haydon said. "It seemed a pity to miss you after driving all the way out to Denham, and when Mr. Grandis offered to give me a lift down I couldn't resist the temptation to get in a little flying and see you at the same time."

"Mr. Haydon is learning to fly," Mark explained. "He wants to have his own aeroplane when he's finished the course."

"I've only just started, you see," said Haydon, taking up the ball, "and I want to buy something cheap to fly next summer. That gives me the winter to have it overhauled by a couple of mechanics I know who'll do it in their spare time. I was passing through St.-Jean-sur-Saône a few days ago and I saw the Auster you and Mr. Charlton bought. It would suit me admirably, so I'd like to buy it as it stands now."

Well, he had something there—if you discounted the *ifs* of having an old aeroplane "rebuilt by a couple of mechanics in their spare time." But that would be his problem.

"Who put you on to me, Mr. Haydon?"

"The people in France you bought the Auster from," he replied casually. "The Aéro Club de Mt.-Vivaral. Look, I'm prepared to offer you three hundred and fifty pounds for that Auster as it stands. It's just what I want."

It was tempting. Three hundred and fifty pounds was more than a tatty Auster with no certificates was worth.

"Why didn't you go for one of the other Austers there? Bill said there were three altogether, all going at about the same price."

Haydon smiled a worldly smile. "They're not so good as yours. They're going to cost quite a lot to do up—and you've already applied for an export permit, too."

He'd been doing his homework. The French customs people reckon that any aeroplane with a motor rated above 120 brake horsepower is potential war matériel, so they insist on a delay of four months between the application to export and your taking the lethal weapon out of the country. Just what sort of an air force they imagine uses twenty-year-old Austers as its strike arm I can't think, but the Gypsy Major Ten engine is quoted at 130 bhp, so you have to put up with the delay. They probably figure that if you're contemplating starting World War Three someone will be kind enough to bump you off during the waiting period anyway, so they'll collar the money without having to cough up one of the country's major aeronautical assets. Anyway, the Mt.-Vivaral Aéro Club people had applied for an export permit in the middle of April, which meant the four months were nearly up.

I thought for a minute. Something smelled a bit wrong somewhere, but I couldn't put my finger on it.

"Look, I'll give you a check, or even cash if you like, right now," said Haydon persuasively. He started reaching into his jacket pocket.

I made up my mind.

"No," I said, surprising myself. "I haven't even seen this Auster yet. I want to have a look at it first; then I'll consider your offer."

Haydon's face hardened imperceptibly. Not something you'd notice normally, but I was watching him carefully and my years as a reporter had taught me to notice such things. He wanted this Auster an awful lot.

"I'll make it four hundred pounds," he said. "If I'm going to buy it at all, I want to get things moving quickly."

Four hundred was a lot of money for that aeroplane. Common sense told me to take it, and I hesitated. There was excitement in Haydon's eyes. He thought he had me.

And all of a sudden I didn't want to be had like that. Haydon was offering too much money. The smell was getting worse.

"No. I'm going to see it first. I'll be over there in a couple of weeks. I'll let you know when I come back, if you'll leave me your address and phone number."

His face tightened up a couple of notches and his lips compressed. When he spoke, his voice was still smooth, though.

"Very well," he said. "I'll get in touch with you again. No point in you trying to contact me: I'm a bit difficult to get hold of most of the time."

He nodded to me and Mark, stitched an insincere smile on his face, and walked off down the track to the aerodrome entrance. Exit a man who had tried much too hard to get his hands on one decrepit old Auster.

And leaving behind him a man who was wondering why the bloody hell he hadn't taken advantage of the opportunity and unloaded the bloody thing. Maybe the heat of August in the Isle of Wight was getting to me.

I went on wondering about it for the rest of the morning—and by lunchtime I had it.

For one thing, Haydon said he'd got my name from the Aéro Club de Mt.-Vivaral. Which made him a liar, because the Aéro Club wouldn't have it. The deal had been solely in Bill's name. He'd found the kite by himself, and there'd been no reason for him to mention me at all.

Yet Haydon had asked for me by name at Denham. Not Bill—me. So where had he got my name from? I didn't know—any more than I knew why he should want this tatty old Auster enough to offer about twice the going price for it. He hadn't looked the sort of man who makes a habit of overpaying for things.

Well, I wasn't going to solve the silly little mystery by cudgeling my brains over it before Haydon got in touch with me again. If he ever did. So I quit worrying about it and concentrated on the joyride business.

CHAPTER 5

I was right about it being a heavy week for joyrides. In fact, it was a heavy week for living. After Haydon had left, Monday set the pattern, with the public arriving at Sandown Airfield in their droves to be taken for a leap into the wild blue yonder. The yonder remained blue and unwild, apart from the inevitable turbulence caused by heat and the sea breezes getting a dig in the ribs from the contours of the island. We flew from breakfast until dusk using the Auster, one of the Tigers, and the Stampe. In the evenings we washed the kites down, checked them over carefully, dragged our tired carcasses into Sandown for a late meal, then returned to the airfield to collapse into our sleeping bags. We slept like dead men.

Between Monday and Thursday I flew over a hundred trips, stopping for nothing but refueling and snatching the odd Coke. Three people were sick in the Stampe—two of whom had the sense to lean over the side and one who didn't. And John Hawkin nearly had an argument with the propeller of the Auster while trying to prevent an inquisitive cocker spaniel from getting itself filleted. We were collectively and artistically rude to the stout woman who owned the spaniel. On Wednesday and Thursday the joyriding business was slightly hampered by the arrival of several marquees for the fete on Friday. We managed to persuade the Chamber of Trade it was unwise to park their wigwams actually *on* the runway, but as usual no amount of tactful bellowing would discourage the workmen from strolling across the path of aircraft landing or taking off. When they weren't ambling across the airfield on foot with both eyes shut and both brain cells resting hard they were driving across it in lorries, timing their passage neatly to coincide with the movements of the aircraft. By Thursday night, the eve of the show, we were all a bit curled round the edges.

If anything, I was a bit more curled than the rest, because that morning I'd had to give evidence of identification at Bill's inquest. The pathologist who performed the postmortem said that Bill had probably lost consciousness in the air due to the effects of poisoning by staphylococcus bacteria—in other words, simple food poisoning. He'd found the remains of a pork pie in Bill's digestive tract, and examination of this revealed enough staphylococci to put a Panzer division away.

Staphylococcus, the pathologist said, is tasteless and would not necessarily provoke a reaction immediately if it was eaten. The effects could come on very suddenly up to two hours after consumption, as the stomach juices broke down the elements of whatever contained the poison. He mentioned that the poison was that ejected from a wound turned septic. You could almost see the coroner and the jury start thinking about a juicy food-factory scandal.

The path man also said that Bill had died instantly of multiple injuries sustained in the crash: the poison shouldn't have been fatal, and if the attack had occurred on the ground, he'd probably have got away with a swift dose of pethidine and a few days in hospital with a drip feed.

The medical evidence was followed by the farmer who owned the field Bill had crashed in. He said he saw the Stampe fly straight into the ground in a shallow dive, and added that he'd been sick when he arrived on the scene and saw what was in the remains of the cockpit. I sympathized.

The coroner, a neat little man with a fastidious goatee, advised the jury to return a verdict of accidental death. This they promptly did, which gave Goatee a chance to play high-court judge and inquire of the police whether investigations were under way to track down the source of the contaminated pie.

The inspector said they were, Goatee said he was glad to hear it, and it was all over. MYSTERY AIR CRASH SOLVED: POLICE SCOUR COUNTRY FOR SOURCE OF KILLER PIE.

I drove back to the airfield and threw myself furiously into the aerobatic joyrides as an anodyne to the black depression.

Late in the afternoon the proceedings were further cheered up by the arrival of a local undertaker, who came to fix the details of Bill's cremation. There were no relations who wanted the bits, so Ted had decided it might as well be dealt with in Sandown. The man caught me in a bad moment of depression and flight fatigue coupled with the first tired jabs of tension over the next day's performance. I spent ten minutes being rude to him, then topped it off by offering him a free ride in the Stampe. He managed to look horrified and justifiably offended all at once, and stalked off with distaste oozing from every pore.

After our evening meal we sat around talking into the night, swatting at the bugs that flittered round the Tilley lamp and made regular sorties against our persons. We were tired, but there was no joyriding the next day, so we could sleep a bit later in the morning. With my preshow nerves winding up, I was glad no one seemed in a hurry to turn in. It cut down the time spent lying awake smoking cigarettes and staring at the roof of the tent.

CHAPTER 6

I slammed open the throttle of the Stampe and held it down three feet above the well-trampled grass. The carnival float that had pulled stolidly out in front of my landing expanded until it filled the whole world. I had the satisfaction of seeing the white-faced driver stand on the brake a split second before I yanked the stick back, then forward again, to leapfrog Miss Sandown's perambulating throne.

Some people, notably the pillars of the church who run charity sideshows and drive carnival floats, haven't got enough brains to grease a throttle lever. It never seems to enter their tiny minds that it would be a bloody good idea to look *up* as well as straight in front of them when they decide to tool across an active runway. How at least one of us doesn't end up finely grated on top of an aircraft-lorry consommé at least once a show I'll never know.

I held the Stampe down to gain speed, stall-turned at the end of the field, then roared back through the sideshows, lifting my wings to clear the tents. A quick split-ass turn brought me over the runway again downwind, in time to give the float a second dose before it could get clear.

All rather childish and unnecessary, but if there's one thing that infuriates me it's other people risking *my* neck through sheer stupidity. I stall-turned again, slipped it off the top, and landed. No one put so much as a big toe on the runway. I turned at the end of the landing run and taxied up to the parked Tigers with short, vicious jabs of throttle. Then I switched off and the prop went *fub-fub-fub-wishy-washy* as it whipped to a stop. I peeled off my helmet and hauled myself out of the cockpit.

With the blare of the engine still buzzing in my ears, I didn't hear the lorry driver in time to even get out on the other side of the fuselage to him.

He was a very angry lorry driver. He was also the kind of lorry driver who drives a directorial chair most of the year, and only actually gets behind the wheel when the town turns out to watch him ferrying the carnival queen around. This kind of lorry driver often has delusions of self-righteousness. A minute ago he'd been white with fright as I'd buzzed him. Now he was red with rage, and seemed all set to continue the color transmission into deep purple.

"You young maniac!" he shouted. "Are you trying to kill me? What do you mean by driving that aeroplane at me? If I hadn't stopped we'd both have been killed! It's not safe to drive around. I saw you over the town a few minutes ago, too. I'll have the police on you, flying like that over the promenade. No wonder your friend crashed. Your whole outfit's a bloody menace. . . ."

His voice trailed off, either because he'd run out of breath or because he caught the look on my face as I eased myself down off the lower wing. Normally I'm quite happy to engage in a slanging match with the local idiot, especially after I've been performing over a town at the request of the idiot's own Carnival Committee—but that crack about Bill had been unwise: one more squeak out of this guy and he was going to need some expensive dentistry.

We stood there glaring at each other—until a voice from my left suddenly broke the tension.

"Hey, hey," it crackled. "Don't be bloody silly, you chaps. Making bloody fools of yourselves, y'know!"

As a speech it had all the histrionic merit of a dialogue in a prewar

Boy's Own. Furthermore, the voice fitted the words: it sounded like a few yards of well-bred gravel sliding cheerfully off a lorry.

But it served its purpose. My temper ran down from the red line, and the moment was past. It had the same effect on Sandown's number one lorry driver—so I risked a glance at the owner of it.

He was an old, old man. A short, round, grizzled old man, bald as a flying helmet and about as leathery. He wore baggy flannel trousers and several layers of shapeless sweaters. A massive clasp knife hung below his topmost cardigan on a chain from his belt, giving him the appearance of an incredibly overage Boy Scout.

The resemblance disappeared when you looked at his eyes, though. Old he might be, but those eyes still snapped and sparkled. And under the wrinkled skin his jaw had that determined, confident set that only years of command can bestow. One of those men you automatically say "sir" to.

"You!" he barked at the lorry driver, who visibly jumped. "Haven't you got enough sense to look where you're going when you drive across a runway? Hey? You're lucky you didn't get y'self killed. Go and find y'self something useful to do."

Thirty seconds ago I'd have bet anyone saying that to our one-man wagon train would have been in grave danger from flying meat and hair as the man blew up with rage. But now his big moment was past. Under the influence of the old boy's major-general eye and with interested spectators beginning to arrive, all he could do was snort a couple of times and stalk off in a stiff-legged fury. I tried not to grin too openly.

"Thank you," I said to the old man. "I . . ."

"You're a bloody fool too," he interrupted. "You were all set to hit that chap, weren't you? You'd probably have got choky, y'know. Sort of man who'd have contacts. Have to put up with fools sometimes, y'know. Can't lose your temper every time. Not worth it."

I jacked my mouth shut and tried to think of something to say. Nothing appropriate presented itself.

"Like the way you fly, young man," he said, changing the subject abruptly. "Useful pilot when you keep your temper. Got time for a beer with an old flyin' man? Me name's Jedrow, by the way."

We shook hands, and I looked him over again with new interest. He hadn't introduced himself fully—but perhaps he found Wing Commander James Jedrow, DSO, DFC and Bar, MC, too much of a mouthful for everyday use. I'd never seen him before, but I'd heard a bit about him here and there. And read about him, too. Flew an aeroplane for the first time in 1915 after one forty-minute lesson. Royal Flying Corps fighter pilot, one of the very early pelicans who first invented war in the air. Started off with four machine guns tied to the undercarriage of a BE2C in the Mesopotamia campaign. Adventurer between the wars, starting an airline in Siam and an airmail service in India, and finding time in between for various unsuccessful attempts at some of the aviation records that were being set up and broken left, right, and center around that time. A contemporary of Bert Hinkler, Alan Cobham, Kingsford-Smith, and all those. Never really made the big time—but on the other hand he was still around, which most of the legendary names aren't. He'd even been a circus pilot for a while, I seemed to remember. Then back to the RAF in the Second War, flying reconnaissance Spitfires and the like and ending up a wingco. Still kept in touch with the aviation world just enough so you heard the odd Jedrow story from time to time, which was mainly how I knew of him. Flying in England's a pretty small world, especially our kind of flying.

The last I'd heard of him was a newspaper story about how he talked his way into a "joyride" in a Victor by twisting a few influential arms at a squadron reunion dinner. The story had made much of him being 78 years old. That was a few years back, so he had to be over 80 now.

Eighty or not, he was a bundle of energy. He whisked me off to a beer tent, disappeared into the thick crowd round the bar, and returned with two cans before the rest of the customers realized he'd jumped the queue. We took our beer outside into the sunshine, and Jedrow promptly sat down crosslegged on the grass. I flopped down after him and leaned my back on a guy rope. Holland's left leg doesn't like being crossed, and a sore hip—or a sorer one than usual—would be about as helpful to me this afternoon as a hole in the head.

"Saw your chum Reeves," said Jedrow abruptly after a short silence. "Tells me you're all going to Lyon for a show next weekend. Want to go to France meself for a holiday. Get bored sitting around nowadays. Thought I'd tag along with you if nobody minds. Like to see a bit of flying again. Reeves seemed to think it was okay. Quite willing to muck in and all that, of course. Don't want anything out of it, but I'd like the holiday and the company.''

It took a second or two to let that sink in. The old boy talked like a telegram. When it did trickle through, though, I was all for it. Old he might be, but only in years. Having him along should keep me away from my own thoughts for hours.

"That's good news, sir," I said. "I've heard a lot—"

"Don't call me sir," he interrupted. It didn't seem my day for finishing sentences. "Me name's Jedrow. Everyone calls me Jedrow. Just plain Jedrow.''

I got the idea. He wanted to be called Jedrow.

"Don't like being called sir or wingco" he went on, "because I've never been a sir and I'm not a wingco any more. Lot of nonsense, these old ranks and things. Now you'd better push off, because y'show starts soon and Reeves told me not to keep you. We'll have another beer later on.''

I pushed, reflecting that Ted was a wily old bird for shooting Jedrow at me just before the show when I most needed something to break the tension. Which made Jedrow another wily old bird for making such a good job of it. You don't meet many characters like that.

Had I known what his "mucking in" would lead to, I'd sooner have welcomed a ticking bomb.

Ninety minutes and most of the show later, I finished zipping up a suit of bright yellow overalls and sat down on the grass with my back against the XK's front wheel. Overhead, Mark and Ted were twisting and turning in a mock dogfight. The snarl of engines was punctuated with the clatter of machine-gun fire and the sporadic *whoof-bang* of our "flak," courtesy of Brocks Fireworks. I peeled back the elastic overall cuff and looked at my watch: three minutes to go to the start of the finale. I lit a cigarette with unsteady hands and tightened the buckle on my crash helmet for the fourth time. To stop myself counting the seconds, I turned to studying the crowd.

I saw her almost immediately.

Even as my heart missed a beat I knew I had to be wrong. Janie was way behind me, and the last thing she'd do would be to come to our show. But the girl in the crowd, looking pert and lovely in shorts and a white blouse, was so much *her* that the shock hit me like a slap in the face. It was several seconds before my brain got into gear again and I realized this was just another girl with long brown hair, beautiful legs, and small, firm breasts. And a happy-looking boyfriend with a possessive arm round her waist, the way I used to put my arm round Janie.

The girl was wearing an engagement ring. They were probably on holiday together. I wondered if the girl made love like Janie. . . .

Angrily, I snapped myself out of it. The blues were getting worse. Big, brave Holland thinking himself into the grave. I dragged my eyes away from the couple and found myself studying a a man in a flowered shirt and sunglasses who was standing a few rows behind them. I felt sure I'd seen the face behind those glasses before. For a second it seemed important tnat I should remember where—and then the sound of the crowd drawing in its collective breath made me turn toward the runway. I was in time to see Ted's Tiger, smoke vomiting from the engine, pull out of a steep side-slip just above the ground and land bumpily. The Tiger taxied past me tail-up, smoke dying as Ted turned off the tap that let pressurized diesel fuel into the exhaust manifold.

Irritated, I levered myself upright against the XK's fender, stumped round to the driving seat, and turned the car to follow the Stampe which had landed behind Ted.

I would have to stop this mooning during the show. I pushed the girl I remembered too well and the man I couldn't remember at all out of my mind and sent up twin plumes of grass as I accelerated down the field.

Mark and Ted had stopped side by side at the far end of the runway. They got out as John taxied the other Tiger up, and I skidded the XK to a stop beside them. Mark flung off his helmet and goggles and jumped in the car. Ted swapped places with John, and I pulled myself up on to the Tiger and stood on the sides of the front cockpit, facing backwards and leaning against the fuel tank in the center section of the top wing. Ted settled himself in with a flurry of straps, and then the slipstream was whipping me as we taxied out in front of the crowd for the last stunt of the show.

Behind the tail I could see the XK following us, and above the blatter of the Gypsy Major I could just hear Lyn Mallet's voice over the PA system.

"Finally, ladies and gentlemen, we have for you the most dangerous trick in the history of flying. One that has rarely been performed before in all the years of aerial showmanship. Ken Holland, who you see standing on the fuselage of the Tiger Moth which is about to take off, will be climbing down a rope ladder in flight and throwing himself into a car moving at nearly sixty miles per hour. One slip, the slightest misjudgment, and he will plummet to his death. I must ask you to make sure that children and dogs are kept under especially tight control during this performance. The slightest distraction could be the cause of a terrible disaster."

The faces of the crowd turned towards me as we taxied slowly up the runway. I grinned and waved, feeling hollow in my stomach and hating the eyes that watched. This was what they'd really come to see—Holland squashed and broken, killed on the runway before their very eyes. Individually, they wished me no harm; but roll a lot of people together, entertain them for an hour with the spice of danger, and at the end of it you've generated a mob desire for the sight of someone's blood. Mine, for instance.

At the end of the runway we turned and Ted lifted his thumb. I repeated the signal, and tightened my grip on the center-section struts. He opened the throttle. We left the ground halfway along the strip, and I waved to the crowd again as we growled up the sky. Ted did a gentle one-eighty and we flew downwind over the runway at about 100 feet. I looked over the tail and watched the horizon bouncing gently and the small movements of the elevators as Ted corrected for the turbulence. Hanging on there in the gale I winked unconvincingly at Ted and tried not to think of the hungry eyes below.

We turned again, and as we neared the crowd I lowered myself down carefully from my perch on the fuselage and stood on the catwalk of the lower wing, clinging on to a center-section strut. The roaring hands of the slipstream tore at me, plastering the overalls solidly against my body and demanding careful premeditation to every slow, hampered movement.

Transferring my grip to a bar set in the side of the fuselage, I knelt down on the wing and reached behind the trailing edge. My groping hand found the ring, and as we passed over the runway again, I pulled it. The rope ladder obediently unfurled itself below the aircraft, fluttering venomously backwards in the slipstream. I fancied I could hear the crowd below catching its breath: for a second, they always think it's me falling off when I let go of the ladder.

Stick around, I thought. The next bit's where I fall off.

I pulled myself slowly upright and twisted round against the blattering, thundering slipstream as we ground past the crowd again. The gale pulled my cheeks back into a death's-head grin.

Then I started shuffling my feet gingerly backwards along the catwalk. As usual, I tried to tread on nothing with my right foot while I thought I still had at least a shuffle and a half to go. Nothing isn't very substantial. I bent my left knee, turned my right foot under the fuselage, and started groping for the first rung of the ladder with it.

The hazy horizon tilted in front of the nose as Ted banked for the next turn. I flexed my foot over a bigger arc.

Where was that bloody rung?

I'd just come to the conclusion that the bloody rung had dropped off, along with the rest of the bloody ladder, when my toes finally encountered it. I got it firmly under my instep and transferred most of my weight on to it. My left hip gave a twinge of relief.

A few seconds later I had both feet on the ladder. I moved them down a few rungs, keeping hold of the grab rail on the fuselage. The slipstream howled and shrieked in the earpieces of the crash helmet as my head came down to the level of the airflow over the bottom wing.

As we ground past the crowd again, I took my eyes off the horizon and twisted my head so I could look upwards at the rear cockpit. The sky and ground arced dizzily over as I moved, but vertigo was an old acquaintance and I was hanging on tight. The silhouette of the fuselage was interrupted by a leather-helmeted head as Ted leaned over the side to see whether I'd fallen off yet. He grinned encouragingly when he saw I hadn't, which is easy to do when you're firmly strapped into the bit of the aeroplane that was designed to accommodate you. I turned my attention back to the business of getting the rest of me on the ladder and down to the bottom of it before the muscles of the screeching wind sapped too much strength from the muscles of Holland. One of my nightmares is getting down to the bottom of the ladder too exhausted to get back up if the transfer should go wrong.

Two minutes later, after a lot of ultracareful hand-swapping, I was down there. I hooked both legs over a couple of rungs, locked an arm round another two, and told myself to relax. Myself remained unconvinced.

I could see the white faces of the crowd turned towards me as we passed in front of them at 50 feet. The field seemed near enough to reach out and touch. The wind howled evenly in my ears now I was out of the battering slipstream of the propeller. The colors of the fields and the big tents underneath seemed especially vivid as we wheeled around in a slow turn, the ladder swinging gently wide of the aircraft.

Risking vertigo again, I looked up at the Tiger ten feet above my head. From where I was it seemed rock-steady, fixed stationary in the blue background of the sky by the steady blattering of the engine, but I could feel the bumping and see the control surfaces making tiny movements as we growled through the turbulence. I looked forward again between the 2000-pound nylon ropes, and tried to ignore the nothing all round. The angled horizon bobbed gently—and then we were rolling out of the turn and the runway was ahead again. I swung to the left and then the right, a human pendulum, as Ted yawed the Tiger on to the exact centerline.

The snarling exhaust muted slightly and we sank towards the ground and the XK, which was waiting on the runway threshold. I could see Mark's face as he looked over his shoulder, judging our approach.

As the gap closed to 100 yards, his head swung round and the car lurched soundlessly forward, back end twitching and plowing twin tracks of wheelspin.

I shifted to a handhold that would let me drop away cleanly and unwound my legs from the rungs. From now on my continued existence depended on Mark's driving, Ted's flying, and my own judgment in timing the drop. I kept my feet on the bottom rung and shifted my hands one rung lower than they had been: that way I could let myself down and get a toehold on the car to stabilize myself before finally letting go.

As we passed over the car I was about 10 feet above the ground. Above me, the Gypsy barked harshly as Ted juggled the throttle to hold exact height and airspeed. I stared over my shoulder and watched the bonnet of the car creeping up.

The 100-yard marker flashed past the tail of my eye.

The bonnet slid beneath me, mere feet away, then dropped back.

The 200-yard marker. Come on, Mark, or we'll have to go round again.

The bonnet was underneath again, then the passenger seat almost below. I took a foot off the ladder and reached for the grab bar with my toes . . .

And the Tiger's engine stopped.

For a second I heard the bellow of the XK in low gear. Then the car braked. My feet thumped on the bonnet as it whipped away behind me. For an instant I hung on the ladder, staring up the runway. In the slow motion of disaster I remembered I must hang on until my feet hit the ground: it's height that kills you, not speed.

Hang on, then. Hang on. . . .

Numbing, thudding impact. Taste of dirt and grass. Dragged along. Flaying . . . *Let go, fool.* Fingers breaking . . . world turning wild somersaults . . . can't stop them . . . thundering crash on the head, sickening neck wrench. Crash on arm and hip, face ground into grass, fragments of glass in my mouth from broken goggles . . .

Rolling. Fingers bent back again . . .

Then suddenly, blessedly, everything still. Everything except the thundering in my ears and the wild rocking of the world as my jumbled senses struggled for balance.

Then a crunch like a lorry driving over a tea chest. The sound a wooden aeroplane makes when it hits something solid.

Blindly, the world still rolling, pitching, and yawing, I staggered to my feet. The wreckage of the Tiger was a hundred yards away, over the fence at the end of the field. The tail was sticking up. I saw a figure leap out and run clear.

The grass came up to meet me.

There was pounding in my head and the taste of blood in my mouth as I tried to rise again. I saw the man in the flowered shirt and sunglasses running with the rest of the crowd toward the wreckage.

Everything went black.

The first thing I knew was the voices. I was floating in a warm red-black limbo and everything was peaceful except for those voices, going on and on a long way away. Slowly, they focused.

"Give him room to breathe . . . doctor . . . on the stretcher . . . bleeding badly. Get him straight to hospital."

Hospital? I'd been to hospitals before. I hadn't liked it, any of the times. The loose, sharp pain of broken bones. The smell of ether and death. The thrumming of stitches going in. I didn't want to go. Best to tell them that. I tried to move and the effort sent a buzzing shaft of dizziness through my head.

I stopped trying. Perhaps I *ought* to go to hospital after all.

54

"Get him on the stretcher."

Gentle hands started moving me. I was interested, but didn't have the energy to help. Maybe I was dying.

"Am I dying?" My voice startled me.

"Don't be silly, son." Deep, reassuring words from somewhere in the red blackness. "You're only knocked about a bit. Don't worry about a thing. We'll soon have you back in shape."

It seemed I did have something to worry about, somewhere, but it wasn't worth the effort. I went to sleep again.

CHAPTER 7

The next morning at ten o'clock I stumped gingerly past the hospital reception desk, opened the door, and moved a few paces forward into a patch of sunshine at the top of the steps.

I ached all over from more abrasions and bruises than I had so far been able to track down. There was a whole new line of stitches down the left-hand side of my face and under the left eye, and an interesting tramline pattern of grazes running over the rest of my face. My left hip produced an all-time high in bubbly pain every time I moved. One day I'm going to thump my right hip and balance myself up.

Worst of all was my left hand. The thumb and index finger stuck out of a massive bandage which enveloped all the rest of the hand from the wrist downwards. I had three broken fingers in there, currently holding a contest to see which one could throb the most. I thought the little finger was winning, which it was entitled to do since it was nearly severed at the base and broken again halfway up, but since the pain was spreading itself generously over the entire hand and forearm, the question was largely academic.

56

I stood there in the sun, being careful to avoid moving anything that hurt—which meant just about everything—and watching the nurses going to and fro across the hospital quadrangle. Some of them were very pretty. A few of them looked curiously at me as they passed into the building. I didn't bother turning my head. That hurt my stiff neck.

After I'd stood there for five minutes, Ted arrived to pick me up. He had to be driving the XK, of course. I winced. The man has all the delicacy of a charging rhino. Among the Morris Minors in the hospital car park, the XK looked like a stripper arriving at a convent.

Ted was not quite at his best, but pretty near it. We might have lost half our aircraft in one week and he might have been worried to death about it, but he kept it to himself. The only visible evidence of yesterday's crash was a small piece of sticking plaster on his cheek.

I lowered myself carefully down the steps, and he bounded up to meet me.

"Hallo, Ken," he boomed. "How's me old mate Ken? You look as though you bounced all right again."

"Hallo, Ted. You all right?"

"Yeah, I wasn't doing any sort of speed at all. Nearly made the next field, but it wouldn't quite scrape over the fence. Caught me wheels on it, and it tipped the aeroplane in. I just caught meself on the compass, that's all."

I wanted to ask about the Tiger, and whether he'd found out what caused the engine failure, but first of all I wanted to get away from the hospital. I opened the passenger door awkwardly with my right hand and sat down slowly and painfully. Ted hovered over me, wanting to help but knowing from past experience that if he touched me he was certain to get hold of the biggest bruise I possessed.

We nearly made it. I had my right leg inside the car and was formulating a workable plan for getting the left in after it when the doctor came down the steps, white coat flapping and indignance all over his face.

"Mr. Reeves? I'm Dr. Arnold, and I must tell you that Mr. Holland isn't fit to be leaving this hospital. I've told him that I won't take the responsibility of discharging him. I'm asking you to bring him back in. He

57

ought to stay in for another two or three days at least.''

Ted narrowed his eyes, staring at the doctor, and appeared to consider. I continued Operation Left Leg, made it, got the door closed, and started groping around for the spare pair of goggles we carried in the car to make up for the absence of a passenger-side windscreen. Ted contemplated the bottom step judiciously, then raised his eyes to the doctor's face.

"I take it Mr. Holland discharged himself, then?''

"Yes. I wouldn't consider discharging him for a moment.''

Ted swung round to me. "Would you rather stay here?''

"No,'' I said. "I'm all right.''

"Okay, then.'' The piercing eyes swiveled back to the doctor. "You heard what he said. Ken's probably had more broken bones than you've ever treated. He knows whether he's fit or not. He knows when to change the dressing on his hand and when to go into hospital and have the stitches out. If I were you, mate, I'd let him sort it out.''

The doctor looked sandbagged. Evidently he wasn't used to people whipping patients away from under his nose. Ted walked round the car and got in. He switched on the ignition and looked up at the doctor again.

"Besides that,'' he said quietly, "he's got me to look after him.''

He pressed the starter, the engine *whoop*ed, and we pulled out of the car park with a little *squip* of wheelspin from the back tires.

Out on the road, Ted turned his head and gave me the benefit of his penetrating gaze.

"You really feel okay, Ken?''

"Yeah, sure.''

"Well, you say if you're not feeling well anytime.''

He looked back at the road. Subject closed—but not forgotten. I'd only got to go half a shade paler than usual in the next few days and Ted would have me in front of a quack before I knew what hit me. Those piercing blue eyes didn't miss a thing, and whenever I got hurt he watched me like a father. He was getting quite good at it: practice, I suppose.

The road to the airfield unwound, and the cold passage of air stung the scratches on my face. I wondered what we were driving back to.

"The Tiger's a write-off?"

" Fraid so. But the engine might be all right. It'll need a crack test, though. The prop was still turning when she went in."

That was a nuisance. In the eyes of the Air Registration Board there are two kinds of crash, enginewise—one where the prop stops and the other where it doesn't. In the first case they'll let you use the motor again after the crankshaft has been checked to make sure it's still running true; but if it was going round at the time, they insist on the engine being stripped for crack tests on the crank and rods, which is expensive.

It was unlucky that this prop should have been going round. If the engine fails due to fuel or sparks trouble—the usual causes—the prop keeps windmilling until you get down to near the stalling speed; then it stops. Ted had obviously been right on the stall trying to get over the fence; yet this prop had kept turning. Dead unlucky.

"Did you find the cause of the failure?"

"No. We haven't looked properly yet, though. Been a lot of other things to do. The Chamber of Trade people were all over the place last night, and we didn't get up this morning until just before I phoned you."

We turned into the airfield. "What are we going to do?" I asked.

"I don't know yet." Little lines of worry chased themselves across his face for the first time. "We can carry on with what we've got for a while if we modify the show a bit. I just hope the insurance people cough up okay. Losing two on the trot is going to play hell with the rates, but I don't see any way they can wriggle out of paying. We'll have to scrub the French trip, though, I think. That's about the only thing. It looks as if we'll be too busy sorting everything out to go on that."

Ted was more worried than he was admitting. There isn't a fortune in flying-circus work, and all our kites have to be underinsured or the rates would be ridiculous. So replacing two machines would make a nasty hole in us one way and another—and it might be months before the insurance came through on the wrecks. The fact that he was prepared to miss the French trip was a bad sign—we'd been trying for a long time to get some Continental contracts, and this was the first. If we didn't turn up it would be ages before anybody else booked us abroad again, if anyone ever did. It would depend upon just how much influence the outraged organizers of the Meeting Aérien de Lyon had on the rest of the aviation scene over there.

On the other hand, Ted was obviously remembering that we'd cut our quote to the bone to get the job, and a non-profit-making trip was something we needed right now like a hole in the head. Come to think of it, holes in the head we already had. My head, anyway.

We turned into the airfield gate and bumped up the entrance road. The workmen were taking down tents all over the place, which seemed to involve even more chaos than putting them up. The remains of the Tiger were partially covered with a big tarpaulin, with one of the top wings sticking out like the arm of a corpse that has gone stiff before it could be laid out properly. Our party was sitting around the small tents, drinking coffee and looking like the aftermath of Hiroshima. Mark opened the door of the XK for me, and I heaved myself painfully out.

"Morning, Ken," he said. His eyes wandered over my latest crop of body repairs. "I see you've bounced again."

No one grinned, least of all me. It was an old joke, dating from the time I tried wearing a padded suit and dropping off a very low-flying Tiger on to half a dozen old mattresses. Constant repetition of the phrase had worn it into a sort of good-luck catechism, but there were times when it seemed a mite out of place. Like the second time inside half an hour on this particularly stiff and painful morning.

"Anyone looked at the Tiger yet?" I asked. No one had. Furthermore, no one seemed particularly anxious to, which was hardly surprising. Everyone felt he'd had a gutful of broken aeroplanes of late.

"I'm going to have a look at it now," I announced. "I want to find out what made the engine stop. Gave me a nasty moment, that did."

I stumped off towards the shrouded wreck. John drained his coffee cup and followed me. By the time I'd made the 200 yards to the Tiger, my head was throbbing with piercing stabs. Each thump felt as if it was about to burst the doctor's needlework in my face. I felt sick and dizzy, and I could see the nearest workmen watching me curiously.

60

The Tiger was a mess, but nowhere near the sort of mess that Bill's Stampe had been. Both bottom wings were pretty maimed, but the fuselage, being metal-framed, had merely crumpled a bit instead of breaking up. The starboard engine bearer had snapped at the fire-wall bulkhead and the motor was skewed to the left. The cowlings were the usual mass of alloy buckled up round the engine, but a few minutes' wrenching by John had them clear enough for me to look at the works.

I spotted it almost immediately.

We hadn't had an engine failure at all.

What we'd had was the throttle rod coming adrift so that the throttle closed on us. That explained why the prop had still been turning when Ted went in: the engine had been ticking over happily and uselessly with a closed throttle.

I examined the linkage more closely. The throttle levers in the cockpits of a Tiger are connected to a rod which runs through the fire wall and moves a bell crank, controlling both the throttle and the magneto advance. The union between rod and bell crank consists of a clevis pin held in place by a split pin—and the clevis pin was missing entirely. It couldn't have been knocked out in the crash, so it must have dropped out in the air. Which meant, in turn, that the split pin hadn't been in place.

And that was more than bloody odd.

I straightened up and pointed silently at the rod, hanging guiltily off the bell crank. John bent down to examine it closely.

"That was it," he said. "The bloody split pin must have come out, and the clevis pin vibrated out afterwards."

I nodded absently: I was thinking hard, and it wasn't doing my headache any good. I looked back down the field, watching the workmen without seeing them. Their voices floated distantly across to me.

"Hey, Don," one of them shouted, "grab that bleedin' guy rope for Chrissake."

And all of a sudden I knew what I was going to do.

I was going to France to see our Auster. And to find out why a certain suave gentleman had tried to kill me.

Ted, understandably, was not very impressed with the idea. I waited until evening to bring it up, knowing it would be folly to introduce such a subject when he was preoccupied. He's the sort who says "no" to everything he hasn't got time to think out, and then it's hell's own job to make him change his mind.

So, feeling rather guilty for dropping it on him during the first time he'd relaxed all day, I waited until the dinner plates had been cleared away in the low-beamed graystone pub we had chosen for our final dinner on the Isle. The tensions of the last two days were beginning to evaporate from all of us under the influence of a few beers and a decent meal, and old Jedrow, who had been hanging around constantly, was helping to unwind the screws by keeping up a nonstop patter of humorous tales.

I waited until the old boy paused for breath, then said: "Ted, I want to take a week's holiday. We won't be on the go again for a fortnight, and I can't do much while I'm messed up like this. I'd like to have next week off, if you wouldn't mind."

Ted's eyes slitted into the familiar glare and swiveled on to my face like a pair of gun barrels. The silence was beginning to ache before he spoke.

"No, mate," he said slowly. "I can't let you go. We might not be working for a couple of weeks, but we can't have people buggering off when they feel like it in the middle of the season. We might get a film job, or anything—and anyway, I'll need you around because there's going to be a lot to do at Denham. Sorry, but you can't do it. I'm surprised you thought about it."

I leaned forward and brought up the big guns.

"Now, listen, Ted, I've got an idea how I can help us with my holiday. If I take the Stampe to France and have a few days' holiday there, I can drift down to Lyon for that air show there. If Rick and John load up the XK with enough for two or three stunts and meet me there with it, we can at least put in some sort of appearance. We're not going to get any more Continental jobs if we don't go at all, and you know it."

It made sense—up to a point—but Ted wasn't liking it. I knew why, too.

"You haven't thought this out, mate," he said gently. "It's going to take eight or ten flying hours to get to Lyon and back. That'll cost us over fifty pounds alone. Then there's the ferry fare for Rick and John and the XK, say another twenty-five, plus all your expenses out there—Christ, we won't get away under about two hundred pounds, whatever you do. And by the time we've finished apologizing to the people for not turning up full strength, we can hardly charge much more than that for just two or three stunts, now, can we? No, mate—we just can't afford it. Sorry."

Oh, well, I hadn't expected it to be easy. I prepared to play my best card—and then Jedrow's gravelly voice shoved its way in.

"Wait a minute, wait a minute, wait a minute," he said. "Do I understand that you want to take this aeroplane out to France, Ken, have a holiday, and do a bit of a show at Lyon?"

I nodded.

"Well, look here: you'll have an empty seat if you do that, won't you?"

I nodded again.

"Well, look here, Ted. Look here. I told you I wanted to go to France, didn't I? Well, how would it be if I paid all the flying expenses for this jaunt and went along with young Ken meself? That way you'd put on something of a show for these blasted Frenchmen, you'd cut your expenses right down, and we'd both get our holiday. How about it? Eh?"

I closed my mouth, since Jedrow had taken the words out of it. Sixty quid's worth of words at that—because I'd been just about to make exactly the same offer myself.

You had to hand it to the old boy—open cockpits for a holiday at 81!

Ted's screwed-up eyes stared down at the tabletop. I kept quiet, since anything I said would most likely harden his refusal. The silence stretched out for a couple of minutes. Finally his eyes unwrinkled and he looked up.

"Okay," he said. "You can do it that way."

BOOK TWO

CHAPTER 8

Jedrow and I took off from Lympne two days later. We flew over the Channel, keeping to the Light Aircraft Corridor, and crossed the coast a mile or so south of Cap Gris Nez. The sea and the cloudless sky merged into a vast white haze on all sides, with a milky blue roof and a wrinkled pale blue floor. Five minutes off the Kent coast I found it easier to fly on instruments than trying to imagine a horizon in the mist, and for the rest of the twenty-minute crossing the Stampe ground through a glaring white bowl a million miles from the rest of the world. I was glad when land showed up again: I don't like sea crossings in nonradio single-engine aeroplanes. From Cap Gris Nez we turned south and followed the coast to Le Touquet, where the control tower kept us running round the sky for ten minutes with furious light signals: revenge for me carefully forgetting to tell them we were nonradio when I rang up from Lympne before we left.

The customs men had evidently had a bad day too. A brace of the airport's nastiest specimens decided to search us from the ground up in case we were carrying a Chieftain tank in our spare socks. They didn't find a Chieftan—but there was much excitement when I declared one of the circus Sten guns. Producing my Firearms Certificate and pointing out that the barrel was semiplugged so it would only fire blanks failed to convince them we weren't about to start a revolution. They rattled away in French at full climb power, then popped us in a small cream room with a gendarme to guard us while they fought the telephone system to Lyon to confirm our story.

The gendarme was a young, eager-looking specimen who kept his hand on his holster and looked disappointed when I started dozing and Jedrow just went on being Jedrow. Probably he'd expected us to reach for the death pills as soon as the door closed.

I was quite happy just to doze for a while, though. I'd had a very busy couple of days, what with the flight back to Denham and all the preparations for the trip and the revised Lyon show. Only by going full chat from dawn to dusk had I been able to squeeze in time for sorting out Bill's belongings and a few other little things. I hadn't been able to find the papers relating to the Vivaral Auster, which was odd, but I did manage to see Bill's estranged wife and buy his share from her—so papers or no papers, that aeroplane was now mine. After that I'd done a little checking on a sudden wild hunch: I had a chat with the lads in the control tower at Denham, and later on found an excuse to whiz over to Redhill in the Tiger.

Then finally I'd shot up to London to see a back-street chum of mine, and come back to Denham via a couple of hours spent with a lathe and a short length of very ordinary-looking metal pipe in a workshop belonging to another chum in Watford. The collective proceeds of that round trip were currently stashed in the port undercarriage fairing of the Stampe— well away, I hoped, from the prying eyes of officious customs men.

The captured-desperadoes bit went on for about an hour, at the end of which the customs men returned, very disgruntled, with the gun. They'd checked with Lyon and found we *were* putting on a show there, so now would we kindly take ourselves, our gun, and our aeroplane away so they could get on with their work? I yawned, stretched, and ambled out on to the tarmac carrying the Sten and feeling like Ché Guevara. We got ourselves strapped into the Stampe—and naturally, the engine decided it didn't feel like firing on the air starter, so I had to get out again and swing the prop by hand. It coughed into life after about five minutes of sweaty effort, and I fully expected the undercarriage fairings to drop off as we taxied out. They didn't, however, and eventually we got a reluctant green light and snarled off towards Orléans-Bricy, our intermediate fuel stop.

We slipped down on to Lyon's vast runway at seven o'clock in the evening, and parked the Stampe on the grass amidst bustling preparations for the air show on Saturday. It took half an hour for me and my ten words of French to catch up with the show organizer, but eventually we collared him while he was directing the erection of the control tent. He turned out to be a fat, deeply tanned little man called Merlin.

M. Merlin had, of course, been told why half our troupe wasn't turning up, and he seemed disposed to take it out on me until he got a good look at my head and hand. The fact that I'd flown out from England in this state seemed to take the wind out of his paunch a bit, and in the end he became quite helpful. He fixed us up with a place to pitch our tent, arranged for us to hire a rather sad-looking Simca 1301, and even bought us a muscat in the airport bar.

At six o'clock the next morning the weather was crisp, bright, and sunny—which was more than I was. I ungummed my eyes and scribbled a note to Jedrow, who was very sensibly still asleep, telling him I was going to St.-Jean airfield to meet my Auster. Then I fiddled with the Stampe for a while, dragged my aches and pains into the Simca, and headed off south.

I got to Mt.-Vivaral just before eight. In the fresh brightness of the morning, it was the most beautiful little town I'd ever seen. Fourteen hundred feet up in the mountains of the same name, it lies in a tiny verdant valley, creeping up the mountainside a little at one end. The road from

Lyon stitches itself in Alpine hairpins over the hills, running past St.-Jean airfield, in the Saône valley, on the way. I didn't even pause at the airfield, but chugged right on up to the village, arriving just as the last of the morning mist dissolved in the crystal sunshine. The place was enchanting, the houses a light gingerbread gilding on the fresh green loveliness of the scenery. I trundled the Simca round the village square and started looking for street names.

CHAPTER 9

Vingt-huit rue d'Avignon proved to be a large, solid, detached house in a "good" neighborhood—not that they have any other kind of neighborhood in Vivaral—and M. Paul Sante, secretary of the Aéro Club de Mt.-Vivaral, proved to be a small, floppy man.

He was obviously a little disconcerted by the unexpected arrival of a secondhand-looking Englishman in the middle of *petit déjeuner,* but he ushered me into his orderly little study with a show of Gallic affability. At that hour of the morning the affability was probably sheer professional habit: a small plaque on the gatepost proclaimed him to be an *avocat,* and he had the jolly-uncle manners that all the shrewdest lawyers seem to carry as part of their stock-in-trade. He also had a brand-new Jaguar XJ6, the first French-registered one I'd seen, parked in his driveway. The law business must be good in sleepy little Vivaral.

We established that he *parle'*d *anglais* "a leedle," that I didn't desire coffee, and that it was *un beau jour.* Then I got down to business.

"My name is Kenneth Holland," I said, speaking slowly and clearly. "I was the business partner of Mr. Charlton, who bought an Auster from your Aéro Club a few months ago. Mr. Charlton has been killed, and I have come here to see you about the Auster.''

Monsieur Sante's mobile face registered sympathy and puzzlement together.

"I 'ave ear of the terrible tragedy of M'sieur Charlton," he said. "I di'n' know he 'ad a business partner, but I mus' extend to you my condolences over 'is death.''

I grunted suitably.

"But this Auster," he went on. "I cannot understand why you are 'ere. The men who buy the Auster from M'sieur Charlton 'ave already got 'ere, and soon they will be taking eet away. They are working on eet at the aerodrome two days, and probably today still.''

I sat back in the chair and absorbed that, trying to think fast and clearly. I'd half expected something along these lines, which was why I'd called on Sante at his home at sparrow-burp instead of tooling gaily on to the airfield during the day. Sante sat behind his solid oaken desk and watched my reaction, suspicion already beginning to edge out the puzzlement on his face. For all his rubber expressions and Gallic hand-waving, Sante was no fool.

I leaned forward in my chair. "Monsieur Sante," I said carefully: "These men who have come for the Auster are not the owners. I had a half share with Mr. Charlton in this aeroplane, and I certainly didn't sell my share to anyone. I have no reason to think that Mr. Charlton sold his share, either. In fact, I bought his share from his widow, so I am now the legal owner of the aircraft. These men have no right to the machine at all.''

It was the wrong thing to say. Sante's face closed up with an almost audible snap.

"But M'sieur 'Olland, I am afraid there must be some sort of . . . of mistakening," he said. "M'sieur Charlton did not mention a business partner to me. These men—M'sieur 'Unt and another man—they 'ave all the documents of the aeroplane. They 'ave the engine and airframe logs and the Journey Book I geeve M'sieur Charlton when 'e pay for the machine four months ago, and also they 'ave the customs clearance I send M'sieur Charlton only recently. They also 'ave a letter—a receipt, I think you say—signed by M'sieur Charlton to say they 'ave bought eet. 'Ave you any documents, please?''

I knew I was wasting my time, but having started, I had to plow on.

"These men got the aircraft documents by stealing them from Mr. Charlton's belongings after he was dead," I said. "If they have a receipt from him, they forged it."

I dug into my wallet and produced a hastily scrawled receipt from Jean Charlton. "Here is the only document I can produce: a receipt from his widow for his share of the aircraft, which went to her after he was killed."

It sounded weak, even to me. Weak the way someone had intended the truth to sound. It evidently sounded weak to Sante too.

"M'sieur, I am very sorry, but I don't think I am goin' to be able to 'elp you. If what you say is true, then these men 'ave committed a crime in England, and it is for the English police to . . . what is the word? . . . arrest them for it. 'Ere in France, I cannot do nothing. They 'ave come 'ere with the correct documentation for this aircraft, and I cannot see a way of stopping the deal."

I couldn't really blame him. From his point of view I was a total stranger he had never even heard of, turning up with a story that looked as though it might involve him in a tremendously complicated trans-Channel legal wrangle if he took any notice of it. I had no real evidence to back myself up, save one handwritten missive purporting to be a receipt from a woman he'd never heard of. There was no reason why he should have known that Bill was married. And I knew Bill hadn't mentioned me in his negotiations with the Aéro Club. If I'd been in Sante's shoes, I wouldn't have wanted to get involved with me either.

Without much hope, I had a final stab.

"I appreciate your difficulty in this, Monsieur Sante. But with regret I must insist that you at least prevent this aircraft leaving St.-Jean Aerodrome until the matter has been investigated by the English police. I am

73

prepared to go to the *gendarmerie* and request their cooperation. I give you my word that a fraud has taken place, and I must have time to prove it."

Sante looked unhappy, and treated me to an eloquent shrug of regret.

"M'sieur, I am sorry. M'sieur 'Unt 'as all the papers for the aeroplane. So far as we are concern, 'e is now the owner. 'E 'as even paid for the use of . . . what is the word? . . . 'angar space for disassembling the aeroplane at St.-Jean. I couldn't 'old the aeroplane because it is not now our aeroplane anymore. If you 'ave a case, the gendarmes will undoubtedly arrest . . . hold . . . the machine while the business is investigate. But me, I cannot do this. I suggest you go to the gendarmes, like you say."

Like hell I would. A man who doesn't speak the lingo is always at a disadvantage when it comes to convincing local cops of anything, and if I got them to move at all the Auster would be long gone by the time they'd taken me seriously enough to impound it. Besides which, I wanted to speak to this "Mr. 'Unt" without the law underfoot. It looked as though the interview with Sante was over.

"Very well," I said distinctly. "I shall do as you say, Monsieur Sante. You should be hearing from me or the gendarmes soon."

He treated me to a small worried smile and wished me luck: he didn't think I'd get far with the cops either. I stood up to go, and he rose to see me out.

At the door I turned.

"One other thing, Monsieur. Just to help me, would you mind telling me how long the Aéro Club has had this Auster, and who they bought it from? It may have some bearing on the matter."

Sante paused, frowning. Probably wondering if the information could possibly rebound and hold up the deal.

"The gendarmes are bound to want to know the background of the aircraft," I said helpfully.

After a moment Sante evidently decided that the information couldn't come under the heading of state secrets. "We bought it in 1957," he said.

"A man named . . . er, M'sieur Miere, I think it was: 'e fly it 'ere one day and is killed in an accident on the road the nex' day. It is *tragique*. The aircraft, she is registered in Spain. She belong to M. Miere and there are no relatives. By the time his—what is it?—his possessions 'ave been dealt with by the Spanish authorities, the aircraft 'as been with us a long time. There is a 'angarage bill, an' eet is no longer in its Spanish—er—like the Révision, whatever they 'ave. We make an offer to the Spanish authorities, and they accept."

"You had to give it a Révision Générale before it could be registered here, then?" I asked. The French Révision Générale is the equivalent to our own Certificate of Airworthiness check, or other countries' Annual Inspections: in all cases the aircraft is ripped apart, at considerable cost to the owner, in order to make sure that nothing has broken, is breaking now, or is thinking about breaking at some time in the future.

"*Mais oui*. We use the aircraft until 1965, when we are stopping using Austers as they come up for their *révisions*. It 'ave four *révisions* with us altogether." He opened the door for me, and I moved as far as the step.

"Thank you, Monsieur," I said. "You have been very helpful. You obviously have all the facts at your fingertips. I suppose Mr. Charlton asked you the same thing?" Holland being crafty.

"*Non*," he replied. "M'sieur Charlton did not ask about that at all. 'E was only interested in the work we 'ad done on the aircraft. But other people interested in our old Austers 'ave asked me not long ago, so I 'ad to look up our records then. There are a lot of people buying old aeroplanes now."

There were indeed. I wished Sante good day, collected another sad Gallic smile, and left, walking carefully round the XJ6.

Then I stumped back to the Simca as fast as my hip would stand, and hurled the car along the steep winding road out of the valley and over the hills.

Twelve minutes later I walked into a lonely café near the entrance to St.-Jean-sur-Saône Aerodrome; ordered a cognac; bought a loaf, some cheese, and a bottle of wine; and got back into the Simca. I drove along the dusty roads round the outside of the airfield until I came to the only clump of trees in the vicinity, parked the Simca as far in the wood as I could get it, and settled down to spend the day watching the field.

That Sante would telephone the airfield and tell them of my call was the most natural thing in the world. In fact, I was counting on it. It was one of the reasons I'd been to see Sante as early as I could.

And if that phone call flushed out a dismantled Auster on a trailer, I wanted to see where it went.

The day slowly unfolded from morning freshness to heavy anti-cyclonic heat. I sat with my back against a tree and fought drowsiness and the flies. The hazy sun beat down out of a blue-white sky and steadily jacked the temperature up to around 90 in the shade. At first I kept awake by swatting at the flies, but after banging my injured hand on the tree I gave that up and let the bites keep me awake instead.

Time after time I caught myself dozing. I'd drag myself upright, stagger around for a few minutes, then flop down again aching in every limb and pouring with sweat. When you've had very little sleep for about a fortnight there's nothing so exhausting as doing nothing on a hot day and trying to keep awake while you do it. My hand throbbed evilly, and as the hours wore on a tension headache wound itself up to pneumatic-drill pitch in the back of my head.

The morning dragged into a broiling, sultry afternoon. I realized foggily that I probably had a touch of infection in the cut on my head. My eyes refused to focus properly on the shimmering hangars, and the noise of aircraft came and went in waves.

The afternoon seemed to go on forever—but at long last the brassy sun sank down on to the mountaintops. The screaming heat climbed down with it, easing my headache and letting my eyes work properly again. The air remained still and humid, but after those ten terrible hours the relief from the hammer blows of the sun was like being born again.

Shortly after sunset the light faded rapidly, the way it does in the southern mountains.

Throughout the day there had been no sign of an Auster on the ground or in the air, and no one had left with a lorry or trailer big enough to carry even a model aircraft. The day's vigil had been a waste of time. The thought cheered me up like a dose of strychnine.

As the hangars faded into the gathering dusk I prized myself off my tree, stretched a few of the kinks out, and rinsed my mouth with luke-warm wine. Time to move.

Thunder growled over the mountains to the west as I stumped to the car.

CHAPTER 10

The storm, born of sullen masses of hot air trapped under a temperature inversion and nurtured by the orographic effect of the mountain range, cracked and grumbled its way nearer as I did my Red Indian bit round the hangars. The distant cu-nims bounced the last shards of day from the sides of the hills, adding an eerie purple tinge to the dying twilight. The air was heavy and electric, gathering strength for the storm. Forked lightning danced on the peaks as the clouds unburdened millions of volts of static.

I tried the two biggest hangars on the field and drew two blanks. The third one contained two bedraggled Austers in pieces, nestling behind a couple of big old Moranes and an immaculate Stampe. Investigation by cigarette lighter, since I didn't want to advertise my presence by switching on the hangar lights and I hadn't had the *nous* to bring a torch, showed that neither of the registrations was the one I was looking for.

The last hangar was the smallest of the lot—little more than a shed with just room enough for one aircraft. The air stirred and the first big drops of rain fell. I waited for a roll of thunder to cover any noise and eased myself in through a small side door.

And there it was.

It had its wings, tail, and undercarriage removed and was lashed down in kit form on a racing-car trailer all ready to be towed away.

Using my lighter, I examined it as best I could. It didn't look much—certainly not enough to arouse hot, covetous passions in the average *Homo sap*. The blue and silver paint on the fabric was cracked, faded and blotched with birdlime; thick layers of dust covered everything, smeared messily by the fingers of the men who had dismantled it. The cockpit, dimly visible through the grimy windscreen, had the musty look that only an aeroplane long out of use can achieve. Squinting into the cowling revealed that the engine had at least been roughly inhibited, but the wings, lashed alongside the fuselage, seemed to be in a very sorry state. The paint was crazed, and the fabric was ripped in all sorts of places.

Ripped? There was something odd about those rents in the fabric.

I examined them by lighter-light, cursing my stupidity in not bringing a torch as the blasted thing started to run out of gas. It gave me just enough light to examine several of the slits. They had all been made by a knife—and made recently, too.

When you buy an old aeroplane, it's not unreasonable to cut slits in the fabric here and there. They are easy to repair, and they enable you to poke an eye inside to have a look at the main structure. An ARB inspector will often ask for just such cuts to be made, so he can examine a spar or whatever. But there was something odd about these cuts. They were dotted around seemingly at random. Climbing on to the edge of the trailer and peering over the wings at the tail, stashed alongside the fuselage, I could see in the dying flicker of my lighter that similar cuts had been made there.

I stood there in the dark absorbing this for a while. The first tentative drops of rain had graduated to a steady, purposeful beat on the tin roof, and regular flashes of lightning were making sudden blue-white squares of the single window. Thunder rolled and crashed continually.

I was lucky to hear the small scrape outside in time to sink back into the nearest corner before the door started to open. The dark shape of a man came through, and he pulled the door shut behind him.

The Sten submachine gun has numerous advantages. It is cheap, rugged, and comparatively light to carry. It accepts practically any 9mm ammunition you can cram into the magazine, and deals it out at a cyclic rate of thirty rounds in 2.4 seconds. It suffers from the usual submachine-gun disease of hauling up and to the right as you fire it, but with thirty nine-mils between you and the aggravation, some small inaccuracy is rarely critical.

If you take the barrel out, a three-minute job, it turns out to be no more than a very ordinary-looking pipe about eight inches long. You can plug it and drill a tiny hole in the plug to give you recoil, and it will then become an ideal circus prop firing wadding-free plastic-nosed blanks made by Messrs. Parabellum. And if you know the right man in Watford he will get busy with his lathe and make you up a new, unplugged, barrel which can easily be hidden in the undercarriage trouser of a Stampe, ready to convert your circus prop into a lethal weapon whenever you have ten minutes to spare. Live 9mm ammunition to fit a Sten can be bought without a certificate from several of London's more unscrupulous firearm dealers.

Another advantage of a Sten is that when you cock it, it sounds like exactly what it is. It doesn't go *snick* like a menial pistol: the heavy piston group goes *ker-chook-wuk,* and commands the undivided attention of your audience before you even open your mouth.

It certainly commanded the attention of my light-footed visitor. When I pulled back the cocking lever, there was a sudden total stillness on his side of the shed. I could imagine him crouching rigid in the darkness, adrenaline pump running at high boost and brain slowly beginning to think again.

"All right, friend," I said softly. "Move over by the window."

Nothing happened. He didn't want to be standing in front of the only light source in the shed, even if it wasn't producing very much light. I heard a tiny rasp of cloth on cloth just as another peal of thunder cleared its throat before the full-scale bellow.

"Don't try it," I shouted.

The thunder crashed.

I fired.

The noise of the Sten in that confined space was earsplitting, although it probably couldn't have been heard 100 yards away beneath the thunder. The flashes lit up my opponent with a weird stroboscopic effect. As I fired above his head I had a slow-motion Charlie Chaplin impression of him diving for the floor, with something metallic coming up in his right hand. I stopped shooting and jumped aside, managing not to collide with anything. There was the flat *bang* of a heavy pistol.

He missed.

The thunder stopped.

The silence thudded on my ears as we both crouched motionless in the dark, trying to work out the next move. I let the tension build up for a while, then slowly turned my head and spoke into the nearest corner of the shed so he wouldn't be able to tell exactly where my voice was coming from.

"Friend, you have five seconds before I start raking your end of the shed with this gun. The only way you can stop it is to take your torch out and shine it very carefully on your gun hand. If it shines over here for the smallest instant I shall start firing. I won't count. You can add up to five as well as I can."

There was a deafening silence while he thought about it. The fact that he hesitated at all made him a very courageous man: he now knew I had a machine gun, and the characters in the world who will let their last few seconds of life tick away while they calculate the chances of beating an automatic weapon with a pistol in a darkened room must be very few and far between.

I meant what I said. I wasn't taking chances with this customer. My silent count reached five, and I was starting to squeeze the trigger when he spoke.

"All right," he said—quite calmly, in the circumstances. The voice was what the books describe as "cultured English." "Don't shoot. I'm taking my torch out of my pocket now."

I kept my finger pressure on the trigger.

"I've got the torch out now," he said carefully, "and I'm going to switch it on . . . now."

The torch snicked on, pointing downwards, and slowly moved until it shone on his left hand, which held a squat revolver pointing prudently at the floor.

"Now bend down slowly and put the gun on the ground," I told him. "Leave the torch shining on it. Then walk over to the window. Slowly."

He did as he was told, and I moved cautiously round the trailer, pocketed the pistol and perched on the wheel. I held the torch awkwardly in my bad hand, and shone it full in his face.

"Well, then, Mr. Haydon," I said. "Since you seem to want my aeroplane so badly, it's time we continued our chat."

Outside, the mummy and daddy of all cu-nims moved over the top of the airfield and let go its watery contents. Thunder rolled and crashed, and rain drummed down on the tin roof like an armored division on the move. I had to shout to make myself heard. Haydon's face remained immobile in the torchlight.

"For instance," I said, "you can tell me why you wanted this machine so badly. What's special about it? What's hidden in it?"

In the bad light I couldn't be sure if his face moved, but his silhouette certainly remained concrete. He said nothing. I tried again.

"You are probably imagining that I won't do anything to you if you keep your mouth shut." I had to shout over another peal of thunder. "I assure you you're wrong. In fact, I shall start shooting your feet to bits if you don't talk very shortly and lucidly."

The silhouette stirred slightly. But he was still a brave man.

"I don't know what you're talking about," he said evenly. "I bought this aircraft from Mr. Charlton, and I have the papers to prove it. You can't prove I was carrying a gun, and the police will certainly be very interested in you attacking people with that thing.''

This was getting us nowhere. I thumbed the firing catch of the Sten to Repeat. It made a *click* that was audible above the rain.

"Haydon, you tried to get me killed in a crash. You tried to steal my Auster. If you don't tell me why right now, I'm going to start shooting at your feet during the next clap of thunder.''

In the yellow light I watched him thinking it over, calculating his chances of making a break. He seemed to come to the conclusion, quite rightly, that he didn't have any.

Above the drumming rain came the beginning rumble of thunder. I lifted the Sten.

"All right,'' he said, speaking fast and clearly, "perhaps we can come to an agree—'' A crash of thunder drowned his words.

It nearly drowned the very un-stealthy opening of the shed door, too. Nearly—but not quite.

I swung round and a small searchlight caught me full in the face. The sudden movement cost me my perch on the wheel. I kicked out my left leg to stop myself falling and my hip gave way with a sharp stab of pain. As I fell I heard the crash of a gun and felt the hot whip of a bullet by my ear. I pulled the trigger of the Sten, aiming wildly at the torch coming at me from the doorway. Set on Repeat, the gun banged once. Out of the corner of my eye I saw Haydon diving from the square of the window. I thumbed the Sten back on to Auto and tried to bring it to bear. . . . Then something crashed into my head right above the stitches.

No pain. Just a sticky, jarring impact with a nasty distant quality about it. The torch beam in my face contracted to a pinpoint as a thin voice miles away cried, "Don't shoot, he's out.''

Then the blackness closed in.

It didn't stay closed in for long. Consciousness filtered back first of all as noises, the sounds of men moving around somewhere a long way off. Slowly they got nearer, and finally focused as feet scraping on the floor near my head. I opened my eyes. Darkness. Think about that. Must be lying on my back looking at the roof. I tried to move my head. The effort didn't seem to produce any result except an appallingly violent wave of nausea. I surrendered myself to lying completely still and thinking out what had happened. Thoughts weren't good for a man in my condition, but they were a lot better than moving.

Haydon had evidently hit me while I was trying to bring the Sten to bear on him. I didn't know what he'd used, but by the feel of it, it couldn't have been anything bigger than a double-decker bus. I seemed to have a slight dose of concussion: the nasty disjointed feel of everything and the sickness were all too dismally familiar. No breakout bids by Holland just for the moment.

For a while there was nothing but the sounds of the two men working, as they completed lashing the Auster to the trailer.

The waves of sickness came and went. My head started to throb very determinedly from deep down, as if it was setting in to ache for the next decade or two.

After a few aeons I heard a couple of ancient doors creak open. From where I was facing, which was upwards in a dark corner, I couldn't see a thing. But I felt the cold wet night come into the shed. Then an engine started up, making the flat muscular rumble of a low-compression petrol engine. When the vehicle reversed towards the shed I caught a familiar transmission whine. A Land-Rover, almost for sure. Nothing surprising about that. Good towing vehicle. Might have chosen it myself for the job in hand.

It backed up until the exhaust was beating strongly in the enclosed space, then stopped. There were sounds of the trailer being hitched up to it. Then the voices again, and footsteps coming towards me. I closed my eyes. The retinal color changed from black to red as someone shone a torch on my face.

" . . . leave him here," Haydon's companion was saying. "We'll have to do something with him."

"All right, we'll take him." Haydon's voice this time. "But we'll have to kill him and make sure no one finds him. I'm not leaving him on the loose. He's a nasty bastard. Get him in the Land-Rover and cover him up.''

Ungentle hands grabbed me under the arms and twisted me round. A great bubble of pain burst in my head, but I stayed conscious as more hands clamped round my legs just below the knees and I was lifted into the air. The pain rolled around sickeningly as Haydon and Co. carried me to the Land-Rover; then the world went into a inverted spin.

When I sorted that out, I was lying curled up in a heap, my legs bent under me and my head cushioned on my left arm. A damp tarpaulin landed on me like a ton of bricks, and the Land-Rover bobbed as someone jumped off the back.

The rain drummed like a funeral dirge on the canvas roof. I couldn't stay in that position, so I had another go at Operation Movement, beginning with a cautious attempt to shift my legs. The effort brought bile to my throat, but the worst of the nausea was backing down to give the headache a chance. I started to push my feet out from under me.

Then Haydon's voice came again, speaking softly and so close that I froze.

''It's coming towards us,'' he said. ''I think it's someone on foot with a torch.''

Another pause, another crash of thunder, and under its cover another stealthy attempt by Holland to unravel himself before the blood gave up trying to get round all the corners. The thunder stopped, I stopped, and Haydon spoke again.

''It's probably the airfield manager seen us moving out. If he'd heard gunfire he'd have sent for the police, and they wouldn't be walking towards us with one torch. Look, I'll go out there and talk to him. When you see the torch stop moving, give me a couple of minutes and then drive up to us. That'll give me time to talk to him—I'll tell him I was just coming over to his house to say good-bye—and when you drive up I'll just get aboard and we'll be away. Make sure Holland's still quiet. If there's any difficulty we'll have to get out any way we can, so be ready. With him in the back there, we can't afford to be stopped.''

The other man grunted, and I pushed my foggy brain into top. ''Make sure Holland's still quiet'' sounded as if Holland might be due for another crack on the head just by way of insurance. In fact, I expected Haydon's little chum to leap in the back of the Land-Rover and bean me with a gun butt immediately. But he didn't, so I waited for the next installment of thunder and dragged myself into a kneeling position under the tarp. The black world rocked, and a Gypsy Major started up in my head and ran on three cylinders.

The thunder stopped, and I heard a soft movement outside. I tensed myself for Holland's Last Stand, the tarp sliding down my back with a slithering crackle as I twisted to face the open tailgate.

No sign of a man with a blunt instrument.

I wondered what was keeping him. A flash of lightning lit up the opening at the back of the Land-Rover and revealed the Auster on its trailer hitched up behind. I waited for the thunder, and when it came I perched my backside on a wheel arch and slid a cautious eyeball round the canvas side. The rain drubbed on my head.

Nothing but blackness. Not even the torchlight Haydon had been so concerned about. Very confusing.

Then another fork of lightning zapped hungrily across the field and for a second the place was lit up with electric-blue brilliance.

I got a snapshot glimpse of Haydon's partner standing with his back to me about five yards away—and then the lightning was gone and it was blacker than ever. The rain thumped into the canvas with renewed vigor, and the crack of thunder sounded the closest yet.

I hesitated. Could I rely on the watcher outside neglecting his responsibilities long enough for me to stroll off into the blackness beyond hope of being found? It didn't seem likely—particularly since the way I felt I wasn't about to crawl very far, let alone stroll. But on the other hand I didn't really feel up to leaping on him unarmed and tearing his throat out, either. I was still cogitating blearily when the decision was taken out of my hands.

The patch of darkness in front of me suddenly became more solid, and I had a confused impression of a head and shoulders in front of me and a gun coming up. I made a desperate grab for it, catching it with the knuckles of my right hand. He made an unbalanced left-handed swipe to fend me off.

And, miraculously, the gun fell out of his hand. It clanged against the trailer tow bar as it dropped.

I dived off the back of the Land-Rover at him, and he threw a punch that caught me hard under the right ear. I fell on the tow bar like a sack of potatoes, head ringing and flaring with pain. The bar ground agonizingly into my back—and he landed on my chest. A bulldozer came down on my head and consciousness started fading. My left hand dropped behind the tow bar.

Straight on to the gun.

Punches rained on my head and neck, but I hardly felt them anymore. I was caught in an immense concrete mixer and I'd never get out again.

. . . Lord, just let it ease for a moment so I can get my finger into the trigger guard. . . . Bandaged hand fumbling, nearly dropping it—and then I had it. Finger in the trigger and thumb round the butt.

The world swam.

I brought the gun up to about the level of my ear and pulled the trigger.

There was a deafening *bang* and the man jolted under the impact of the bullet. He hit me full in the face—and I fired again, so close to my head that I felt the sting of hot powder on my cheek and all sound cut out under a dull ringing.

His weight came off me.

Then lightning flared again and I saw him silhouetted. He was still on his feet and reeling back towards me with his head tucked down like a charging animal.

Blackness again. In weary slow motion I transferred the gun to my good hand and fired as fast as I could into where I'd last seen him. I heard the bangs distantly, and in the gun flashes I saw him jerk as the bullets hit him.

The last time I pulled the trigger there was no bang and no thumping recoil. But by that time it didn't matter.

Consciousness coming and going in waves, I prized myself off the tow bar. Whatever Haydon was doing, he'd have heard the shots, and would be along hotfoot any second to find out What the Hell. I didn't want to meet Haydon with an empty gun in my hand, so it was time to be moving.

The question was, where to? No good running: I'd collapse before I got ten yards. I thought of searching the body for more bullets, or searching the Land-Rover for my Sten, but decided I didn't have time. Staggering drunkenly and grasping the Auster for support, I lurched my way round the back of the trailer and rolled underneath it. As a strategy it was about on a par with Custer's Last Stand—but at least Haydon might not think of me doing anything quite so daft. Anyway, I didn't have the energy to do anything else.

I was right about him rushing up hotfoot. No sooner was I more or less under the trailer than he arrived at a dead run. Careless of him—for all he knew he might have been rushing straight into the arms of the gendarmes, or worse still, me with a loaded gun.

He even had his torch switched on. I saw the light bobbing up and down as he ran, then steady suddenly as the beam picked up the body of his pal. I fervently wished I *had* got a loaded gun: in the reflection of the torchlight he was a sitting duck as he knelt by the remains.

He stood up after a moment, and the torch scythed around as he looked for me. I steeled myself for the inevitable discovery.

But instead of continuing the search he bent down again, picked up the remains of his partner in an awkward fireman's lift, and dumped him in the back of the Land-Rover. Then he jumped into the driving seat, started up, and drove off with his lights out as fast as a Land-Rover laden with corpse and Auster will go.

I was so surprised I didn't duck down quickly enough, and the rear chassis member caught me yet another crack on my long-suffering head as he pulled away.

The last thing I heard before I passed out was a deep *boom* from the far distance.

A grating voice was saying, "Ken. Come on, Ken" about twelve kilometers away.

I went through the depressingly familiar routine of floating up from the bottom of a morass, senses crawling back one by one, until I finally achieved a semblance of consciousness.

Everything was red. I tried to reason this out, but my brain wasn't up to thought yet, so I opened my eyes to find out firsthand. A torch was glaring full in my face. I shut my eyes again. The grating voice continued, more urgently, and a second later something passed between my lips. I choked and spluttered, sending stabbing pains up behind my eyes.

Scotch. Didn't whoever-it-was know that Scotch was bad for people with concussion?

"Don't give me alcohol," I said. "I've got concussion."

At least, that's what I tried to say. What with my general condition plus a throatful of whisky and a mouthful of bottle, it came out like the last bit of bathwater running away. Anyway, it achieved its object. The bottle was removed, anointing my neck with Scotch on the way.

A familiar gravelly voice said, "You all right now?"—and I recognized it. Jedrow. Little round ebullient wonderful old Wing Commander James Jedrow, DSO, DFC and Bar, MC.

"What the hell are you doing here?" I mumbled.

"Don't talk. We've got to get moving. Can't stay here all night, can we? Friend of mine's here in a car. We'll have to walk over to him. You lean on me. Okay?"

It wasn't okay because I didn't feel like anything nearly so energetic as walking. But on the other hand, he was right: we couldn't stay there all night. It was still raining like hell, for one thing.

He got to his feet and pulled me up after him. I hung round his neck and we lurched off across the black airfield with the rain beating down on us. I kept bumping against something hard in one of his pockets.

After what felt like ten miles we stumbled on to a concrete surface.

Jedrow's creaky voice bawled out, "Hulloa" as if he was summoning a pack of hounds after a fox. The sidelights of a car flicked on a few paces ahead.

I heard a door open; then another pair of hands grabbed me under the armpits, and a few seconds later I was inside the car. It was a big Citroën, and in the courtesy light I got a quick look at Jedrow's friend. He seemed to be a tall man wearing an old raincoat and a black beret.

I wondered vaguely who he was and what he had to do with Jedrow, and what Jedrow was doing here anyway and what the hard lump was in his pocket, and then the warmth and dryness of the car took over and my thoughts tailed off. I didn't even feel us start moving.

CHAPTER 11

I clung to the rope ladder with all the strength in my hands while the earth pinwheeled crazily below. I looked up at the spinning Tiger and Ted leaned over the side and said, "It won't come out until you've got back in." I tried to climb back up the ladder but it was flailing round on the outside of the spin and I couldn't do it and the ground was getting nearer. I hit the ground and the Tiger spun down on top of me, the fuselage getting bigger and bigger and finally hitting my head.

I screamed and woke up.

Consciousness came suddenly and clearly. I was lying in a white bed in a white room and someone was touching my head with something cool. The someone was a pretty girl with long black hair. She had deep blue eyes and a wide mouth. They were right after all: there *is* a Heaven. Then I remembered about me: if there's a Heaven, I won't be going to it. So this had to be old Mother Earth, in which case I ought to say something.

"Hello," I said. A brilliant opening, Holland. Doubtless to be followed by further stunning repartee.

"'Ullo," said the girl. "Keep still awhile."

She had a lovely voice, too. English spoken here with a delightful French accent. I kept still. She stopped touching my head, and I had a glimpse of a wad of blood-soaked cotton wool moving away and out of my field of vision. I watched her while she sat back and carefully fashioned a pad of lint, stuck it on two strips of plaster, and bent forward to place the result on my forehead.

"Where am I?" I asked. Stunning repartee didn't exactly describe it, but the point was beginning to bother me. If I was in a hospital there might be some explaining to do, in which case I'd better have a quick relapse while I thought out what I was going to say.

"I am Louise Lubec," said the girl. "You are in my father's 'ouse. You came with the Wing Commander an' my father. I fetch the Wing Commander now."

And without the smallest trace of a smile, she picked up a bowl from beside the bed and was gone.

I lay there with my brain in neutral. If Jedrow was here he would explain, and until then there was no point in my pounding the brain cell. It had been pounded quite enough of late. I looked round the room. It was clean and neat, in white with a cream ceiling. There were a few pictures on the walls, mainly landscapes. The exception was a painting of an aeroplane, a very accurate reproduction of a prewar Morane Parasol two-seater in Armée de l'Air markings.

Jedrow came in ten minutes later. He was wearing his usual baggy flannels and cardigans. I looked at his trouser pockets. No hard bulges.

"Hullo, young Ken," he said cheerfully. "You bounced again, then?"

I looked at him sourly. The aches and pains were limbering up as the last dregs of sleep drained away. I felt as if I'd bounced down the north face of the Matterhorn without missing a single pebble on the way. I dragged myself into a sitting position.

"I want to thank you for picking me up last night," I began.

He waved an airy hand.

"I also," I went on, "want to know how you found me and how you managed to get rid of the assembled company with such dispatch."

The old boy grinned from ear to ear as if he'd just bluffed me out of five quid with a pair of twos.

"I'll tell you how I came to be there if you'll tell me why you were after that chap Haydon with a machine gun."

I felt my jaw drop foolishly. So much for Holland the Cunning, with his gun barrel and ammunition stashed away in an undercarriage leg.

"How did you know about that?" I asked stupidly.

"Ruddy obvious," he told me cheerfully. "That thing could have gone in the XK—there was no reason for you squeezing it in the Stampe unless you wanted it for something special. Then it was gone when you disappeared yesterday morning, so you had to have it with you. And you could only have wanted it to have a pot at friend Haydon—quail's out of season here, y'know."

Ho, bloody ho. I sank back on to the pillows, trying to make head or tail of it all. I was in no state for cat-and-mouse stuff.

"Okay, Jedrow," I said. "I'll tell you my side, and then you can tell me what you know. All right?"

He gave a noncommittal nod and sat down on the edge of the bed, all attention.

"The main reason I was gunning for Haydon," I said wearily, "was because he murdered Bill Charlton."

That shook him. The remains of the grin dropped off his face and he looked as if someone had sneaked up behind and clobbered him with a sandbag.

"Murdered him? *Murdered* him?" He was getting the idea. "But . . . but Charlton died of food poisoning. You went to the inquest yourself. You . . . you . . . What . . .?" He ran out of words.

"He didn't *die* of food poisoning," I said. My voice seemed to come from a long way off. "He was only taken ill with food poisoning . . . he *died* in the crash." I paused for a moment to get it all straight in my mind, then carried on.

"I'll start from the beginning. When Haydon tried to buy that Auster

93

from me he offered too much momey—and he told me a lie. I didn't realize it while I was talking to him, but later on it dawned on me that he said
he'd got my name from the people at Vivaral—when he couldn't have.
They didn't have it. So then I wondered where he *had* got it from. I checked at Redhill and found he'd been talking to Bill there the afternoon of the
crash. Pete Haig at the Tiger Club said he'd seen a man of Haydon's description eating with Bill in the clubroom. That was when he slipped him
the poisoned pie: there's no other explanation.''

Jedrow held up a limp hand and said, ''But . . .'' in a weak sort of
voice.

''Shut up and listen. Haydon poisoned Bill and lied to me to cover his
trail. And after that he got at our Tiger and caused the crash at Sandown.
Split pins don't just jump out by themselves—I reckon he or his little
mate got busy with a pair of pliers when nobody was watching the kite.
Again it didn't click till later—but when I was looking at the Tiger after
the crash I suddenly realized I'd seen him in the crowd, hiding behind a
pair of sunglasses and a flash shirt. Watching to see if it worked, the
bastard.''

I stopped to let the old boy catch up. He had that sandbagged look
again. He swallowed hard a couple of times, trying to decide where to
start not understanding.

''But . . . *why?*'' he asked finally. ''I mean, if he wanted to kill you,
why food poisoning and an engine failure? Damn uncertain way of doing
it, eh?''

''Right. That's what I thought at first—that he was being bloody
clumsy. But then it occurred to me that he wasn't trying to *kill* anybody—
he was only trying to keep us out of France. Then it all made sense. Food
poisoning and a crash! Nothing suspicious about that. Just bad luck—but
enough to give us so many problems that we wouldn't go to France for a
while. Actually, it was bloody clever of him at short notice. I wouldn't
have thought twice about it if he hadn't cocked it up by making me suspicious with that lie and the big offer for the Auster. He must have made a
similar offer to Bill, and Bill told him he'd have to talk it over with me.
Maybe Bill was suspicious of him for some reason; I don't know. Any-

way, Haydon must have thought he might not be able to buy the kite, so he poisoned Bill as the first step in the delaying tactic. It was just unlucky that Bill got taken ill in the air and crashed.''

I found my voice had gone cold and hard. I cleared my throat and went on.

''To clinch it, the Auster's papers weren't in Bill's belongings. He wouldn't have lost things like that—so they must have been stolen. So I came out here expecting to find Haydon—and sure enough, he was here with the papers claiming he'd bought the machine from Bill. I checked with the secretary of the Aéro Club. So I went after him—and I had him treed until his bloody mate showed up. I was bleedin' stupid not thinking of that. And the rest you know.''

But he didn't know. I'd left him behind somewhere.

''Wait a minute, wait a minute,'' he said querulously. ''*What* mate? I only saw one bloke last night—where was this mate of his?''

I stared at him.

''I killed him,'' I said bluntly. ''I thought you knew. We had a fight and I shot him while you were distracting Haydon.''

Jedrow went white very suddenly.

''And now,'' I went on, ''I want to know where you stand in this. How you came to be searching for me with a gun in your pocket on an airfield in the middle of the night in a thunderstorm; what I'm doing here instead of in hospital with a copper sitting beside me—everything. Don't waste time hedging: I know you had a gun because I heard you fire it as Haydon drove off, and then felt it in your pocket while you were helping me to the car. So give.''

But he was in no condition to give, not right then. He'd looked sand-bagged before; now he looked as if he'd just caught the Simplon Express in the small of the back. He was silent for a long minute, staring down at the bedclothes while he tried to absorb it all. When he spoke, his voice was more gravelly than ever.

''One thing I don't understand,'' he said slowly. ''Why did you come out here yourself with a machine gun? Why didn't you go to the police about it?''

I almost laughed at him. Almost.

"Go to the cops? With what? I haven't got any evidence—none at all. The poisoning, the crash looked like accidents: like I said, Haydon was bloody clever. The only evidence was the missing aircraft papers—and when I was in England I couldn't prove he had them, and now out here I can't prove he didn't buy the kite from Bill like he said. I'm buggered all round.

"Besides which," I added slowly, "I want the bastard myself. He killed my best mate. Now I'm going to kill him."

My voice had got cold again. It seemed to come from a million miles away. Jedrow just looked at me.

"Yes, I believe you," he said softly. "I've seen people like you before, in the wars. The ones who turn killer."

There was an awkward silence. Not my day for winning friends and influencing people. I lay there and waited.

Abruptly he said: "Okay. I'll tell you my side. But I'll have to get Pierre in on it. I'll be back in a moment."

He hauled himself up and walked stiffly to the door, moving as if he was in the grip of some bad dream. For the first time since I'd known him he looked his age.

He was gone for nearly an hour. I spent the time hurting and drowsing. A bee buzzed angrily against the window, unable to understand why he couldn't fly out into the daylight beyond. I sympathized with him. I wasn't seeing too much daylight either.

I drifted off to sleep.

I was woken by Jedrow returning. He sidled into the room wearing a grim look and trailing a man who could only be M. Lubec. I had a faint recollection of his general features, but this was the first time I'd seen him in circumstances that could be described as moderately favorable.

He was a tall dark-haired man in his middle fifties with a cynical military look about him, as if he'd watched worse men being promoted above him and still resented it. His eyes were dark, and very still. The eyes of an interrogator. He was wearing a crisp open-necked shirt and sports slacks.

The still eyes examined me carefully as he fetched a chair from a corner of the room. He sat with his back to the window, so that his face was in shadow.

Jedrow perched on the bed again. "This is Monsieur Pierre Lubec," he said unnecessarily.

I engaged a small smile and thanked Lubec for having me in his house. Lubec just nodded slightly. Jedrow shifted his weight on the bed, cleared his throat, and looked unhappy.

"I . . . er . . . We've . . . got to . . ." He stopped, looking down at the floor and then round the room, as if seeking escape. After a moment he seemed to steel himself, looked me straight in the face, and made a fresh start.

"I'm afraid I've got to tell you that I might have been instrumental in Bill Charlton's death," he said.

I stared at him.

"You see, I caught him at Denham before he went to Redhill that day," he went on. His voice was low and serious. "I offered him three hundred pounds for the Auster. He said he'd have to speak to you about it. So when Haydon saw him a couple of hours later he must have wondered what on earth was going on with two people wanting to buy the thing in one day. He probably got suspicious, and let Haydon see it. So Haydon realized he wasn't going to be able to buy it, and poisoned him."

Now it was my turn to look sandbagged.

"You . . . *you* wanted to buy it? But why? What's . . . what's. . ?" My voice tapered off. I didn't understand any of it anymore. The whole thing was running away from me down a long, long corridor.

"I'd better tell you all about it from the start," Jedrow was saying. Well, that was an idea, anyway. "It's a long story, so you'll have to be patient."

I found I was propped up on my elbows. I sank back into the pillows. I had nothing but time.

97

"It starts about ten years back," he said. "I was living in St. Kitts, in the West Indies, then. Had a property business. I knew an old boy called Stefan Miere there. Bit of a recluse, but we used to play chess together and so on. Got to be quite good friends. Wrote to each other occasionally after I left the islands five years ago.

"I hadn't heard from him for a long time when suddenly, the other day, I got a notification from his solicitors. Poor old Stef had got killed in a road accident and he'd left me his house and some money and a sealed letter. Didn't have anyone else to leave anything to. It was the letter that started all this business—for me, anyway.

"In the letter he told me the story of his life, just about. I always thought he had the odd skeleton in his cupboard—he never talked about his past—but I never imagined anything like this. It seems he was a member of the Mafia in Paris before the war. You know what the Mafia is?"

I nodded. Who doesn't, these days? I probably knew a bit more than most, too. One of them wanted me to do a bit of smuggling, once.

"Well, old Stef said he'd been the *consigliere* of a big family in Paris in the thirties. You know what a *consigliere* is?"

I nodded again. It's a sort of second-in-command of a Mafia family. Jedrow looked round the room, thought for a moment, then carried on.

"Well, Stef married into this family before he started to work for them. He rose to *consigliere,* and had two sons. Then his wife got killed in a Mafia war in 1937. He said that after that he wanted to get out. He'd had enough. But you don't pull out of a Mafia family just like that. So he bided his time, and finally got his chance in '39.

"He said that when the head of the family thought there was going to be war with Germany, he decided to pull the family out and go to America. They sold all their businesses in Paris—he didn't say what they were in—and then they had the problem of getting all the money out. They couldn't just do it by banker's draft or anything because it was undeclared income. So they had to smuggle it out, and apparently the Don, the head of the family, decided it was best to buy works of art and antiques and

98

things. They were easier to shift than cash, especially since the franc was getting a bit rocky by that time.

"So one of the things they bought was a lot of collections of valuable stamps. Stefan, as *consigliere,* was in charge of the buying. He said he bought a lot in his own name, so that legally the family didn't come into it.

"And on the day when he was supposed to go to America himself, he ran off with them."

There was one of those silences. I shifted my bandaged hand to what I hoped might be a more comfortable position. Lubec just stayed still.

Jedrow coughed and went on.

"Well, he didn't get clean away. A couple of the family's *capi,* the sort of generals, got after him. Stef was traveling south, in a car, with his two boys. The *capi* caught up with him near Lyon and there was a gun battle. The youngest boy was killed, but Stef and the other lad got away.

"Stef was a bit vague in his letter about what happened after that. Apparently he stopped somewhere around here in the middle of the night to bury his son. He must have been nearly barmy with grief, because he divided up the stamps and buried half of them at the same time. He had some vague idea that if the family caught up with him again he might be able to make some sort of bargain—you know, my life for the rest of the stamps, that sort of thing. Anyway, he buried them and then carried on.

"In the end he made it to Spain. He changed his name to Miere and spent the whole war there, selling a few of the stamps he'd kept to keep himself going and pay for his son's education. Then at the end of the war he came to England, sold the remainder of his stamps in one go, and beat it to the West Indies. He liked St. Kitts—Christ knows why—so he stayed there."

Jedrow looked at the bedclothes again for a moment.

"The funny thing was, he never collected the stamps he buried in

France. He said in his letter that he didn't want to go near the little boy's grave again. I think he must have been a bit nuts, meself. Brooding about it, and so on. Anyway, he reckoned he had enough money to live comfortably from what he got for the stamps he'd taken with him, so he never went back for the others.

"They might have just stayed there in the ground forever—except for his other son, Roberto. After the war he sent Roberto to England to finish his education, and of all things the lad went into flying. There was no future for low-time pilots in England in the early fifties, so Roberto ended up back in Spain, where he'd spent six years of his boyhood. He spoke Spanish fluently, of course, and he got a job at a flying school and charter outfit near Barcelona. He was pretty successful—got to be chief instructor, and bought his own Auster.

"Anyway, one day he turns up on his father's doorstep in St. Kitts. Early in '57, this was. He said that the company he was working for was going bust, and he had a chance to buy them out very cheaply. He wanted about twenty thousand pounds. Stefan didn't have twenty thousand to spare by this time, but the lad had brought over the company's books with him, and Stef looked them over and thought the thing was a good investment. So he told the boy about the buried stamps and in the end the two of them flew back to England together. Stef stayed in London, and Roberto went back to Spain, then flew from there to St. Jean in his Auster. The idea was that Roberto would collect the stamps—Stef still didn't want to go near the place—and smuggle them into England in the Auster, and Stef would sell them in London. He knew quite a lot about the stamp market from selling the first lot.''

Jedrow stopped talking for a moment. His gravelly voice was getting hoarse. He took a few deep breaths and cleared his throat. I lay still and waited.

"Well, the boy got the stamps from their hiding place all right. He sent Stefan a telegram saying so. Then the next morning he was knocked down by a car right outside the aerodrome and killed.

"Old Stefan didn't know anything about it for ten days. He was nearly mad with worry. The boy had never told anyone about his father, just in case things ever went wrong with Stefan, so no one knew about him to notify him as next of kin. In the end Stef went over to France himself to find out what had happened. At first he thought the Mafia family might have caught up with Roberto, though he couldn't think how. But it turned out that the accident was just that—a genuine accident. They'd buried Roberto in the local churchyard. Stefan looked in the old hiding place and in the hotel Roberto stayed at, and he even had a quick look in the aeroplane, but he couldn't find the stamps, so he gave up and went home. He didn't care about them anyway, he said. He was ill for a long time after that.

"Anyway, so far as he was concerned that was the end of it. He said he had intended to let the story die with him, but in the end he decided to let me know after his death so I could have a search for the stamps if I wanted to. He said that as far as he knew they'd never come on to the market again, so he reckoned they were probably hidden in the aeroplane. He never claimed it or anything. He sent me a list of about a hundred of the stamps that he could remember. He said there were about two hundred and fifty all told."

Jedrow stopped for breath again.

"I checked with Stanley Gibbons and one or two other London firms," he went on, "and from what they told me it looks as if the ones Stefan named, alone, are worth something over a million pounds on the open market today."

There was a long silence, led by Holland. The bee had given up butting its head against the window and was crawling around on the ledge looking stunned.

A million pounds sterling. I saw a lineup of Stampes and Jungmeisters and Pitts Specials and First War replicas. Big tents with static displays. Ambling round the world during the off season. A Ford GT40 for getting about and a D Type Jaguar for sunny Sundays . . .

Slowly the pictures dissolved and I was back in the little white room. Jedrow and Lubec were both watching me: Jedrow looking interested in my reactions and Lubec just looking.

"Now I see it," I said slowly. "You traced the aeroplane, found the Vivaral Aéro Club had got it but had sold it to Bill, and went and saw Bill. Yes?"

"Yes, that's right." Jedrow looked unhappy at the mention of Bill again. "I got Pierre here to help—we'd worked together in the War—and we had a look at the machine. We couldn't find anything in any obvious places, so we thought the only thing to do was to buy it and take it apart piece by piece."

"I see." I was slowly coming out from under the ether of a million-pound dream. "So why didn't you tell me this before? It's *my* bloody aeroplane, for Chrissake."

Jedrow looked even more uncomfortable. It was Lubec who answered, in correct, slightly stilted English.

"We didn't know what to make of you, Ken," he said. "When you refused to sell the aeroplane to Haydon at a handsome profit we thought you must know something about the stamps—but if you *did* know about them, we couldn't understand why you hadn't done something about it before."

The planes of his face were hard, with the light behind him. It was impossible to see his expression.

"You see," he went on, "we knew someone else was after them. Someone had been to see M'sieur Sante, the Aéro Club secretary, before we did. And then Haydon made that offer to you. We didn't know how they knew about it or how many different people there were, or whether you were one of them or not. We didn't know anything. There was nothing we could do about Haydon—but you seemed happy to let Jedrow come along with you, so we thought that was the best thing to do. For Jedrow to come along and keep quiet and see what happened. But when you were away all of yesterday, with the machine gun with you, we got worried. So we took my gun and came to look for you. We found you, too. Jedrow was most brave, shooting at your friend Haydon."

I nodded wryly to Jedrow. "I'm most grateful," I said. "But if you'd told me what was happening before that it wouldn't have been necessary —and we might still have the bleedin' aeroplane." Only might, of course. I'd probably have found some way to screw it up even if I had known the whole story.

There was a long silence all round. Jedrow was thinking and I was thinking and Lubec was just sitting still.

"I guess we have to face it," I said eventually. "The opposition is Miere's old Mafia family."

If I'd expected a big reaction I'd have been disappointed. Jedrow just nodded his head glumly and Lubec smiled his cynical smile.

"We think the same thing," he said. "There really isn't anybody else it could be."

There was another of those silences. I thought about the stamps. A little box or packet worth a million pounds hidden in a rotting old aeroplane. *If* we could find it again. And, come to think of it, *if* we could sell them if we *did* find it.

"Hey," I said. "What about the ownership of these stamps? Don't valuable stamps have to have pedigrees and histories or something? Can we get rid of them if we get hold of them?"

Probably a stupid thing to worry about, since we didn't even know the whereabouts of the Auster, let alone whether they were really in it, but one has these silly thoughts at times.

The same silly thought had obviously occurred to Jedrow.

"We'd be all right there," he said. "Remember, they were bought in Stefan's name. His old name, actually—Fiore, it was. There won't be any trace of Fiore after 1939, so no one's going to be in a position to shed doubts about a claim of ownership arising now.

"He wasn't a blood relation of the Mafia family—he only married into it. All the stamps in the collection that could be identified individually are believed by philatelists to have been lost during the war. If we get them we must have them checked and authenticated by a committee of experts like the Royal Philatelic Society. We'll also have to think up a damn good watertight story about how we got hold of them, too, 'cause the Scotland Yard Philatelic Squad check into the background of stamps that turn up like this with a fine-tooth comb. But since they were never reported stolen, and the last known legal owner is dead or disappeared, we

103

should be all right if we're careful. We could probably tell the truth to some extent, actually: say you found them in the Auster and leave out the bits about the fighting and so forth. I can't see the Mafia people being able to kick up a fuss: after all, what sort of evidence could they produce?''

I didn't have any answer to that, although from what I'd heard of the Mafia a little thing like legal evidence wasn't likely to stand in their way. Still, if they didn't even know what the stamps were it was difficult to see what they *could* do: they could hardly stick a gun in the back of every stamp seller in the next five years on the off chance that he might be pushing *the* stamps.

If they didn't know what the stamps were. I wasn't convinced about that.

I tried another angle.

''Anyone got any ideas about *how* they got on to it?''

No one had, of course. More pensive silence. The bee was sitting on the window ledge peering out at the hills beyond. Probably thinking about the mystery of glass.

After a while, Lubec shifted his position.

''The question is,'' he said, ''what do we do now?''

I didn't know. Nobody knew. We talked it over for a while and reached the profound conclusion that the only thing we could do was find the Auster again.

Unfortunately, no one had any constructive thoughts on how to go about it.

We chewed the problem over for an hour, until the pain in my head and hand put an end to our fruitless cerebrations. Then Jedrow left Miere's letter with me, and they tiptoed out as I slipped into half-consciousness.

The last thing that penetrated was Lubec telling me that I mustn't mention anything to Louise.

CHAPTER 12

I stayed in the blackness until Louise brought me coffee, *croissants,* an omelette, and fresh bandages the next morning. She bustled about cleaning up the room while I ate the omelette, then changed the bandages with hardly a word. I guessed her smile must be very nice, but since she didn't choose to exercise it I didn't have the opportunity of finding out firsthand. I wondered vaguely why she was so hostile, but no glaringly obvious reason presented itself. Anyway, her medical care, as before, was professionally deft.

After unsticking the bandage from my head with lukewarm water, she peered closely at the gash and said I ought to have the stitches out. I said go ahead, and she produced a pair of nail scissors and started in on them.

Stitches are funny things. Sometimes they come out with a slight *thrum* and that's that, and sometimes they hurt like hell. Maybe they hurt if you don't take them out at the right time: if that's the case, this wasn't the right time. They hurt like hell. Probably been there a bit too long.

Even with Louise's practiced touch, each one was a red-hot needle in my head. I could feel the blood running, and Louise had to keep dabbing it away. The pain made my eyes water, but with so much cold unfriendliness around I wasn't going to say anything. After about two centuries she was finished. Fourteen bloody little wisps of catgut, or whatever they use nowadays, lay in the enamel bowl beside the bed.

Then she bandaged a new pad to the swollen wound, packed up the medical supplies with efficient little movements, and left the room. I felt unaccountably lonely.

After a while I started to read Miere's letter. Reading between the lines of his old-fashioned English, I felt quite drawn to the poor bastard. The thread of loneliness weaved through his words as clearly as if I'd seen him myself, hunched up alone over a desk in his beautiful house, writing to his last friend, who was 4,000 miles away.

I could also see the man, thirty years before that, crying tears of desolation as he dug into the good French earth to bury his little boy. The despair of the years of waiting in Spain. The liberation to the West Indies and at the same time a shutting-away of all his past. The reopening of old wounds and fears when his remaining son needed money. The courage he had to find to leave his comfortable shell in St. Kitts to help his son sell the stamps—and then the final agony of Roberto's ironic death and the lone fight with depression after the blind, automatic journey back to his island.

It took me an hour to read the long letter, and at the end of it I was convinced that the story was true. All of it. I'd have believed it even without the corroboration of Roberto's death. Old Miere was certainly a bit unbalanced by the years of solitude, but nobody reading that letter could have doubted the truth of it.

After reading the letter I turned my attention to the list of fugitive stamps that Miere had provided. It wasn't complete—he said there were about 150 he couldn't remember the identity of. But the 100 or so he described, even in the stilted phrases of the stamp world, made impressive reading. Whoever his Mafia family were, they'd plenty of money—but then that wasn't surprising. Miere's family would have been the genuine article—dyed-in-the-money secret-society characters probably straight out of Sicily, much more dangerous than the blurred mixtures of genuine

Mafia and latecoming Italian Cosa Nostra families you get around nowadays. I wasn't looking forward to running into them again.

The most valuable item in the collection was an 1847 "Post Office" Mauritius penny and twopenny in a mint-condition unsevered pair. Jedrow had added a scrawled note in the margin to the effect that the most expensive single philatelic sale on record was some guy in New York buying a folded letter with a twopenny Post Office Mauritius on it for a cool £158,000. Christ knows what that made this pair worth; Jedrow's scribble said that some London dealer had estimated about £120,000 at auction. The world has a funny sense of values sometimes: that little scrap of gummed paper would not only appreciate as time went on, but would always be far more stable than any of the world's currencies.

The next one was only worth a humble £80,000 or so. This was a used block of four 1851 Canadian twelvepenny blacks. At roughly the same bidding were a Ceylon 1857 fourpenny "dull rose imperforate in mint block of four" and a French 1869 five-franc gray in "mint tête-bêche pair." Jedrow had scribbled that "tête-bêche" meant an unseparated pair joined vertically and with one of the pair inverted. A sort of cross between mirror-formation flying and *soixante-neuf*.

Then there were a British 1869 "sixpenny mauve, plate eleven, used," which was estimated at £25,000; a Hawaiian Islands 1851 "Missionary" three-cent red unused which might fetch £60,000; and a Western Australia 1854 one-shilling brown "with centre inverted" weighing in at another £15,000-odd. Barbados contributed what was described by Miere as an "1878 mint pair 1d on half of five shillings with surcharge double, one inverted." Jedrow's notation explained that these were five-shilling stamps perforated down the middle and overprinted on each half to be used as penny stamps. The double surcharge and inverted bits meant some clot had overprinted each side twice by mistake and then compounded the error by printing the "1d" upside down on one side. He may have got bawled out for it in 1878—but the stamp was worth about £15,000 now.

Of the 100-odd that Miere remembered, 35 or 40 were reckoned to be worth over £10,000 each on today's market, and the rest anything from about £5,000 downwards. Miere mentioned that those he couldn't remember the identity of were the least valuable, but added that the lowest price he paid for any item when he was buying was the equivalent of about £300 sterling. And that was before the last war. . . .

All in all, quite a collection of miniaturized king's ransoms. And I still didn't have the slightest idea how to get my hands on them.

That evening, Friday, Jedrow and Lubec came to the bedroom for another conference. We all hoped the others might have had some ideas—but nobody had. We kicked the thing around for half an hour and in the end degenerated into wondering what we were going to do tomorrow. That much, at least, I'd thought out.

"I'm getting up," I said. "Rick and John have either arrived or will be arriving tomorrow morning, and we've still got a circus performance to do. We'll have to tell them something to account for these"—I indicated the new cuts and bruises and bandages—"but that shouldn't be too difficult. Christ—with my record of late it'd probably take more explaining if I *hadn't* had some sort of prang since they last saw me."

The others seemed shocked that I should think of such a thing as work at a time like this—but since it would only create unnecessary complications to back out of the Lyon show now, we eventually agreed that Lubec would run me out to where I'd left the Simca at nine o'clock the next morning. Jedrow raised a halfhearted objection on medical grounds, but it wasn't he who was bent, so I soon dealt with that.

After the conference Louise brought me a steak, a small bowl of salad, and a cup of coffee. She also carried fresh bandages, scissors, and the enamel bowl for the debris of the old dressings. She evidently wanted to get me all over and done with in one go, because she sat in a chair beside the bed, waiting while I ate. She hardly said a word: just sat there, looking at her hands in her lap, while I picked awkwardly at the meal with my one operational paw. She was wearing a pair of faded skin-tight jeans and a white tee shirt. Even in the pale electric pool of the bedside lamp, the contrast between the white shirt and her black hair was very attractive. In fact, she was very attractive all round.

Eating with one hand while lying propped in bed is an awkward business. It took me some time to finish the meal, and by the time I got round to tackling the coffee the stony silence was getting on my nerves. I may not exactly be Buckinghamshire's gift to Continental girls—or any other girls, come to that—but I don't have two heads or anything, and I couldn't imagine what I'd done to engender such obvious dislike.

"How old are you, Louise?" I asked.

She almost jumped at the sound of my voice. She looked at me quickly, then down at her hands again. "Twenty-two," she said.

Try again. I felt ridiculous making such an awkward attempt at conversation with someone who was so familiar with my injuries and weaknesses. "Did you cook this, or your mother? It was very good."

"I did it. My mother died ten years ago. Give me your left hand."

I gave her my left hand and shut up.

She gently removed the bandages and the little aluminium channels that were splinting the broken fingers. Sitting on the bed, she bent her head and peered closely at the fingers. Looking for irregularities in the mending, I suppose. Gentle as she was, the hand hurt like hell. I winced, and clenched my right fist.

She said, "Sorry" without looking up.

"You must be a nurse," I said. "You obviously know what you're doing."

The black hair bobbed slightly, but she didn't look up.

"Yes, I am a nurse at the Clinique St.-Junien in Paris. I am on holiday now."

"Hell, I'm sorry. This is no kind of holiday for you, having to look after me."

She said, "That's all right" without looking up. It obviously wasn't all right. There was more silence. She started binding my fingers back into the splints. Gently, professionally.

I said softly, "Why do you dislike me so much?"

This time she looked up. "I don't dislike you," she said coldly.

"Oh, for Christ's sake!" I was beginning to get irritable. "You obviously can't stand the sight of me. I don't blame you—I don't like myself much sometimes—but what have I done to you?"

This time she looked straight into my eyes. I said, *"Ugh"* right from my stomach as she involuntarily jerked the bandage slightly.

"All right," she said softly. "I'll tell you why. My father an' the Wing Commander brought you 'ere when you 'ad been in a fight. The Wing Commander 'ad a gun. I saw it. I say you need to go to 'ospital, but my father told me to look after you 'ere. There is much talk, but no one tells me what is 'appening. I only know that I never see my father like this before. An' you are the cause of it. I don' know what is going on, but I think my father is going to be in danger. So I am sorry if I cannot like you."

She bent her attention back to the bandage, pinned it neatly, then started unwinding the turban round my head. The only sounds in the room were the rustling of sheets as she moved and the creaking you get inside your head as the dressings come off. After a decent interval, during which Louise poked gently at the wound, I tried again.

"Look, I'm afraid I can't tell you what's going on. It's better that you don't know." I winced at the melodramatic sound of that, but it was true. "But I give you my word on this: your father was involved before I came along, and my being here hasn't increased any danger there might be.

"Also," I added lamely, "I promise that he won't come to any harm if there's anything I can possibly do to stop it."

I *always* say the wrong thing to women.

Louise stopped inspecting the holes in my head and looked straight at me again. Her face was inches from mine.

"I don' believe you," she said. She still spoke softly, but there was real hurt and anger in her voice. "You're worse than my father and the Wing Commander. You'll take chances they'd never take by themselves. They're both much older than you, but that won't mean a thing."

I started to say something, but she cut me off.

"I'm a nurse in Paris," she went on, her voice rising. "I know a little about people. I've seen your body, an' I know how you've hurt it. I know what you do, because the Wing Commander told me. And I know that normal people don' live like that. Normal people are more glad to be alive than to be so . . . so careless with their bodies. When I change your dressings you're not interested in the injuries, in the scars you're going to have. To you, your body's just a machine, and you don' care about it so long as it keeps running. I don' like people like that. They are too ruthless, too uncaring. You don' care about other people, either. I overhear the Wing Commander tell my father that you killed someone that night. But it didn't affect you at all. You'll kill again if you think you need to, and you won't give it a second thought. You're cold—you're completely cold!'' Her voice caught for a moment.

''An'—an' now you're going to have my father with you,'' she finished quietly.

I was thunderstruck. Was that *really* the way she thought of me? Did everybody see me like that? Janie's words came bubbling up from the past. *''There's some quirk in you . . .''*

Louise avoided meeting my eyes. She padded a piece of lint under a folded bandage and stuck it on my forehead with two strips of Elastoplast. Then she was finished. She got up off the bed, put the enamel bowl on the food tray, and cleared up the stray bandages. I could think of nothing to say. She reached the door and balanced the tray awkwardly on one knee while she dealt with the doorknob.

''Louise,'' I said quietly. She stopped fumbling with the knob and turned her head slightly, not looking at me. Her black hair rippled on her shoulder.

''Thank you for what you've done for me.''

It was all I could think of to say.

Her shoulders gave a tiny shudder and she left the room.

It was a bad night.

While I was asleep, Janie came to me. She'd left a little note for me, the way she sometimes used to if I was still asleep when she got up for work.

It said "Ken, I love you. Janie." Just that. I spent a lot of time during the day planning something special for the evening. We went and saw *Hair* and then went and ate at that place with the bits of old coaches in it at the Aldwych. Then home and slow, warm love.

I woke up from the happy cocoon at three A.M.

I lay there for a while, semiconscious, reaching back for sleep and the dream again. In the end I got up, switched on the light, and found my trousers. The fraying piece of paper was still in my wallet.

"Ken, I love you. Janie."

I looked at it for a while. It was a real note. The night at *Hair* and the restaurant had been real too. I got back into bed with the note in my hand, turned the light off, and sat up against the pillows smoking and remembering. It was opening the wounds again, I knew—but then, they'd never closed anyway. In the morning I was going to regret it, but now, in the still of the sleepless night, I couldn't stop myself. My memories were the only things that brought any relief, however temporary, from the loneliness. With the note in my hand, I drifted away in a dream. Her voice, her touch filled the empty night in my mind.

I dozed.

When dawn lightened the window I was still propped up on the pillows. The note was still in my hand. My private world curled at the edges, then became fragmentary.

I found my wallet and put the note away beside her picture.

CHAPTER 13

The scene at Lyon-Bron Airport was typical morning-before-an-air-show chaos. Last-minute preparations are the same the world over—except that the French are noisier about it than most. I drove in through an eastern entrance, which had been specially opened for the Pageant so that the air-show crowds would stay on the far side of the main runway and not contaminate the terminal to the west, and threaded the Simca gingerly between the gangs of men picketing the last rope barriers and marquees. Several people shouted, *"Passez pas par ici"* at me, but I shouted back in nonsensical English and kept going. I was in no condition for walking.

After doing half a lap of the grass area I finally came upon the control tent. Lyon-Bron has a perfectly good modern tower over to the west of the field which would be controlling the aircraft during the show, but the real nerve center would be this little tent. The announcer would be sitting outside it and the tower would take their cues from his words, relayed to them by radio. The main runway at Lyon is a big, wide strip of concrete over 8,000 feet long, running roughly north and south. The tower and the terminal buildings are to the west of the runway, and to the east is a grass area containing a grass runway running parallel to the main one. Today

113

this grass area had been taken over by the Meeting Aérien: new entrances had been opened via the old perimeter tracks to the east, and the area was a stormy sea of excited Frenchmen, ropes, canvas, and color.

I got out of the car and breathed it all in. The day was heating up, and in spite of a limp breeze from the south the distinctive tang of all air shows was already hanging over the field. A mixture of mown grass, oil, petrol, and slowly cooking garlicky hamburgers and hotdogs. The nostalgic hot-oil-on-doped-fabric taint of old aircraft. Voices raised in exasperation. Sweating organizers with red harried faces trotting from crisis to crisis, their OFFICIEL armbands endowing them with demigod powers and cares for the day. Teen-agers in charge of parking waving their arms importantly at taxiing aircraft.

The sweet, even blatter of a Siemens Halse radial as a Jungmeister taxied past drowned the uninteresting drone of arriving Cessnas and Jodels. A purposeful buzz-saw growl made me look up in time to see a black-and-gold Zlin Trener-Master making a long flat approach on its back. It turned lazily right-way-up at the last moment and touched down gently. I read the registration letters: G-ASIM. That was Neville Browning*—as if I needed any confirmation after watching that approach. I was surprised to see the 70-year-old Grand Master of aerobatics at Lyon. Although he was a familiar star turn at air shows in Britain, he didn't often stray this far from his farm in Essex.

I grinned to myself and breathed deeply, shaking off some of the anguish of the night.

I was home.

I found M. Merlin, the show organizer, in the tent. A notice hanging outside said that crews and controllers must assemble for final briefing at 1200 hours GMT. M. Merlin was sweating profusely and arguing loudly in high-speed French with a group of men who looked like fliers. He broke off when he saw me in the entrance, and his face telegraphed an interesting mixture of relief and anger as he bounced clear of the group.

---

*Neville Browning died in his Zlin when he crashed while flying inverted at an air show in 1971. He was nearing his 71st birthday. There will not be another.

"M'sieur 'Olland!" he exploded. *"Mon Dieu!* Where 'ave you been? No word, no notheeng! I 'ave been distracted! I . . . I . . . ." Words failed him.

"I'm terribly sorry, Monsieur Merlin. I was taken ill at a friend's house." I touched the plaster on my head significantly.

Merlin immediately kneaded his rubber face into concern and sympathy.

"But you are well now?" he asked anxiously. "I don't want you to fly if you are not well, but . . ." I got the impression that if I didn't fly he would personally kill me. I hastily reassured him.

"Okay, then," he said, with evident relief. "You are a big attraction since I tell the press you 'ave come 'ere with still your injuries from the las' crash you 'ave. That 'as a lot of appeal—all the crowd will be waiting for you to crash again."

Oh, very funny. I said: "That's nice of them. Thanks very much."

"Is all right," he replied, grinning hugely. He was getting his revenge for my disappearing trick. "Now, look: We 'ave you scheduled for two performances, each fifteen minutes. The exact times will be said at the final briefing. The firs' one we want pure flyin'-circus stuff—wing-walking, guns, ever'thing. The nex' should be much comedy. Okay? *Bien!* Now speak to M'sieur Pourlin, 'oo will be doing the—er—commentairy for your performances."

Merlin made a long arm and hooked a tall thin man out of the crowd in the tent. I spent twenty minutes with Pourlin explaining the commentarial needs of our Poacher and Wayward Joyride stunts, which mainly boiled down to ensuring that he would express the right amount of horror at the right moments, then left in search of the rest of the Continental Division of the Old Time Flying Circus.

I found them, and the travel-stained XK, next to the Stampe. John, a heavyset character of 32 with a cherubic face, was sitting on the catwalk of the aircraft and staring moodily out across the field. Bundled up in his inevitable roll-neck sweater and baggy corduroy trousers, he resembled nothing so much as a large despondent Teddy bear. I followed his gaze and found he was looking at Neville Browning's Zlin. Probably wondering if he knew Neville well enough to ask him to fly the Stampe if I didn't turn up.

Rick, in contrast, was twitching like a first solo in a thunderstorm. About average height, very good-looking in a swarthy sort of way, he normally plays the clown parts in the show. Today was to be his first live performance as a wing-walker, and he must have been steeling himself for the ordeal all through France. And now the time had come—but his pilot hadn't. He was finding the experience unnerving, flitting round the Stampe checking and rechecking, jerking cigarette smoke out of his mouth and nostrils as he went.

He visibly jumped when he spotted me stumping towards him.

"Where the *bloody* hell have you been?" he exploded. "You were supposed to meet us last night, you bastard! We've been—"

"Okay, *okay*!" I held up my hands to stem the flood. "Sorry, but I got held up. Now, relax, eh?"

Rick looked as if he wanted to relax by busting Holland on the nose. He took a deep breath for a few more what-the-hells, but subsided as John shambled up and dropped a hand on his shoulder. John was a mountain of calm. He studied me for a moment.

Then he said: "Hello, Bruv"—everyone is "Bruv" to John— "what happened? You look as if you've got a couple of new bruises here and there."

"Yeah. I had a slight incident. I'll tell you about it later. I'm sorry I didn't turn up last night, but right now we'd better start thinking about the show."

I hadn't told anyone about taking the Sten before I left England, so they'd brought another prop Sten along for the performance. I looked at it longingly as we unloaded the props from the XK. My kingdom for another unplugged barrel and a few rounds of live 9mm. . . .

Not, unfortunately, that I knew where to find anyone worth shooting. . . .

Two hours later I was fighting down the hollow ball of fear in my stomach and listening to a still small voice in my head saying for the thou-

116

sandth time that there must be an easier way of making a living. I agreed with the voice: I always do when I'm about to stick the Holland neck out even further than usual.

And I *was* about to stick it out, too. About ten miles, at a conservative estimate. We'd done the Poacher and the Farmer stunt, with Rick doing the wing-walking like a pro, and now I was nearly through with the Wayward Joyride act—the finale to which is most definitely *not* a good life-insurance proposition.

The multicolored speckles of the crowd, 1,000 feet below, slid under the starboard lower wing. Looking over the side of the cockpit, I kept my eyes on the control tent. When it disappeared under the leading edge, I promised the still small voice—as usual—that I'd do it just this one more time and then quit; then I slammed the throttle shut and shoved the stick hard forward.

The Stampe dropped away instantly. The sickening hand of negative G pushed me up into the straps as the nose clubbed downwards—and then the tent was just to the right of the engine cowling and the wind noise winding itself up to a thundering howl as we dived vertically.

I held her pointing straight down for several seconds. Then, when the tent and the grass and the white faces began to swell rapidly in the optical illusion that parachutists call "ground-rush," I hauled back on the stick.

The nose reared up. The tent flicked past. I snatched a glimpse at the airspeed—around 140—then banged my wheels quickly on the ground, pulled up sharply, and did a brisk power-off aileron roll.

As the wings came level, the airspeed flicked around 50. I dipped the nose for an instant, then eased the stick back into my stomach. The Stampe settled on the grass in a neat three-pointer.

I breathed out in a long, shuddering sigh.

There was sweat on my palms and under my goggles—but the ball of fear was gone. In its place was the tingle of elation. I'd done it again; it was all over—until the next time. The still small voice had nothing to say.

The roar of the crowd was music in my ears as I stood up in the cockpit to take a bow.

117

CHAPTER 14

An hour after the last turn I was still unwinding. M. Merlin, sweating profusely as he moved around in the perpetual jog trot adopted by air-show organizers while their air shows are in progress, had made a special detour of at least 100 yards for the sole purpose of congratulating us on our performance. The show's resident doctor had arrived a few minutes later and rebandaged my hand for me. Rick and John had wandered off to mingle with the crowd in the hope of bumping into some stray unattached women who spoke English. I hadn't gone with them because in the first place I *never* bump into beguiling birds at air shows, and secondly my left hip was bubbling evilly every time I moved. So I lay down in the shade of a wing with a bundled-up flying jacket as a pillow, and let my mind nibble at the how-to-find-Haydon problem.

And that was how they found me.

The first thing I knew of them was an American voice coming from just behind my head.

"Don't move, Mr. Holland," it said softly. "Don't do anything I don't tell you to do, because I have a silenced gun pointing right at your heart. Now turn your head slowly to the left and look at me."

At the first words I'd gone rigid, tensed up ready to jump. Now I thought about what he'd said for a moment, and in the end did the gentlemanly thing and turned my head cautiously to the left.

He was a rather obvious American tourist with a wide college-boy face, short fair hair, and completely expressionless blue eyes. He was carrying a raincoat over his left arm and hand, and under the folds of the coat I could just discern the muzzle of a silencer. He was right. It was pointing straight at my heart.

"I want you to come along with me," he said conversationally. "But before we move I ought to tell you a few things. Firstly, in order to save you from speculation, I have been sent by Mr. Haydon, who wants to speak to you. Secondly, Mr. Haydon said if you wouldn't come, I am to kill you. Now, don't think you can get away with anything. I could shoot you here, put your jacket over your chest, and be gone in ten seconds. If you try anything when we start moving I could shoot you, call out to the nearest passerby that you're ill and that I'm going to fetch a doctor, and again be gone and lost in the crowd in seconds. I speak French quite well enough for that. I'm telling you this because it would be silly for you to die unnecessarily, but I assure you I don't give a damn one way or the other. Now I'm going to stand up. When I have, I want you to get up slowly and walk over to the white Mercedes you will see parked a short distance away directly behind your aircraft. I will be behind and slightly to one side of you, out of your reach. You know what will happen if you do anything I don't like."

His words were somehow doubly menacing because of the way he said them—his voice was a flat, almost bored monotone, and his facial muscles never moved. I thought about it for a moment, and found I was quite sure he'd do exactly what he said. The face and the raincoat with the gun in it moved back out of my field of vision. I relaxed my muscles from their jumping-on-people red alert and got up slowly just like the man said. Viewed from a normal standpoint he proved to be over six feet tall and

119

well built to boot. Not the sort of *Homo sap* it would do Holland much good to jump on at the best of times. And, of course, there was that silenced gun.

I picked up my flying jacket and walked towards the car.

The 1969 Mercedes 280SE is a good solid Teutonic hunk of motorcar. Probably solid enough, I reflected as I walked, to stop a bullet from a silenced gun if one was to dodge nimbly round the boot so as to put the car between oneself and the course of the slug. It would be a pretty desperate gamble, but I had a feeling that once I was off Lyon Airport my position was going to be pretty desperate anyway. The only trouble was that College Boy and the man I could now see in the driving seat of the Merc had carefully parked the car well out in the open. If I got round the other side of the car, which was a fair-sized *if* in the first place, there was nowhere to go except to run for the main car park, which was a good 50 yards away. The way I run with my hip, College Boy could roll a cigarette, light it, and then set off in pursuit and still have time to club me gently behind the ear with the butt of his gun before I'd got halfway.

Unless, of course, he simply got tired of the game and shot me.

''Get in the rear right-hand seat,'' he said softly as my steps faltered.

I opened the door and got into the car, vaguely noting that the man in the driving seat was black-haired and impassive and had both hands on the wheel. I made a performance of pulling my right leg in, as if it was hurting me. Everybody notices if you have a limp, but very few people notice it enough to tell which is the bad leg unless they stop and think about it. I started rubbing my leg, leaving the car door open.

College Boy stepped up to shut it.

I twisted in the seat and kicked with both feet just as his hand reached the handle. The door flew open and the top rear corner of the window frame hit him square in the face.

I catapulted myself out of the car and dived for his gun hand as he staggered back. He fell over backwards and I landed on top of him, desperately grabbing his arm. He caught me on the side of the head with his free hand, but there was no force behind it. I tried to get under the folds of the raincoat to the gun, felt the metal of it—and then something small and

120

hard ground viciously into the back of my neck.

"Don' move any more, boy," snarled the voice behind the hard object. The voice was vicious and commanding, and the hard object unmistakable. I froze.

"Get up."

I got up.

College Boy got up after me. His face was a mask of blood and hate. He reached into the pocket of his sports jacket with his right hand and produced a handkerchief. He spat blood and wiped ineffectually at his mouth and nose; all the time his eyes never left my face, and the gun, still under the raincoat, pointed steadily at my heart.

He spat red again, then said very softly, "I'm gonna fuckin' kill you, you bastard."

The words were slurred by his thickening lips, but I had no trouble understanding. The raincoat rippled slightly about where his trigger finger was.

"Cut it out, Harvey." The voice of the dark man behind me was still hard and vicious. "Someone's gonna see us if we don' get movin'. Leave it till later."

There was a long second or two while the college boy called Harvey wound himself down from immediate murder. I kept very still and breathed very softly. The dark man's gun ground into the back of my neck. Two Jungmeisters, their wing tips not more than six feet apart, both cut their engines at exactly the same instant on top of a loop. It was suddenly very quiet.

Then Harvey said softly: "Okay, Holland, get in the car. Very slowly and carefully."

The gun muzzle removed itself from the back of my neck. I got in the car. *Very* slowly and carefully. Harvey got in the front passenger seat, and the dark man slid behind the wheel. His right hand flickered under the left lapel of his jacket and out again, leaving the gun behind. Very neat. The dark man was a fast and dangerous animal. Far faster and more dangerous than me.

Harvey twisted round in his seat, and the barrel of his silenced gun poked gently over the seat back. I looked into his eyes—and actually felt my skin crawl and the hair prickle on the back of my neck.

"Now, understand," he said hoarsely, "that if you make the very slightest wrong move again I really will kill you. This is a Colt forty-five automatic, and even with the silencer on I can shoot clear through the seat back and into you, and you won't recover. If you so much as look twice at a copper on the way out I'll shoot you and enjoy it. Even if the cops see what happens they won't catch us because we'll have a running start. And don't think about throwing yourself out, because the child locks are set on the rear doors. Also, don't think of grabbing my friend while he's driving: I assure you you won't live long enough to see what happens. You got all that?"

I nodded. Slowly. The gun muzzle disappeared and Harvey shifted so that he appeared to be sitting in the natural half-sideways position of a person in the front of a car who's holding a conversation with someone in the back.

The swarthy man glanced back at me and grinned. A tight, nasty grin.

"You seem to've upset Harvey," he said. "I wouldn't move a muscle, I was you." He had a nasal, near-American voice.

I cradled my throbbing left hand, which had got clobbered when I jumped Harvey, and decided to take his advice for the moment.

It wasn't a difficult decision.

We made it out of Lyon Airport, past all the gendarmes directing traffic, without a quiver. Harvey sat and snuffled, holding a handkerchief over his mouth and nose to hide the blood and keeping his eyes fixed firmly on me. I was careful to make no sudden movements. My hand throbbed like a two-cylinder compressor.

Once out of the airfield we followed the ring road, then the Route Nationale south for a few miles, and turned off west at Givors on to a narrow road winding into the foothills of the massif. The road straggled through a couple of small villages, first Rive-de-Gier and then St.-Chamond, looking ancient, clean-painted, and very French in the late-Saturday-afternoon sunshine. Out of St.-Chamond we turned right on to an even smaller road which took us through hilly farmland.

After a total of about fifty minutes' driving, in complete silence, we turned into a bumpy farm track. The last sign I saw before that pointed to a place called St.-Galmier. We rocked along the track for a mile or so, and finally turned from that on to another short track, at the end of which we came to a stop outside a large tumbledown wooden barn.

The driver got out first and came round to my side of the car. His hand flickered under his jacket again, and he was holding a little snub-nosed revolver that looked like a .38. Harvey mumbled that I should get out very slowly and stand quite still once I was out there. I did as I was told. Harvey sounded as if his mouth was hurting and he wasn't in a good mood. He got out after me and went and rapped on the barn door—three knocks, a pause, then two slow knocks—and after the door opened he came back to the car. He told me to walk slowly into the barn, and the two of them followed me to make sure I didn't fall over backwards and hurt myself.

CHAPTER 15

The light was poor in the barn. I stopped just inside the door to let my eyes adjust. Haydon, wearing light slacks and a blue windcheater open to the stomach, was standing in a Fidel Castro posture, one foot on the arm of a multicolored folding picnic chair. He had a short cigar in his mouth and my Sten gun cradled in his right arm.

Behind him, and fitting much better into the musty interior of the barn, were the Auster, the trailer, and the Land-Rover. This was no surprise, because I'd seen the distinctive tracks of the Land-Rover and the wide-track trailer among the other wheel marks on the dirt road. Nor was it any particular surprise that the Auster was scattered all over the barn, no little dismembered. Little piles of discarded fabric, panels ripped from the framework during the search, had been laid alongside the skeleton of the aeroplane. They'd even cut through some of the steel tubes of the fuselage and stripped the rocker covers and most of the ancillaries off the engine.

I finished my inspection of the premises and went back to looking at

Haydon. We stared at each other for a minute or so, and then he said, "Search him and tie him to a chair."

Four willing hands frisked me, found nothing—I don't carry things in my pockets during a performance—and then yanked me down into another picnic chair. I sat in silence as my ankles were lashed to the front legs of the chair and my thumbs and wrists to the rear. They used heavy string, which is easy to get good knots into, and they knew their jobs. Hands tied tightly by wrists and thumbs are peculiarly useless right from the start, let alone after half an hour or so when the tightness of the bindings has had time to put a significant crimp in the circulation.

Harvey had been on my left, so the bindings on that side were particularly tight. Harvey didn't like me.

Haydon watched the trussing operation in silence. At the end of it he seemed to feel safe from a Holland insurrection. He placed the Sten gently on the floor and spared an expressionless glance for Harvey's bloody face.

"Put some lights on, Rico," he said.

The swarthy man went to the back of the Land-Rover, which was fast becoming hidden in the gathering gloom in the barn and came back with two small economy-sized Gaz lamps. He put one on the floor on each side of my chair, very close to me, and lit them. As they hissed into life I could feel the heat from them, and everything outside the light became several shades blacker.

Harvey moved out of the penumbra, and I heard the sounds of a tin being uncapped and water splashing as he set about removing the traces of Holland's Last Stand.

Haydon perched his right thigh on the arm of his chair and let me stew for a while in the heat of the lamps. Eventually, he broke the silence.

"I'm going to level with you, Holland," he said in his neutral BBC voice. "We both know we're looking for a packet of very valuable stamps, so I'm not going to beat about the bush. We have, as you can see, taken this aeroplane apart very thoroughly. They weren't there. My conclusion is that someone else has them, and you and old Mr. Jedrow are the obvious suspects.''

He paused for effect. I tried to look suitably impressed.

''Now, I want to know where the stamps are,'' he went on. ''I also want to know how you and Jedrow knew about them. I'm not going to tell you not to lie to me, because it will soon become apparent that if you do, you'll only prolong things for yourself.''

I said nothing. Watching me from the shadowy edge of the light, he reached into a trouser pocket and produced a small plastic cylinder. He flipped the cap off it with his thumb and shook four pills into his other hand.

Without looking round, he said ''Harvey, bring a cup of water.''

Then he raised his eyes to a point above my head and said, ''Open his mouth.''

An instant later, the sky fell in on me. I felt the meaty smash just over my right ear as if it were miles away. The blow was so totally unexpected that I had the ridiculous slow-motion thought that my neck must be breaking with the whiplash effect. Everything was humming and singing, and my eyes were out of focus.

Then something clapped over my forehead and yanked my head back. My mouth opened involuntarily, and strong fingers immediately hooked into my bottom lip and hauled savagely downwards to keep it that way. Something dropped on to the back of my tongue. I tried to gag—it was like having a spoon pressed down your throat to make you sick—but couldn't because of the position of my head. More fingers clamped over my nose, and water splashed into my mouth and ran down my neck. I struggled frantically, trying to retch, trying to breathe. A voice shouted in my ear.

''Just swallow and we'll let go.''

I swallowed.

They let go.

Slowly, the roaring and pounding in my head subsided. My eyes came back into some sort of focus. Haydon was back in the shadows again, and

126

his voice floated down to me from several continents away as I reentered the world.

"You'll have to excuse Rico," he said. "The poor man thought you might bite him if he didn't hit you first."

From behind me, the poor man chuckled the sort of chuckle that would go with his nasty grin. Huge joke. Very bloody funny.

The world gradually stopped rocking, and I became aware of a sharp localized ache in my right temple and a funny taste in my mouth. The taste seemed somehow familiar. Suddenly I found I was thinking about the nights just after Janie was gone and washing down sleeping pills with a slug of Scotch before dropping into the friendly blackness. . . .

Mandrax! That was the taste! Haydon had just given me Mandrax sleeping pills. *Four* of them!

I started laughing weakly. Haydon's outline in the shadows didn't move.

"You've given me four Mandrax pills, haven't you?" I said. "You . . . you of all people. The bloody chemistry expert. The bright bastard who puts staphylococci in meat pies. What's up, mate? Run out of scopolamine? No LSD handy? Four bleeding Mandrax pills! You know what they'll do? They'll put me to sleep for bloody hours! I won't be able to talk to anyone till this time tomorrow. You must be right off your 'ead . . . head . . ."

I realized I was babbling, so I shut up. The pills were already taking effect. I could hear voices from far, far off, but they weren't interesting. The welcoming blackness opened and I was slipping, slipping. . .

Suddenly I was awake again. Not completely awake, but something was dragging me slowly from the sea of blackness. There it was again. I woke up a bit more. . . .

Then I knew what was overcoming those four Mandrax pills.

It was Rico, standing behind the hissing lamp on my left. He was kicking my injured hand.

I groaned as he did it again.

Haydon's face was suddenly very close to mine, reddish and ghostly in the wavering light.

"That's right, Holland," he said, "they're Mandrax tablets." The voice wasn't suave now. The veneer was cracking, the way it had that night at St.-Jean Airfield. Now it was almost a snarl.

"Mandrax tablets so you're so tired you can't think straight enough to lie. So tired that you can't think about anything but answering me and sleeping. I don't need scopolamine or staphylococci for you. All I need is four little sleeping pills and Rico to work on your hand to make sure you don't actually drop off. Do you understand me, Holland? I broke your hand once, and now I'm going to have it done again. How badly it gets broken this time depends on how quickly I'm satisfied that you're telling the truth."

I nodded vaguely, beginning to slip into the blackness again. Dimly, somewhere in the recesses of my mind, I realized that Haydon had just tacitly admitted both poisoning Bill and causing the crash at Sandown—but even that didn't seem worth staying awake for.

Then Rico kicked my hand again. Haydon slapped me twice round the face.

"Where are the stamps?"

I slid back towards sleep. Haydon's image wavered in front of me, drifting in and out of focus.

"I . . . dunno," I mumbled, truthfully. I knew he wouldn't believe me, but I was too sleepy to care. I tried to add "Bugger off," but I don't think I got it out.

The next time I came round was to a sharp pain in the base of my left thumb. Blearily, trying to focus, I found Rico kneeling down on my left. He must have felt the leaden movement of my head, because he looked up at me. His dark face glistened in the lamplight. I could see beads of sweat on his forehead. His teeth flashed as he spoke, and I caught a whiff of garlic on his breath.

"You better talk damn quick," he said softly, "or I'm really gonna hurt you." Judging by his performance to date, I was prepared to believe him.

There was a quiet *zwip* from down by my left hand, and suddenly it was free. My eyelids, which weighed a ton each, started to shut again.

I felt my hand being lifted gently on to the arm of the chair; then a jabbing pain like a knife cut made me jerk my eyes open again.

It took a week or two to get my head turned and my eyes focused on my hand, but when I finally managed it I found that the pain had felt like a knife cut because it *was* a knife cut. Rico had slid a wicked-looking switchblade under the bandage on my hand and twisted it.

Having ripped away the outer bandage, the knife flicked among the bindings that held the individual fingers in their aluminium channels. I felt blood running down my wrist as the blade nicked me again, but the pain of the cut was totally lost under the jabs of agony that lanced up my arm as Rico pulled the splints away from my part-knitted fingers.

Rivers of sweat ran down my temples and dripped off my chin as I fought to keep my eyes focused on what he was doing. I couldn't think why I wanted to watch him, but somehow it seemed important. He placed his knife on the floor and took my hand almost gently in his own. He looked into my eyes and grinned his nasty grin.

Then he squeezed my fingers.

I arched my back and strained as every muscle in my body went rigid. Over the hoarse rasp of my ragged breathing I heard a thin animal howl. It was several seconds before I realized the noise was coming from my throat. Then Rico relaxed his grip and my body sagged. Haydon's face swam in front of my eyes.

"Next time Rico is going to break your little finger again," he said conversationally. "So don't be foolish and make things worse for yourself. *Where are the stamps?*"

I focused blearily on his face.

"I dunno, I tell you. Chris', they're s'posed to've been in th' bloody aeroplane for thirt-thirteen years." Fuzzily, I pushed each word through the cotton-wool layers round my brain. "I've only ever seen the bloody thing for a few minutes before tonight. Why the 'ell should I have them? Any-anyone could have the bloody things by now.''

Haydon looked at Rico and nodded.

Rico bent my little finger slowly backwards until it broke. It snapped on the old break near the base of it. I heard the crack.

Then he wriggled it around so that the broken ends ground together.

I found I had all my weight on the tips of my toes and the bindings round my right wrist. My rigid body was arched completely clear of the chair. My eyes were clenched shut, sweat was running into my ears, and my breath was coming out of my throat as a thin screaming noise.

Rico seemed to have stopped moving my broken finger about, because the red-hot agony was slowly easing off a few points. Very gently, I brought my head forward and lowered my weight back into the chair. The screaming stopped. Haydon was standing in front of me with his arms folded.

''Nobody else has them, Holland,'' he said distinctly. ''If anyone else had found them they'd have sold them, and we'd know about it. *So where are they?*''

In the back of my mind some small cell, still functioning, nagged me that Haydon had just let something important drop. But I couldn't place it, and after a second it slipped away.

''Who's 'we'?'' I heard myself mumble. ''W'ish family?''

Haydon didn't reply. He just glanced at Rico again.

Rico squeezed my hand and a red-hot lance shot clear up my shoulder. The double pain pushed back the mists in my head a little.

''If you get the stamps *you'll* sell them; then I'll be able to check an' find out who you are.'' I didn't really know why I was pushing the stupid point. Maybe I had some woolly notion of keeping Haydon off subjects that got my fingers broken. If that was the idea it wasn't conspicuously successful.

''We don't give a damn what you find out once we've got the stamps,'' he said coldly. ''I'll ask you again: *Where are they?*''

130

I closed my eyes, trying to think through the fog in my brain. I realized vaguely that as soon as I told Haydon all he wanted to know I'd be dead. He'd shown every indication of being willing to rub me out on two previous occasions, and nothing about his actions since then had led me to believe that he'd had a major change of heart. No—once I'd talked it would be a quick bullet, probably from Harvey, and a shallow grave somewhere in the French countryside. I shivered.

"Where are they?"

I came out from the fog again as Rico squeezed my fingers in his fist. If I hadn't had the Mandrax pills inside me I'd probably have fainted from the pain, but under their sedatory effect Rico's agonizing ministrations were having the opposite effect of keeping me awake. Just as Haydon wanted it: awake, but too pain-wracked and dozy to start inventing cohesive lies.

"I dunno where they are. If I had 'em I wouldn' waited for you that night, would I? . . . *Aaargh!*"

Rico was kneading my fingers in his big fist. He didn't seem to believe me.

"All right," said Haydon. He suddenly squatted so that his face, ruddy in the lamplight, was very near mine. His eyes held a feral gleam, and his nostrils flared slightly as he spoke.

"All right, we'll start somewhere else. Who told you about the stamps?"

"Wha' stamps?" A real bright reply on my part.

Rico balled my fingers into a fist and squeezed. A deep groan pushed itself up from my stomach, and I fought against being sick. More tears of pain ran down my cheeks.

"That wasn't intelligent, Holland," hissed Haydon. Well, he was right there. "I'll ask once more: Who told you about the stamps? Mr. Jedrow?" .

"I dunno. . . ." Rico squeezed again. "Okay . . . okay . . . Yeah, Jedrow."

"How did he know about them?"

"Dunno . . . *Aargh!* . . . Man tol' him."

"Obviously. What man?"

"Can' remember name. . . ."

"Miere?"

"I don' . . . *Yeah* . . . Stop . . . Yeah, Miere."

"When did Miere tell Jedrow about them?"

"Don't know. . . ."

"*When?*" Haydon's voice lashed out at me. Rico squeezed again. I retched dryly, the taste of vomit rising to the back of my throat.

"Gimme . . . drink of water. . . ."

"No. When did Miere talk to Jedrow? *Answer!*"

"Di'n' talk. Miere left letter. Miere dead. I jus' wanted my bloody aeroplane. So Jedrow told me about it. But I di'n' find them. . . ."

"You're lying. *Where are they?* Answer me!"

There was a small silence while I fought down the rising nausea and tried to think of a new way of saying I didn't know. Into the silence poked the distant growl of a car on the track. Everyone froze and listened.

The noise came nearer.

Haydon straightened up. To Rico he snapped, "Put that light out."

He took a step forward and put out the one on my right himself. The hissing of the gas stopped, and the light faded quickly through eerie red into blackness as the mantles cooled. Haydon's voice came crisply out of the dark.

"That should be Toni and Pete. Harvey, come outside with me. Rico, watch Holland."

A dark blue square appeared in the blackness to my right as Haydon opened the door. I saw his silhouette, followed by Harvey's, move out into the night. Rico was still crouched down on my left, in the position he'd been in when we'd first heard the car.

I waited until I could hold it no longer, then turned my head towards him and vomited explosively in his face.

Rico bounced to his feet shouting obscenities. I retched again, loudly, this time to my right. A figure appeared in the doorway, and Haydon's voice said, "What the hell's going on?"

"The fuckin' bastard's puked over me." Rico's voice shook with rage.

"Well, just keep him quiet. We can see the car lights in the distance. They should be giving us the signal in a minute if it's them." I saw the outline of the Sten in his hand as he turned and left. A very careful man, Anthony Haydon.

I could hear Rico, still swearing under his breath, stumbling his way to the Land-Rover, presumably in search of a rag. I retched again, leaning forward as far as I could and trying to ignore the fresh stabs of agony in my fingers as I sent my left hand on a frantic search of the floor near the front leg of the chair. I tried to use just forefinger and thumb, but the rest of the fingers dragged and every movement sent a bolt of red-hot flame up my arm. My head rocked and the blood sang in my ears.

Then something moved under my fingers—and I had it.

The little razor-sharp knife that Rico had left on the floor after using it to cut my bandages.

I gripped it firmly between thumb and forefinger, then straightened up and let my arm dangle slackly by my side. Consciousness dimmed and lapped back again with the effort of straightening, but the realization that the knife represented my last chance made me keep hold of it.

The only thing was, I still didn't know how I was going to use it. I thought, muzzily, of trying to reach across my back to cut my right hand free, but threw that one away because in the first place my right hand was too numb to be any use anyway, and secondly I'd look bloody silly if Rico happened to come back in the middle of the operation. The way he felt about me now, he'd probably just stand three paces back and blow my head off with that stubby little gun. I was still woozily trying to plan some sort of intelligent move when steps from the darkness indicated that Rico had finished the ablutions.

Because I couldn't think of anything else to do, I closed my eyes and let my head drop on to my chest, feigning sleep. Being sick had, in fact, woken me up considerably: apart from anything else, I'd probably retched up a lot of the Mandrax along with the rest of my guts. Or maybe it was just a combination of the pain in my hand and the sour sting of vomit in my throat and nose that was keeping me awake.

The steps stopped in front of me and there was an aching silence. For the second time that day, my skin crawled. What was he doing? Had he spotted the knife in my hand? The silence went on. Then I heard the car again, much nearer now.

At any moment Haydon and Co. would come back and my chance, however small, would be gone for good. Desperate with the need to do something, anything, before the chance slipped away, I did the only thing I could think of on the spur of the moment.

I moved my head weakly and said "Water . . . p-please, water. . . ." My voice was a dry, painful croak. That was genuine enough, anyway.

"Balls to you," hissed Rico.

I gave no sign of hearing, and he did what I hoped he'd do. I heard the slight rustle of clothing as he bent towards me. There was a small whiff of garlic, and his voice rasped very close to me.

"Balls to you. Get your own fuckin' water."

I half-opened my eyes. He was standing, bent at the waist, with his head thrust forward so that his face was about a foot from mine.

Outside, the car was slowing down.

I stabbed desperately upwards with the knife. The blade slid easily into his neck.

I imagined I saw a look of surprise on his face. He uttered a small gurgling noise as I pushed the knife sideways, cutting his throat. Blood gushed warm over my hand and splashed on my face and legs as the blade sliced through the carotid artery.

Then his reflexes jerked him backwards and he sat down heavily, legs straight out in front of him. His shirtfront instantly blacked in the gloom as the rushing blood soaked it. He tried to move his hands to his throat—

then died. The top half of his body fell back, his head hitting the floor with a loud *thump*.

The whole thing was over in seconds. I looked at the body for a moment before twisting round to cut the string that held me. My fingers sent new lances of fire through me as I sawed through the bonds of my right hand.

I supposed I ought to feel horrified at what I'd done, but the only thing I did feel was the nausea of reactive shock and the hope that he'd had time to realize what had happened to him before he died.

I still feel that way.

CHAPTER 16

As soon as I was free I tried to get up from the chair. My legs, completely numb from the knees down, promptly collapsed like a couple of wet noodles and I ended up kneeling on the floor. The fall made my head swim, and my feet and right hand started to throb agonizingly as circulation got under way again.

Outside, the car engine stopped and a couple of doors opened and shut.

For the space of perhaps a minute I was completely unable to move, and the suspense of waiting for the whole party to come trooping in while I was totally disabled brought me near shrieking point.

Finally I dropped on to my right elbow and pulled myself up the length of Rico's blood-soaked body, then pushed myself to a kneeling position beside his shoulders. My right hand still wouldn't answer to the helm in spite of an apparently infinite capacity for transmitting pain; so I sent my left hand under his jacket to find the gun. The agony from my broken fingers as they rubbed on the cloth at least served to put the cramps into perspective.

But I got the gun. He was carrying it in a spring-clip holster just above his hip. I drew it out very carefully between thumb and forefinger. All I needed was to drop the bloody thing and to have to waste time groping for it in the darkness.

As soon as I could flex my right hand enough to pull a trigger I transferred the pistol to it, ensuring with elaborate caution that the butt was firmly nestled in the still-numb palm.

Then I held the gun up to my eyes. All I could be sure about in the near-dark was that it was a revolver, probably a .38 Smith & Wesson, with about a two-inch barrel and a very short-eared hammer. I pulled the hammer back and it cocked with a satisfying *snick*.

I pointed it vaguely at the doorway and felt a whole lot better, which wasn't altogether logical since Haydon still had my Sten and two or three armed assistants. Still, after my recent straits I was easy to please.

Nothing happened.

After about a minute of kneeling there ready to start blasting, it finally struck me that something was wrong. If the car was one of his, Haydon should have been back in the barn by now. Furthermore, everything was unnaturally quiet out there.

I decided that the least I could do was shift myself to a better tactical position than the middle of the floor. The cramps had finally run down to several severe cases of pins and needles, so I pushed myself on to my feet and limped as quietly as I could to the nearest wall, then worked my way round to the doorway. My head pounded and my vision blurred in and out of focus as I moved.

I knelt down beside the doorjamb so I wouldn't present a head at normal head level, then poked an eye and my gun hand out together.

There was a second white Mercedes pulled up alongside the one I'd been brought in. Both of them were about 30 yards away, and pointing at the barn. In the rapidly deepening twilight I could see Haydon and another man on one side of the cars while Harvey and a fourth party stood in the small gap between them. The newcomers were presumably Toni and Pete. All four of them seemed to be listening to something.

Then I heard it too: the throaty ululation of a powerful car engine, coming nearer.

Haydon evidently didn't like it.

"Harvey, get behind that old plow," he snapped. "Toni, you go behind the barn. Pete, you've got a silencer? Right—back in the car and keep those two quiet. Stay down out of sight."

He leaned towards one of the rear windows of the car himself, holding the Sten in front of him as if for emphasis. "You two crouch below window level," he said. "One squeak out of you and Pete'll shoot you both. Got that?"

There was no response from inside the car. Haydon crouched down beside it, so that both cars were between him and the track leading to the barn, and I ducked smartly back as the one called Toni ran to his position behind the barn. I looked out again just in time to catch a glimpse of one of the occupants of the car as Pete got in and the courtesy light came on.

It was Jedrow.

I was trying to absorb that when a throaty *woofle* from the track, off to my right, announced the arrival of the car everyone was worrying about. Headlight beams brushed across the two Mercs as it turned the final corner leading to the barn. The engine growled again—and with a second shock I recognized the noise.

It was the distinctive rumble of my XK.

I thought frantically, trying to catch up with the situation as the headlights wavered and brightened. Everything was getting away from me. The only thing that really registered was that Rick or John or both were driving straight into a trap.

Warning them was *urgent*.

For the second time that evening I did the first thing that came into my head. I leaned out of the doorway, pointed the pistol a long way above the oncoming headlights, and pulled the trigger.

The short gun went off with a huge *crash*.

For a second the whole world seemed stunned. Then everything happened at once.

The Jag engine *whoof*ed and the rear wheels spewed up a hail of gravel as the car was wrenched into a sliding U-turn.

138

Haydon leaped up, shouted, *"You fucking idiot."*—and loosed off at the XK with the Sten.

The roar of the gun was incredible. Bullet flashes danced on the white roofs of the Mercs as he fired over them. I shot at him twice and missed, but the second one came near enough to make him dive for the ground behind one of the cars.

I'd moved him, but not soon enough. The taillights of the XK swerved wildly, then stopped and went out. The engine died.

For a moment there was a ringing silence.

Then Haydon shouted, "Rico?" There was a note of doubt in his voice. He'd been thinking again.

I threw myself outside the barn door and rolled, terrified of being bottled up when they got themselves organized. Haydon either saw me or finished his thinking at the same moment.

"Holland!" he yelled. "Toni—get Holland!"

I twisted in mid-roll and ended up on my stomach facing the corner Toni had disappeared behind. I heard a distant scream—my own—as my left hand got ground underneath my body.

Toni dived out from behind the barn, about ten yards away, and I fired at him. By some miracle I got him in the body and he half-turned, fell against the wall of the barn, and slumped to the ground.

Shots converged on me, and a bullet plucked at my right shoe. I shot forward instinctively, yanking the ground behind me with toes, knees, and both hands. A new, slower machine gun started up somewhere.

I ended up face to face with Toni.

He was half-sitting against the wooden wall. His lips were drawn back over his teeth in a ghastly grin of agony. I'd got him in the chest, and he was clutching the wound with a hand already black with welling blood. But he was still conscious, and the other hand, with a gun in it, came up in slow motion as the grinning rictus of his face turned towards me. I pushed my revolver at the face—but then his gun hand dropped into his lap and his body sagged tiredly forward.

My stomach churned and I took several deep, wracking breaths. As the world stopped going round, the two machine guns roared briefly. The slower gun kept firing a moment after the nearer thunder of Haydon's had stopped—and in that second I recognized the distinctive sharp hammering of one of our circus Stens.

Firing blanks, of course.

The noise was convincing enough to Haydon and Co., who wouldn't expect to be shot at with pretend-guns—but it also meant that the two bullets I had left in the Smith & Wesson constituted the entire firepower of the Holland regime. In the momentary lull I tried, unsuccessfully, to think of something constructive to do with them. I could hear liquid sloshing from somewhere in the region of the barn.

Then the humming silence was broken by a dull *whoomph* as the far end of the barn erupted in an enormous gout of oily red flame.

I turned and rolled, instinctively trying to get away from the heat and the light. More shots crashed, seemingly from all around, and I hugged the earth, desperately trying to get a grip on what was happening.

The barn burned like tinder, the flames leaping and crackling hungrily and bathing the scene in a red glow. I looked for Haydon, but he must still have been behind the cars because I couldn't see him. But I did see Harvey, his flickering red shadow rising up from behind the ancient plow off to my left. Stupidly, it didn't occur to me that he could also see me until his gun hand came up. He pointed the Colt .45 at me at arm's length, steadying his aim by gripping his wrist with his other hand.

I brought up Rico's revolver and fired the last two rounds at him. They missed. I rolled desperately to one side, hearing a heavy *boom* as I moved.

And then nothing.

After a moment I raised my head. Harvey had his arms in the air, and seemed to be stretching slowly like a man who's just got out of bed. I stared at him stupidly. He slowly arched his back and let out a deep, wrenching groan which I heard above the crackling roar of the flames. His hands reached tiredly towards his back; then his knees buckled and he slid forward in slow motion, pitching face-down across the plow.

I stayed where I was, completely at a loss. Did Rick or John have a real gun after all? I couldn't imagine them digging one up in the time—and even if they had, they weren't the types to start blasting away without knowing who they were shooting at and why.

The mysterious gun boomed again, and glass fragments exploded from the Mercedes furthest away from me, the one with Jedrow and Pete in it. A door flew open and Pete dived out into the gap between the cars. The blank-firing Sten opened up again from down the track to my right—and Pete was joined precipitately by Haydon, who catapulted himself into the gap with the Sten in one hand and a heavy automatic in the other. Suddenly I realized the Sten might be out of ammunition. They only had one magazine, and one Sten mag doesn't last long if you fire it in family-sized bursts. Then it takes time to load it up again—always assuming you have more ammunition for it anyway, which Haydon might not have.

Watching Haydon and Pete in the red firelight, it finally occurred to me that I was bang in line with the gap between the two cars—and thus right in Target Alley for them if they happened to look in my direction. They could hardly miss me, silhouetted against the roaring flames.

I gathered my legs under me and threw myself to my left, out of line with the gap. My feet hit something slippery and shot out from underneath me. I put my left hand out to save myself and landed—of course—on my broken hand. My scream of agony was lost in the thunder of the fire as I collapsed on to something soft which grunted with the impact. I almost retched again as I realized it was Toni. The grunt was air being expelled from his body as I landed on his stomach. I rolled off him, shuddering—and suddenly remembered that he'd had a gun. I scrabbled around for a moment, and found it near his hand.

It was a big, heavy Browning automatic. I felt around with my thumb and found the hammer drawn back.

Now I was ready to shoot someone again.

At that moment the roof of the barn collapsed with a splintering *crash*, throwing up a new column of roaring flame and an explosion of smoke. A flaming splinter fell on Toni's body, setting fire to his jacket. Several sparks landed on me, and I smelled singeing cloth as I rolled over again to get out of the way.

I rolled on to my feet and whizzed round the Mercedes on the left. If I could get round the back of the two cars I'd be in the dark, with Haydon and Pete silhouetted in the firelight in the gap between them. As I passed the back of the Merc there was another heavy *boom* over the roar of the flames, and something cut the back of my left leg like a hot knife while the car echoed with a metallic crash. My mind registered the thought "shotgun" as I threw myself forward and to the right, rolling over and coming up in line with the gap.

Haydon and Pete, alerted by the shotgun blast, were turning towards me as I started shooting. The Wild West stuff was purely a reflex attempt to finish the job I'd started out on, so I wasn't surprised when I didn't hit anybody. Pete came up from a crouch in Haydon's way and pointed a gun at me. I fired a couple more rounds, missed again, and wondered why he wasn't shooting.

I couldn't hear anything over the roar of the flames, but his hand jerked once or twice, and then something hit a stone near my head and went whining off into the distance—and I remembered about Pete: he was the one with a silenced gun. I rolled frantically out of the way as the shotgun boomed again and he dropped down.

For a moment there was silence, the roar of the fire seeming insignificant after the thunder of guns.

My last roll had taken me out of line with the gap between the cars, and I wasn't too anxious to move back again now that Haydon and Pete knew where I was. Pete might or might not have been hit by the last shotgun blast—but Haydon was certainly still a going concern.

I was still thinking about it when the Land-Rover's tank went up. It blew with a dull, earth-shaking *thump,* spewing a red fireball from the heart of the inferno. Everything was lit up with the eerie scarlet glow of burning vapor. Tendrils of flaming petrol rained down.

In the midst of the fireworks two car doors opened and slammed shut. The Mercedes on my left—the one I'd been brought in—*whoop*ed into life. Even with the exhaust beating practically in my face, the thought of danger from that direction never occurred to me. I was thinking in terms of guns. All I saw was Haydon getting away. I leaped up to shoot into the car—and the movement saved my life because I was able to turn it into a dive to one side as the car shot backwards in a welter of wheelspin. Even so, I didn't dive quite far enough; the right wheel seemed to nick my broken fingers. I got a flash of Pete's white face and gun hand leaning out of the rear window as he tried to bring the silenced pistol to bear on me— and then his arm jerking upwards as Haydon shifted into a forward gear and dropped the clutch again.

The wheels spun crunchingly and spat stones in my face. The Mercedes shot forward, skidded broadside, straightened out, and hurtled off down the track. The bright colors of the XK, slewed in its own skid marks where the track widened out into the barnyard, stood out in the yellow headlights for a second before Haydon swerved round it in a spume of dust and stones.

After the car vanished round the bend, I could hear it thumping along the rough track.

As the sound diminished, a shocked silence descended. In spite of the pistol-cracking of the flames, my ears rang with the quiet.

I retched once, dryly, then dragged myself over to the remaining Mercedes and slid down with my back propped against a rear wheel.

CHAPTER 17

Jedrow, inevitably, was the first to come to life.

The rear door of the Merc opened and he eased himself cautiously out.

I said, "Hello, Jedrow" from my leaning post beneath him, and he jumped a good three inches off the ground.

"Good Lord!" he croaked. "You all right? God, what a mess."

He fumbled in his pocket, produced a box of matches, knelt down beside me, and struck one. He dropped it immediately. "My God, you've been hit! You're . . . You've . . ." He petered out, obviously at a loss to know what to do with a dying Holland.

"No, I'm all right."

Well, more or less, anyway. Apart from a mangled hand, a shotgun crease in the leg, and a stomach that felt as if a horse had kicked it. I raised my right hand and found I still had a gun in it. I put the gun between my knees and drew the shaking hand across my brow. My fingers came away wet and sticky.

I puzzled vaguely over this for a moment, but forgot it as another door slammed and footsteps came round the back of the car. I found I had a handful of gun again, and was pointing it at Lubec as he appeared around the rear fender. I lowered it sheepishly: I would have to kick this habit of pointing firearms at everybody. Lubec was holding his right arm with his left hand, and his white sweater was wet with blood. He recoiled when he saw me.

"*Est-il vivant? Mon Dieu!* Where are you hit, Ken?"

"I'm only nicked," I said. My voice rasped out of my dry throat, but in fact I was beginning to feel better. I could detect the beginnings of a Mandrax high, the intoxicated feeling you get if you've taken a couple of pills but still can't get to sleep. Maybe Mandrax and adrenaline together do that to you.

"What about you? You look as if you've hurt your arm."

"I think it is broken. I try to get out of the car and the one called Pete shot me. It is a simple wound, though. But you . . . you are covered with blood. . . ."

I investigated the sticky wetness on my right hand. It seemed to be blood. I wiped my face again. There was more of it. I started feeling around for holes. There was a hail from the darkness and Rick and John arrived, breathing heavily. Rick was carrying the prop Sten and looking very guerrilla in the red light of the now-dying fire, while John, more practically, had a torch in his hand. He shone it at me and joined the startled-exclamations club.

"Jesus Christ," he said. "Ken, we'll get you to a hospital right away. . . ."

"Hold it, hold it." I'd finally worked out where all the blood was coming from. "It's not mine. I stabbed somebody in there"—I jerked my head at the barn and wished I hadn't—"and he bled over me. I'm not hit at all."

Everyone looked disbelieving. To prove the point I pushed myself upright, hanging on to the car for support, and tried to look like a party in the full flush of health.

"How about the rest of you? Jedrow, John, Rick—you all okay?"

Miraculously, everyone seemed to be, apart from Lubec. We examined his arm in the torchlight, and it turned out to be quite a nasty mess. It was certainly broken, and the only good thing about it seemed to be that the bullet had gone right through, breaking the forearm en route, without lodging anywhere. He was bleeding copiously, and Jedrow put a tourniquet on his arm and started bandaging it with a handkerchief and some strips off John's shirt. I remembered telling a worried girl that I'd look after her father. She'd been right not to believe me.

While Lubec was being patched up as far as possible, I asked Jedrow what had happened to them.

"Those two blokes picked us up at the airfield," he said. "We were looking for you. They came up behind us and stuck a gun in my back and said they'd shoot me in the spine if we didn't both go with them. They made us get in this car and drove us out here. The one who was watching us kept telling the driver he thought we were being followed." He looked at John and Rick. "I suppose that was you two?"

"That's right." John, holding the torch beam on the medical operations, took up the story. "We saw you being hustled into the car. We were already wondering where the hell Ken had got to. We knew there was something strange going on so we grabbed the XK and followed you."

"I picked up the Sten," Rick chipped in. "We thought it might be useful. Bloody well was, too, though I don't mind telling you I was frightened bloody stiff when that bloke started shooting with a real machine gun." His voice held a mixture of nervous reaction and pride. Well, he had a right to feel proud. So had John. It must have taken a lot of guts to stick around and make flying-circus bangs in the face of the genuine article.

Talking about the genuine article reminded me . . .

"Hang on a minute," I said. "Did either of you bring a shotgun?"

They both shook their heads.

"Didn't either of you set fire to the barn, either?"

"No, we didn't," said John. "I thought you had, or they had. . . . Look, just what the hell *is* going on, anyway?"

"Hold it, hold it a minute. If you didn't have a shotgun and you didn't set fire to the barn, then there's someone else around."

146

Quick-on-the-uptake Holland again. For the last five minutes I'd forgotten all about the shotgun-and-fire mystery. The unknown quantity could have a double-barreled 12 lined up on the back of my head right now for all I knew. . . .

I sprang around, waving the automatic in the general direction of the darkness behind the car. Nobody stepped out to be shot at.

After a moment I started thinking again. If anyone *was* lurking there waiting to blow us apart he'd probably have done it by now, especially since I'd been presenting the back of my head as a nice stationary target for some minutes. I lowered the gun, feeling silly and wondering just what the bloody hell *was* going on. . . .

The others were looking at me curiously, obviously coming to the conclusion that I'd finally thrown a rod. Maybe they were right, at that. John was taking a breath to start asking questions again, but I said, "Wait a minute" and limped round the Merc to where Harvey was sprawled over the old plow.

In the dying red glow of the fire I could see a tight group of little tears in the back of his brown sports jacket. The jacket was darker round the tears. A shotgun victim—but I'd already known that. I turned him over to see if I could find something I hadn't known.

John came up behind me with the torch as I was one-handedly going through his pockets. All Harvey had on him was about a thousand francs in notes and some small change, cigarettes and a book of matches, and a holster which dangled inside his trousers on his left hip. There were two spare Colt magazines, fully loaded, in little pouches on the holster belt. He hadn't wanted them in his pockets to collect fluff and tobacco fragments. Careful type.

Just out of interest I yanked back the collar of his jacket and then inspected the inside pocket. No labels.

I pocketed the francs and helped myself awkwardly to one of Harvey's Gitanes. He didn't seem to be needing them. I fumbled around with the book of matches, trying to get one out one-handed, until John stepped forward with a lighter. I dragged smoke deep into my lungs as John swung his torch over the barn. The beam lit on Toni's legs, sticking out from the debris of collapsed wall. John walked over and kicked the smoldering planks off the body in a shower of sparks. He bent down for a look at the remains and immediately turned and retched. What with my bullet and the fire, Toni was very dead. Silently, we rejoined the group around Lubec.

John wiped his face with a dirty handkerchief, then blew his nose hard. "Did . . . did you do that?" he asked shakily.

I nodded. "You might as well know there's another one in the barn too. He's dead as well."

There was a pregnant silence.

"You, man . . . you've killed three people?" Rick's voice was querulous, willing it to be untrue.

"No, I killed two. The bloke with the shotgun got the other one. Don't worry about it. These are the people who killed Bill and made Ted and me crash at Sandown."

"*Killed* . . . Bill?" Rick sagged against the car. He looked stunned. I threw away my cigarette, shook another one out of the pack, and carefully fitted the book of matches between my left thumb and forefinger so I could use my good hand for tearing out a match and striking it.

Rick found his voice and said slowly, incredulously, "Bill was *killed*? But he . . . he crashed, didn't he? How on . . .?"

His voice tapered off. His eyes had dropped to my hands, fumbling with Operation Match, and now he was staring with sick fascination.

"Oh, God . . ." he said.

I looked down myself.

The little finger of my left hand was gone, the root sluggishly oozing blood.

I stared at it blankly. There was very little pain from the hand now I wasn't bashing it on something every few seconds. Just a dull, rhythmic throbbing in time with the welling seepage of blood. For a moment I couldn't believe I'd actually lost the finger. I blinked hard, half expecting it to be back when I opened my eyes. It wasn't.

Then, stupidly, I found I was looking at the book of matches in my hand. The cover, smeared with blood, said HÔTEL D'AUVERGNE, MONTCEAU-LES-MINES.

Harvey wasn't such a professional after all.

John gently took my left hand and examined it by torchlight. He tore more strips off his shirt, spat on a pad of cloth, and very carefully started to clean off the blood and dirt. The others watched dumbly. My loss of a finger seemed to shock them more than anything else, though in fact Lubec's arm was a much more serious wound. Bolts of agony stabbed through me as John worked, but when he wasn't actually touching the root or the two broken fingers the pain wasn't all that bad. Possibly the remaining Mandrax in me was having an anesthetic effect.

I made up my mind what I was going to do.

"Jedrow, would you find me a small piece of wood for a splint for these fingers, please? John, I want you to bind the busted ones up good and tight. Now, Rick—how bad is the XK? Can you get it going again?"

For a moment they just looked at me, still held by shock.

"Come on," I snapped. "We can't stay here all bloody night."

That got through to them. Jedrow found a splinter about half an inch square by six inches long, John switched on the Mercedes' headlights to illuminate the bandaging and Rick went off with the torch to investigate the XK. He came back just as John tied the last knot. I was sweating with pain as he finished, and blood was already soaking the bandage around the stump.

"The Jag's okay," said Rick. "Your friends put a bullet through the nearside rear tire, which is why we stopped, but apart from that there's only a few bullet holes in the body which don't seem to be serious. The aero-screen's smashed—that's about the only other thing."

"Is the spare all right?"

"Yeah."

"Okay. Now, John and Rick, you change the wheel, then get everyone in the XK—you can do that at a squeeze—and head back to . . . er, I guess you'd better go to Monsieur Lubec's house." Lubec, looking very strained, nodded. "Yeah, go to Monsieur Lubec's house. I'm taking the

Merc, and I'll join you at the house not later than—let's see—this time tomorrow evening.''

"Now, hold it," said John firmly. He was looking stubborn. "Just wait a minute. Aren't you going to bring the police in?"

"Jesus, no! D'you want me to be charged with murder? The cops can make what they like out of it: there's nothing to connect us with this lot once we're out of here. You know what the Mafia is? Well, that's who these people were. Their mates aren't going to call the cops in. If you do it I'll get held on suspicion of murder, at least, and you'll be with me as accomplices or accessories. The circus'll fall apart, the other two bastards get away, and we'll have this goddamn Mafia family round our necks again as soon as they've got themselves sorted out.''

I turned to Lubec. "They think we've got the stamps," I explained quickly. "They won't leave us alone after this."

He nodded.

I looked back at John. "Trust me. The two that got away are the buggers who killed Bill. Jedrow and Pierre here'll tell you all the details. Just forget the cops and get everybody back to Pierre's place. You'd better do something about those bullet holes in the car, too. Patch them with glass fiber, or something. You can't drive it back to England looking like something out of a Hollywood gangster film.''

John wasn't having it. His eyes narrowed with rare anger.

"Christ, Bruv, you don't want much, do you? We *still* don't know what's going on, yet you want us to hide a triple killing from the police, take your car back through customs with umpteen bullet holes in it, and sit on our backsides for twenty-four hours while you go off on some mysterious goose chase in"—he nodded at the Merc—"a stolen car. Just what the bloody hell *is* happening? *Who* killed Bill? And how? And why? And what are you going to do?''

"The blokes who killed Bill are the ones who got away in the other Merc. The whole mob is part of a Mafia family who wanted the Auster Bill and I bought, because they thought there was something very valuable hidden in it. They killed Bill because he wouldn't sell; then they

150

started on me. Jedrow and Pierre will give you all the details.'' I looked at them and they both nodded.

''They were torturing me before you turned up because they thought I'd nicked the stuff out of the kite when I had a run-in with them at St.-Jean Airfield a few nights ago. I killed another of them then. Now, for Christ's sake just trust me for the moment, eh? I've got to get *moving*.''

Rick and John looked clubbed as they tried to absorb it all. I could sympathize: when you said it fast like that it sounded unreal. Then I looked at the bodies in the firelight and the bloody bandage round Lubec's elbow and the gap where my finger used to be. It got real again.

''All right.'' John was recovering well. ''Suppose we go along with all that. Where are you going?''

''I'm going to catch up with Haydon and Pete—they're the two that got away. That's why I'm taking the Merc: I don't want the XK associated with anything that happens.''

''*What!*'' John almost visibly staggered. ''You're going to . . . going to . . . *Christ*, you've got a bloody death wish! You can't do that! They'll kill you!'' He pawed limply at the air. ''You . . . you . . . you've got to get your hand fixed up,'' he ended lamely.

''No, they won't kill me. They're not expecting me. The last thing they'll think of is me following them now''—I hoped—''and if I don't go after them they'll be after us—or me, anyway—as soon as they've got themselves organized again. Besides which, these are the bastards that killed Bill! *Do you understand that? They killed Bill!*'' I found I was shouting. ''Now stop bloody arguing and let me get on with it!''

''How do you know where to go?'' Lubec's quiet voice. His face was drawn with pain, but he was thinking.

''Montceau-les-Mines. The Hôtel d'Auvergne.'' I gestured at the book of matches lying on the bonnet of the Mercedes. ''They must have been staying somewhere. I imagine that's where.''

''How do you know they'll go back there?''

''I don't, for sure. But they're professionals. Harvey, for instance— there was nothing in his pockets, no identification on him at all. I'll bet none of the others carried anything, either. So they had to leave things like passports somewhere—and they'll have to collect them again sometime. I'm guessing they'll go back to the hotel. I may be completely wrong on all counts—they might just have had a meal or even done nothing more than buy cigarettes there. If that's the case I won't find them— but I won't lose anything by trying. There's one other thing: the location's right. A pro isn't going to stay at a hotel near the center of his operations. Makes it too easy for people to get on his track afterwards. Montceau, if I remember rightly, is about a hundred miles away. No one'd check the hotels that far out if they were after someone who did something in St.-Jean.''

Lubec nodded, considering. "You may be right," he said doubtfully. "Anyway, as you say, there is nothing lost in trying. But your hand, your head—you are not in a state for such a search."

"I'll go with him," said John quickly. He was getting himself back in gear again.

"No, you won't. If I catch these two I'm going to kill them. If possible, I'm going to shoot them in the back before they even see me. You don't have any part in this yet and there's no point in your getting involved now. It wouldn't help anybody if something went wrong and we both got arrested for murder or something."

"But look . . ."

"No, *you* bloody look! You're not a killer and I don't want to be responsible for turning you into one!" I was shouting again. There was an awkward little silence.

"You, on the other hand, are," said Lubec, very softly.

I looked round the circle of their faces. They were looking at me with strange expressions.

To hell with them. I grabbed the torch from Rick and stumped over to Harvey's body. After a few minutes' searching I found what I was after. His Colt .45 automatic. It had fallen in between the shares of the rusted plow, and I had to kneel down awkwardly to pick it up without using my left hand. A Colt .45 is a big pistol anyway, and with five inches of silencer screwed on to the barrel it looked and felt like a baby Howitzer. Nevertheless, I left the silencer on. One never knows when a spot of quiet might come in useful. I finished the armament program by taking Harvey's two spare magazines. With Toni's pistol stuck in my belt and the Colt in my hand I felt like a perambulating gun shop. As an afterthought, I swept the torch around the wheel marks left by Haydon's departure. Within two minutes I found what I was looking for: a small, dirt-covered lump of gristle and bone. My little finger. I put it in my pocket.

Nobody said anything as I stumped back into the headlight beams of the Merc. I looked at Rick and John and said: "Well, get moving. You're going to be here all night if you don't soon get that bloody wheel changed."

I threw John the torch. He caught it, stared at me with that curious expression on his face for a few moments longer, then turned and walked off in the direction of the XK. Rick followed him.

The pistol I'd got from Toni turned out to be a Browning 9mm, with nine rounds left in the clip. I stuck it in my right trouser pocket and dropped the Colt in the driver's-door cubbyhole of the Mercedes. I made sure there was a road map in the car, then walked round looking for shotgun damage. The right rear door window had been shattered, and the door itself had pockmarks and tiny holes in it from stray shot. The right rear fender was in a similar condition, only more so, from the potshot that had been taken at me. Nothing of functional importance had been hit, but the trouble with shotgun holes in a car is that they look exactly like shotgun holes and not much like anything else. I scooped up a handful of dirt and rubbed it on the rear fender, but it still looked as if it had been hit by a shotgun. Perhaps no one would notice in the dark.

Opening the door to get in, I caught sight of myself in the driving mirror as the courtesy light came on. The vision was appalling: Rico's blood was drying on my face and matted in my hair, the front of my tee shirt was soaked in it, and on top of it all was a layer of dirt and dust from rolling around on the ground. If anyone got a look at me it would certainly take his mind off insignificant things like gunshot damage to the car. I got out again, stumped over to the XK, and fished out the can of water we always carried in the boot. The others watched silently as I soaked a piece of rag and cleaned up my face as best I could. Rick finished changing the wheel as I took a few gulps of the warm brackish water, gargled to wash the lingering taste of vomit out of my throat, and recapped the can.

"See you tomorrow, then," I said to everyone in general.

Rick muttered, "Okay" without looking up, and Jedrow and Lubec both mumbled something unintelligible. Not Old Chums Night for Holland. I thought, Sod you, then, and turned back to the Merc.

John was in the way. He touched my arm as he stepped aside. "Look after yourself, Bruv," he said softly.

I felt a bit better.

CHAPTER 18

I felt better still once I was under way. I like driving—in fact, I like operating any machine that moves—and although my taste in cars runs more to open sports jobs, a Mercedes always imparts a pleasant sensation of smooth silent power. This one, which I imagined must be a hire car, was another 280SE, a six-cylinder 2.8-liter with fuel injection, like the one I'd been snatched in. The left-hand drive felt a bit strange, but having the gear change on the right of the wheel was a feature much appreciated by my busted left hand. I felt alert and almost happy as we bumped along the farm track. This was the result of the Mandrax high, which I knew must be getting near its peak.

The track was mostly dry, with occasional puddles and damp patches. Where it was muddy I could see the chunky wheel marks left by the Land-Rover, with the crisscross treads of the wide-track trailer running outside them. These marks were overlaid in places by the conventional tread patterns of Mercedes tires and the distinctive footprints of the XK's Cinturatos. The only other car tracks seemed to have been made by a set of wide tires with grooves down the middle.

When I got on to the road I turned on the heater to combat the cool night air which rushed in through the broken rear window and sliced through my thin tee shirt. As I got used to the car I stepped up the pace, humming to myself as I set the Merc into bends with the tires muttering on the edge of squeal.

Before long I was hitting up 150, 160 kph on the straights, zipping past the occasional crawling 2CVs and Renault 4Ls. I whipped through St.-Chamond and then Givors, and turned right on the Autoroute du Nord.

The rain started 30 kilometers or so south of Lyon, at just about the time I realized I'd have to make a fuel stop. It started with big, slow, determined drops, as if it was going to make a thorough job of it.

It was.

After ten minutes, water was sheeting down and the windscreen wipers, running at their highest speed, were completely unable to keep up with it. The oncoming headlights shimmered and starred madly in the wavering roils on the screen. I blinked hard and crawled along at 40 kph, using all my concentration to stay on the road. Cars and lorries swept past me, horns blaring, throwing up walls of spray. I realized I was on the downcurve of the Mandrax high, and it was affecting my vision.

Every minute or so I squeezed my eyes tight shut for several seconds in the pious hope that such a treat would get them working properly again. It didn't, of course, but after one such effort I opened them to the sight of an illuminated Esso sign. The pumps were lit, but apart from that the place looked like France's dingiest filling station. Just what I wanted. I was right on top of the turn-in, so I wrenched the wheel to the right. The tail wagged heavily as we shot into the forecourt and slid to a stop in an angry hiss of tires. The attendant, who was in his little glass-fronted hut drinking something from a steaming mug, jumped visibly at my nonstandard arrival.

So did the two gendarmes who were drinking with him.

For a second I nearly panicked and drove straight out of there. I had my foot on the clutch and hand on the gear lever before sanity prevailed. If I hurtled out the same way I came in without waiting to buy fuel, I'd have the *flics* on my tail in seconds. There was a police Citroën parked in the shadows by the attendant's tumbledown hut.

So I froze, seeing the end of it all. Slowly and numbly, I reached forward and turned off lights and ignition. I visualized the arrest, the questioning, being held in custody, and finally the connection between myself, the guns, and the carnage back there in the foothills.

I tried desperately to think of something to do. If only I wasn't so tired. . . .

The attendant held his plastic mac tight round his neck as he moved out into the deluge. Both the gendarmes were wearing the light blue shirts of their summer uniforms. One of them came out of the door behind the pump man, humped his shoulders as the rain hit him, wavered for a second—then turned and hopped smartly back into the dry of the hut.

I found I was holding a pretty ancient breath. I let it go.

Ghostly fingers of tension played up and down my spine as I asked the attendant for *"Quarante francs de premier essence, s'il vous plaît"* in my schoolboy French. Out of the corner of my eye I could see the gendarmes looking at me and talking. I thought about stretching nonchalantly, then remembered it was a better idea to keep my bandaged hand out of sight. The attendant was fumbling around at the back of the car. If he asked me where the filler cap was it would be all over. I could hardly expect to get out of the car, a small limping figure in a bloody tee shirt, and search for the fuel filler without arousing the suspicion of the onlooking law.

Come on, come on . . . surely you've filled up a bloody Mercedes before. . . .

The cap finally opened and I heard the man clunking around with the fuel nozzle and then the sweet sloshing of petrol. I sorted out four tens from Harvey's roll of francs and started breathing occasionally again.

When the man came to the window for the money I said, *"Bonsoir, Monsieur, et merci"* in what I hoped was a casual voice but suspected was a dry squeak, then took my time over starting the engine, switching on lights and the wipers, and driving gently out of the forecourt.

I wanted to scream. I could feel the gendarmes' eyes on the back of my head as I waited for a gap in the traffic. Had they spotted the rear window, and wondered why it was open in a thunderstorm? Had they seen the shotgun damage on the rear fender? It was on the side of the car nearest to them. I sat there while a leisurely flurry of northbound traffic ambled past.

Sweet Jesus—come *on*! Every other French vehicle hurtles along at maniac pace, and you lot choose this moment to crawl! I wanted to throw the Merc into the traffic and race away from there as fast as the car would go. Instead I sat, engine idling, waiting. The rain rumbled on the roof. After about a fortnight the traffic passed.

I eased the Merc out on to the road.

Nothing pulled out after me.

I drove into Lyon twenty minutes later, just going along with the traffic flow in the hope that it would eventually wash me out to the north.

There were several white Mercs among the cars parked outside the restaurants on the riverfront, and it occurred to me to wonder whether Haydon's might be one of them. It was possible, I decided, but improbable—and I could hardly stop and check every white Merc I saw between St. Chamond and Montceau. Mercs are a common car in France, and white is a common color for Mercs—so if I tried anything like that I'd be at it until Thursday fortnight while Haydon was long gone. Besides which, my lurching around Lyon on foot covered in blood and bristling with lethal weapons would be likely to arouse comment. No—my best bet was to press on and follow my hunch to the Hôtel d'Auvergne. I found the Autoroute du Nord and kept going.

I was thirty, maybe forty minutes north of the city before I started to take notice of the lights behind me. I hadn't paid much attention before, but as the traffic thinned, the impression slowly grew that one set was there all the time. Was it imagination—or was there someone sitting about 300 yards back, following me?

I watched the mirror more carefully for the next ten minutes. Yellow headlights came and went as I passed the odd lorry or small car.

That one set of lights was still there.

All right: it still didn't have to mean anything. Maybe somebody just happened to be cruising at the same speed as me. Maybe. Taking my time about it, I slowed to around 80 kph.

The lights behind slowed as well.

The cops from the filling station!

They hadn't been so stupid: they were following me, cat-and-mousing to see what I was doing.

My nerves crawled. Any minute they'd tire of the game and stop me. Bonsoir, M'sieur. Just a routine check. You are hurt, M'sieur? This is your car? These are your guns, M'sieur? We regret, M'sieur, but we must ask you to accompany us. . .

One way out of that.

I put my foot down.

The engine sighed softly and the speed wound up. One hundred forty kph. One hundred fifty. The tires made an angry hissing roar on the wet road, and the noise of the wind coming in through the rear window rose to a keening howl. The car behind seemed to be in about the same place. I leaned back, straightened my arms, and opened her up all the way. The howl became a shrieking gale and the car rocked with speed. One hundred sixty . . . 165—a pinch over 100 mph. The rain growled heavily on the windscreen and the yellow lights bored into the darkness ahead. I tried to whip my reflexes into keeping up with the rapidly unwinding road —but it wasn't working: I was behind the car, and I knew it.

I tore past a couple of big lorries which were rolling along in a vast ball of spray. It was like driving through a swimming pool.

A few seconds past them and the road made a slight bend to the left. The Merc started to aquaplane on some standing water. I thought I'd lost it. The back end began to come round, quite gently; then suddenly we were off the puddle and the car lurched sickeningly as the tires struggled for grip on the wet road. I fought down the tail-wagging session by pure reflex, and kept my foot down.

The car rocked with speed and started to drift several times in the next few miles as I clung to the gentle bends and undulations of the *autoroute*. I was driving like a maniac. The adrenaline pump was working overtime, and the hot sick feeling of fear balled up in my stomach.

If the cops were still behind me now they had to be chasing in real earnest. No one would keep up with this kind of driving for fun. I looked in the mirror as the Merc topped a small rise.

The lights were still there.

They were a little further back, probably half a mile or so, and weaving slightly as the car hurtled through a bend. But they were definitely still there. They disappeared from the mirror as I plunged down the other side of the hill.

I saw the sign almost immediately. The silhouettes of a tent and a caravan on a board that said CAMPING 300M.

I made my only really fast decision of the night and stood on everything. The tires bit through the wet and screamed in drawn-out agony. The car slued to the right. I wound the wheel frantically and kept my foot hard on the brake. The car whipped out and slid left. As it got out of hand I took my foot off the brake and hurled the wheel round again. The Merc slid heavily, tires howling; the bonnet shot between the entrance posts of the site and the back end bounced off the one on my side with a bone-jarring crash. I stood on the brakes again and had the lights off even before it skidded to a final halt.

The hissing roar of a fast-moving car came from the road as I threw myself out of the door ready to run like hell. I got a momentary flash of lights bucketing past in a fury of spray, and then it was out of sight behind the hedge.

My left hip gave under me and I sprawled on the ground.

By the time I got up the car was out of sight, though I could hear it in the distance. It was still moving fast. I breathed out in a long sigh.

As the noise faded away, the quiet wet night moved in. The rain muttered softly on invisible hedges and grass, and the place smelled damp and fresh. I found I was shaking like a leaf. I perched on the side of the Merc's front seat, rested my elbows on my knees, and put my head in my hands—and burst into a flood of tears. Pure reaction.

The roar of a couple of lorries going past on the road outside brought me back to reality. A final couple of racking, shuddering sobs and the monsoon season was over. I gripped the doorpost with my good hand and pulled myself very slowly to my feet. I had to get moving—and get moving *now*. Those cops might just work out that I was no longer in front of them, and if they did they might come back and start searching for places I could have darted into. There wouldn't be many bolt-holes like this on the *autoroute,* so it wouldn't take them very long.

You can't tiptoe in a Mercedes 280SE, so I did the next-best thing. Put my foot down. Not to the breakneck speed of a few minutes before, but fast enough so that anything getting bigger in the mirror had to be doing a deliberate job of chasing. For the next few miles I tried to look in eight directions at once—studying the cars I passed, looking into every roadside cranny and byway, and watching the lights tapering away in the mirror.

Nothing got bigger. After 20 kilos I eased off the speed a bit, made a conscious effort to relax, and tried to stop my hands shaking. The cops were either not interested enough or not clever enough.

Half an hour later, squinting through the rain, I nearly missed the Mâcon turning. The French put up lovely big road signs, but very often they put them up *at* the junction instead of before it to give you warning. I passed the turning still braking, backed up smartly, and dived off on the last leg.

I passed through Mâcon almost immediately and put my foot down again outside the town. The road turned out to be one of the better second-class French roads. It was narrow, but had long straight stretches and step-down speed-limit signs with direction arrows to warn you of the bends. I pushed the Merc along fast and alone. At first the road was poplar-lined and ran between fields; then after a few miles it started climbing and entered a wood.

The last right-hander was blind, but the step-downs only said 80, then 60 kph, so I slowed to 70 or so and set the Merc up to start on the left and cut in for the best line. . . .

Just past the apex, another white Mercedes was parked well out in the road.

CHAPTER 19

I straightened for an instant to widen my line, then put my foot down and slued the wheel hard right to stay on the road. The Merc lunged heavily and started to slide. I kept the power on and tried to hold it in the drift, sudden fear punching adrenaline into me like a shock of cold water.

I shot past the other car in a howl of tires, juggling throttle and wheel on the ragged edge of losing it. The left rear wheel crunched momentarily on the roadside gravel, she snaked sickeningly, I clawed her back—and then I had her again and we were out of the bend and running.

It lasted perhaps two seconds.

Then a machine gun blared briefly and appallingly behind me, and the wheel whipped out of my hands. I had time to register *tires* as the car thumped down heavily, lurched, then spun to the right. I instinctively threw the wheel left, but it was wasted effort.

The Merc slid across the road with a grinding screech of metal, hit the ditch on the left, and flick-rolled.

Trees tumbled crazily in the yellow lights; I thought, This is it, and put my fists over my face. There was a tearing, crunching *crash* as we hit. Giant hands grabbed me, slammed me into the seat, and swatted me from side to side. The noise went on and on and on. Something walloped me on the temple; then the hands smashed me to the roof.

I got a glimpse of the ground coming up impossibly from dead ahead, an impression of the bonnet crumpling as we hit again; then the headlights were gone and the car was bouncing through the trees like a giant maniac pinball. Metal screeched and crashed and I was trapped in a concrete mixer. . . .

There was a final jarring *smash*—and suddenly everything was still. The silence rang. Cooling metal ticked.

I opened my eyes. My head thundered. Little points of light swam in blackness. I wondered, stupidly, if I was dead. My left hand thumped fresh pain at me. Would it do that if I was dead? I seemed to be in a funny position. I moved my right arm. Glass fragments cascaded over me with a rushing clatter as the shattered windscreen flopped in. My muscles twitched at the shock of it, but it convinced me I was alive.

Having decided item one, I stared into the blackness and started in to worry about whether I was blinded. Loss of sight is my personal ultimate horror. Panic rose in my throat as I squinted frantically into the dark. Was it just being in a wood on a black night, or was it . . . ?

Then I made out the faint outline of a door pillar and the top of the steering wheel. The panic wound down. I closed one eye and then the other. The dim outlines were still there.

I'd bounced again.

As sense filtered back I realized I was lying downhill across the front seats of the car, with my back propped against the passenger door and my right foot somehow jammed under the pedals on the driver's side. The Merc had come to rest with its nose pointing steeply upwards and lying over nearly on its right side, so that my feet were above the level of my head. It was probably resting up against a tree, I thought. There were altogether too many trees hereabouts.

The rain peckled on the roof of the car, the cooling engine ticked some more, and I supposed I ought to be thinking about moving. Something was digging into my right hip. I shifted slightly, but it still dug, so I sent my hand down to investigate. It was the Browning. It reminded me in a rush that I could be expecting Haydon and Pete along any moment, a fact that I had hitherto forgotten under the press of events. It had been their Merc on the road—and it hadn't been any police car chasing me on the Autoroute du Nord either.

I pulled the gun out, eared the hammer back with my thumb, and tried to think about something helpful. Such as getting out.

Footsteps came crashing through the undergrowth. There was a metallic clatter from the back end and a couple of thumps. The car rocked slightly and I sensed a shadow darker than the rest looming over the driver's-side windows. The catch rattled; then the left-hand front door flew open with a wrenching screech of buckled metal.

Shocking in its unexpectedness, the courtesy light blinked on.

It lit up Pete's head and shoulders at a funny angle in the doorway. He'd climbed on to the wreck and was kneeling on the rear door while he held the front one open. For a second he stared at me.

I raised the Browning and shot him.

The *boom* was deafening in the enclosed space. The flash blinded me for an instant, and the reek of cordite cut across the smell of metal and petrol and wet grass.

It got him in the throat. For a few seconds he stayed where he was. His eyes bulged hideously, and his left hand pushed out vaguely towards me as if to ward off any more bullets. The wound started to ooze dark blood —and then he made a small gagging noise, his mouth opened, and suddenly there was blood everywhere. It splashed out of his mouth, covered his chin, and ran off on to my legs.

Then his muscles relaxed as he died. The body flopped off the car like a coat falling from a peg, his head hitting the door with a sickening *thud* as it went.

I kicked my foot free of the pedals, jackknifed convulsively in a shower of glass fragments, and ended up half-kneeling on the passenger door, shaking with reaction. *Get out of here!* I scooped the Colt out of the driver's door pocket and threw myself out of the distorted windscreen aperture.

The Sten bellowed from somewhere in the darkness, and the car echoed to the crash of bullets going through the side and roof.

I dived round the crumpled bonnet and threw myself flat in the undergrowth, praying that I'd put a few feet of Mercedes between me and the gun. An instant later the firing stopped, so I guessed I must have. The silence rang in my ears.

I found I was holding both pistols in my right hand. I rolled on my back, dropped them on to my chest, snuggled the Colt into my throbbing left hand, then picked up the Browning in my right again.

So now what?

There was a crunch of undergrowth from the other side of the car. My adrenaline pump hitched itself into emergency overboost. I sent my right hand down by my side, found a small fragment of wood, and pitched it gently over the top of the Merc.

It pattered down softly. The oldest trick in the book.

The Sten crashed.

I threw myself to my feet and leaped round the front of the car. Haydon was a dim outline in the courtesy light, turning back towards me. I fired the Browning again and again; then the Sten flashed several times and a giant numbing hammer swiped the pistol out of my hand.

I turned and ran.

I got probably ten paces before I cannoned off a tree, tripped over something, and went down like a piano off a tenth-floor roof. When my head stopped swinging on its hinges I found I was lying on my left hand, which still held the Colt, and wheezing like a walrus as I tried to cram some air into my winded lungs. I started to move—and then saw the dim outline of Haydon, five feet away. He was bringing the Sten up.

I played my last desperate card.

"Way—ugh—wait," I croaked between gasps. "Do a . . . deal . . . stamps . . . here."

He hesitated for a second or two, keeping the gun on me. I gasped and gulped a bit more for local color, then groped for the pocket of my jeans with my numb right hand.

"Here, look . . . Mauritius Post Office . . ."

It jolted him. He obviously recognized the name of the most valuable stamp in the collection. He ought to have blown my head off and gone through my pockets afterwards—but hearing me claim to have £120,000 worth of primary objective on board put him off his stride for a moment. He stepped right up close and bent over me.

I rolled gently to the left, just a little so as not to excite him, and made a show of trying to get the unresponsive fingers of my right hand into my pocket. Under cover of the squirmings I moved my left hand up underneath my chest—then suddenly whipped over on to my back and fired the heavy Colt up into him.

His shadowy form swayed above me, and I kept pulling the trigger as fast as I could. The Colt coughed heavily through its silencer and jumped in my hand so that I nearly dropped it. The Sten banged twice or three times and something stung my ear. I rolled frantically aside. I kept rolling, terrified, until I realized it wasn't firing anymore.

I twisted round and slid to a stop on my stomach, facing him with the Colt held out in front of me. The shadow of him staggered, and the muzzle of the Sten drooped towards the ground.

The Colt coughed and bucked, sending jabs of agony up my arm, as I fired again. He jerked twice, spun round—and dropped the Sten. I stopped shooting. He staggered back a couple of paces, groping behind with one hand as if seeking support, then crumpled up and pitched over on his side.

I let my gun hand fall to the ground and my face sink into the wet leaves. My breath came out in a long, whistling sigh.

I shouldn't have got away with it. I could hear my limbs rustling on the ground as they shook with sheer animal terror. My stomach churned and the taste of bile welled up in my throat. He'd had me stone cold. I ought to be dead.

166

The rain pattered down gently, punctuated by water dripping off the leaves.

After a long time I pushed myself to my feet and limped slowly over to Haydon's prostrate figure. My footsteps crunched loudly through the dripping quiet.

He was doubled up on his side, right hand clutching his stomach and left hand sticking straight out from his body, palm upwards, as if in supplication.

He was still alive. His eyes followed me as I knelt beside him.

The hand on his stomach was covered in a dark glistening mass. There was another dark patch on his trousers, up by his hip, which was spreading slowly. Blood was pulsing gently out of the corner of his mouth.

I leaned forward so that my left forearm rested on the ground with the long silencer of the Colt pointing straight at his forehead. His eyes followed the gun.

I said, loudly and distinctly, "Which family are you from?"

The eyes blinked slowly, and his lips worked a little. I leaned further forward to catch the words.

"Fu' . . . you. I . . . see . . . y'ag'in. Sh . . . Ship'll ge' . . . you."

Then the eyes closed, more blood ran from his mouth, and he slipped into unconsciousness. No plea for help, no asking for mercy. He seemed to think he was dying anyway.

He was right about that.

I thought about Bill and squeezed the trigger. The Colt coughed its harsh cough and Haydon grew a black blob on his forehead. The slug tore off the back of his skull. His sphincter opened with a gasping sound and I nearly gagged on the smell.

Then there was just the patter of the rain.

Feeling infinitely weary, I pushed myself on to my feet again. The Colt dangled from my left hand. I stumbled around until I found the Sten and the remains of the Browning. I dropped all the guns by the car, scooped up a handful of wet leaves, leaned in through the windscreen hole, and wiped the steering wheel, gear lever, door handles, and switches. Then I flicked off the light switch to put out the one remaining taillight, and pulled the passenger door far enough closed to switch off the interior light. The black night closed in. With any luck, the wreck wouldn't be found until daylight.

I picked up the guns again and clanked out of the wood towards Haydon's Mercedes.

CHAPTER 20

Dawn, poking bright and newly washed round the remnants of cold-front cumulus, found me tooling the Mercedes slowly through the back roads near Chalon-sur-Saône. My left hand throbbed, my right hand ached, and my head had two little men in it working with pickaxes on overtime rates. My eyes, gritty and bloodshot, took several seconds to focus on the dashboard clock.

I'd been driving all night: driving and thinking, not daring to stop and sleep in case a prowling cop car found me. I was pretty sure the law wouldn't be looking for me specifically yet—but if the cops happened upon someone in my state in possession of a machine gun they wouldn't even *ask* if I was on the wanted list: they'd just slap me in the hoosegow on general suspicion of starting World War Three, then work out what I actually *had* done at their leisure. So no sleep for Holland.

My first act after pinching Haydon's car had been to put 50 fast kilometers between me and the stiffs in the wood. Then I'd stopped and buried the Colt, the Browning, and the barrel of the Sten in the bottom of a deep wet ditch. Half an hour after that I'd found a stream running by the roadside, so I stopped again, cleaned myself up as best I could, and washed my tee shirt. Then I dug the grisly corpse of my little finger out of my pocket and flung it into the middle of the stream.

At three in the morning, I'd found a roadside telephone in a little village. I rang Lubec's house and told John to pick me up in Lubec's Citroën at 6:30 A.M. three kilos south of Chalon on the Autoroute du Sud. He said okay, worry deep in his voice, and I got back into the Merc and kept moving.

So here it was, just after 5:30—and here I was, a mile or two south of Chalon and a little way west of the *autoroute*. Bully for me.

I found an entrance to a field of waving corn, and drove the Merc into it just as the yellow rim of the sun peeped over the horizon. We jounced down the farm track for about 20 yards; then I trod on the throttle and spun the wheel to the left. The car plunged into the corn, thumped heavily over the furrows, and finally stalled about 10 yards in. I sat for a moment listening to the ticking of cooling metal and trying to summon up the energy to get moving. I was an old, old man this bright morning.

Finally I picked up my tee shirt where it had been drying in the blast of the heater and hauled myself out of the car. It was the same Merc that Harvey and Rico had used to pick me up from Lyon Airport, so I'd found my flying jacket on the back seat. I used the tee shirt to wipe the car clean of fingerprints, then put it on back to front to get the cleanest side to the fore. After that I shoved the Sten magazine down the back of my trousers, put my jacket on, and wrapped the rest of the gun up in the road map. When I'd finished, the result looked exactly like a gun wrapped up in a map and not much like anything else—but it was the best I could do. I tried to stand some of the corn back up behind the car, but it wouldn't stand. Maybe the farmer didn't go down this particular track on Sundays.

The dawn chorus was cranking itself up nicely as I started walking. The air smelled fresh, and the sun on my face felt good after the cold wetness of the night and the dry fug of the car. My hip produced a stab of pain each time I put my left foot down, but I tried to ignore it and tell myself it was a lovely morning for a stroll.

Forty-five minutes later I'd given up kidding myself. It was definitely *not* a lovely morning for a stroll. With my hip, no morning is—and on this particular bloody sunrise, the hip had plenty of competition from various other parts of me. By the time I reached the fence beside the *autoroute* I was lurching along mindlessly, in a state of nervous exhaustion.

I plunked down behind the fence to wait. Within fifteen minutes, Lubec's Citroën rolled slowly along the northbound carriageway. After it went by I gave it a couple of minutes, then clambered over the fence, left the Sten in the long grass, and started walking slowly south, praying that John would come back before any cop cars happened along.

He did. Two lorries rumbled past—and then the Citroën swished to a stop alongside me. I opened the door, said "Wait a mo'," retrieved the Sten, and pitched myself into the front seat. The car moved off almost before I had the door shut.

John, of course, immediately wanted to know What the Hell? I started to tell him to wait until we were all together—and then suddenly the exhaustion, triggered by the final release from the tension of the night, came welling up from my guts and hit me right between the eyes. For the second time in that Citroën, I went out like a light.

I came round, crawling slowly out of a black swamp, to find John shaking me. I jacked an eye open and growled something out of a dry, sticky throat. The shaking stopped. There was a roaring in my ears, a tight pain behind my eyes, and my mouth tasted like an old oil filter. I peered blearily through the Citroën's windscreen and found we were at Lubec's house. The clock on the dash said 10:30.

Automatically, I reached under my feet and picked up the Sten. John

171

helped me out of the car. The front door opened as we lurched slowly up the steps. Rick, Jedrow and Louise were waiting in the hall, a silent row of faces, as we staggered over the threshold, I let the gun drop out of my hand and leaned tiredly against the wall.

For a moment no one said anything at all. No jolly welcomes for Holland.

Then Jedrow cleared his throat, shifted his weight, and said hesitantly: "You . . . ah . . . er . . . okay?"

"Yeah, sure." I quite obviously wasn't, but no one wanted to make anything of it.

"We . . . er . . . Did you . . . er . . .?" His voice tailed off.

"Yeah, I found 'em. Or they found me. They're dead." Oh, smooth, tactful Holland. So delicately put. I turned to Louise, who visibly stiffened. Christ, what it was to be popular.

"How's your father?" I asked her.

She obviously wasn't expecting the question. "He . . . should be all right. The bullet glance off a bone of his forearm and broke it, but it is not so difficult a fracture."

"That's good. Where is he, here?"

"*Oui*—yes. He is upstairs, asleep. The doctor says he ought to go to 'ospital, but he will not go." She correctly interpreted the questioning look on my face and added bitterly: "It is all right—the doctor will not report the wound. He 'as known our family for years, an' my father tell him it was an accident he did not want reported."

I nodded wearily. There didn't seem to be anything useful to say to that. There was an awkward silence. No one wanted to look at me.

And suddenly I was furious. My best chum had been murdered; I'd been tortured, crashed, and shot at—and now my friends, the people I'd been protecting, were frightened to touch me in case they caught something nasty. Rage welled up in my throat like a furry ball.

"You bastards!" I croaked hoarsely. I found I was on the edge of tears. "Don't you get all bloody sanctimonious with me! That was *Bill* those buggers murdered! You remember Bill—you were supposed to be his fuckin' friends! And they'd have been after you next, too—but don't worry about that. Everything's all right provided we all behave like little bloody gentlemen and sit still and take it! All right—*you* fuckin' take it: I'll fuck off so you don't have to touch me!''

I turned for the door. Jedrow shrank back from me. I didn't know where I was going. Then the room and the faces started a slow barrel roll, and sound and vision tapered off into a tunnel of blackness.

I didn't even feel John catch me as I fell.

CHAPTER 21

I was in the cockpit of a spinning Tiger. Janie was standing on the catwalk on the lower wing. The spin got tighter and tighter, and it wouldn't recover because of her weight and drag out there. I shouted, "Come in, darling." She turned her head and looked at me —and shuddered with revulsion. "There's something wrong with you," she said. Then she let go and whirled away from the aeroplane. I tried frantically to get out after her, but I couldn't get the straps undone. . . .

I woke up screaming.

I seemed to be held down by clamps. Something was happening to my left hand.

I screwed my eyes shut for a moment, collected myself, and opened them again. I was lying on a sofa. John was at the far end, holding my ankles. Jedrow was leaning over the back of it using both hands to pin my right arm by my side. I looked up and found Rick standing over my head. He was holding my shoulders down.

Louise was sitting on a stool level with my chest. She had my left forearm clamped between her knees and was winding a bandage around my head.

I said: "All right, you can let go. I'm awake now." My voice was a hoarse croak.

One by one, hesitantly, the hands released me. I must have been threshing around like a maniac. Feeling the brush of cool air on my body, I looked down. I was wearing a pair of underpants and nothing else. There was a big towel underneath me on the sofa, and a bowl of steaming soapy water nearby. Taking stock, I found I had a pad plastered to the back of my left leg where I'd been nicked with the shotgun pellet. There seemed to be something on my face, and I raised my right hand and found another dressing taped over the cut on my forehead.

The girl finished bandaging my left hand and released it from between her knees, taking care not to knock the fingers as she did so. The hand was sore, but the vicious throb was gone.

"Thank you, Louise," I said quietly. "Thank you very much."

To my surprise she said, "That's all right," and even managed a small, hesitant smile. Then she put aside a tray with bandages and dressings on it, picked up the bowl of water and a damp towel, and left the room.

There was one of those awkward silences.

Not without difficulty, I swung my legs off the sofa and got myself sat up. Everyone rushed over to help. John wrapped a blanket round my shoulders. They all looked embarrassed and awkward.

Then Jedrow cleared his throat and said: "We . . . er . . . we. . . sort of want to apologize, young Ken." His gravelly voice was very deep and earnest. "We didn't mean to . . . er . . . ."

"Skip it," I interrupted. I felt thick and muzzy, and my mouth had a mohair lining. "What I want is a cigarette and a Scotch."

Rick whizzed over to the drinks trolley while John produced a Disque Bleu and lit it for me. His wristwatch said 10:15: I'd been out for nearly twelve hours. Rick handed me a generous double, and my mistreated stomach gave a halfhearted heave as the first belt went down like liquid

175

fire. I came awake another two hundred percent and looked around their faces. They looked anxious and awkward—but they still had that sick, shocked look in the back of their eyes. Even Jedrow. It was going to take time for them to get over the fact that I could turn killer.

It was going to take time for me too, come to that.

John perched himself on the stool Louise had been using.

"Well, Bruv," he said, "what happened exactly?"

So I took another gulp of Scotch and told them what happened exactly. Nearly exactly, anyway—I left out the bit about blowing Haydon's brains out after he was down. That was something between Bill and Haydon and me. The rest of the tale produced a stunned silence.

The silence went on for a while after I'd finished. Then John said slowly, "Jesus, you *did* have a night."

I agreed. Rick poured some more Scotch into my glass, and I silently toasted survival. I was beginning to feel the effects on my very empty stomach.

"It was on the radio this morning and television tonight," said Rick. "The car looked a right mess. They reckon the cops've got a nationwide hunt going for the blokes who did it. They've connected the crash with the thing at the barn."

I nearly choked over my Scotch.

"Are they looking for me yet?"

"No, they didn't say anyth . . ." Suddenly he realized what I'd said. His eyes got very big. "Look . . . looking for *you*?" His voice was hushed, shocked. "They won't be looking for you, will they? They won't . . . They can't . . ."

"They can and they will," I said harshly. "The remains of the Auster in the barn'll lead them to Monsieur Sante, the secretary of the Vivaral Aéro Club, and Monsieur Sante'll tell them about me. Any moment now they'll be putting out my description with a wanted-dead-or-alive sign under it."

There was total silence in the room. They obviously hadn't thought of that. Everyone went a whiter shade of pale as they did think of it.

Jedrow, characteristically, was the first to speak.

176

"Does that mean you'll . . . we'll . . . be . . . arrested?" He sounded about 200 years old.

"No," I replied wearily. "Not necessarily. But they'll certainly want me, and probably you, for questioning. They'll question us pretty closely, too, because I let Sante know I was at odds with Haydon. On the other hand, I don't see that they can *prove* anything. Everything I might have left fingerprints on in the barn went up in smoke, and I wiped off both of the cars pretty carefully. I got rid of all the guns except the Sten, and I chucked my little finger away, too."

Jedrow shuddered—but he was thinking again, after a fashion. "Hold it," he said creakily. "Why did you keep the Sten? That sounds bloody dangerous."

"Had to," I said. "When Sante tells the cops I'm English they'll check all the ports of entry to see whether I've left the country yet. Le Touquet are bound to tell them about the gun—and once they know about it, I'm going to look very silly indeed if I try to tell them I've lost the bloody thing, aren't I? Especially since I never reported it lost or anything. No—the only thing we can do is to put the plugged barrel back and produce it with an innocent smile when we turn ourselves in."

"Turn . . . ourselves . . . in?" Jedrow obviously didn't like the idea of that. "You mean we've got to . . . give ourselves up?"

I took another gulp of Scotch. If we got unlucky, that might very well be what it amounted to. But we still didn't have any other choice. I tried to sound confident.

"No," I said. "We'll wait until they broadcast our names . . . or my name . . . as being people they want to interview. Then we'll roll into a cop shop somewhere and say, 'Here we are—what's all the bother?' Play it dead innocent. If we've got our stories straight they shouldn't be able to shake us after that."

I hoped.

"Just a minute, just a minute, just a minute." It was John. He was chewing his lip and looking paler than ever. "What about Rick and me? You say you'll go to the cops—but there's us with four bullet holes in the XK, and Lubec here with a bullet wound in his arm. What about that?"

177

"Have you filled in those holes?"

"Yes, but if the gendarmes look hard enough they won't have any trouble finding them: all we could do was slap a bit of glass-fiber filler in them."

"That's good enough for the moment. You get going and get back home as soon as possible. If Jedrow and I talk our way out of it there's no reason why they should want to question you at all. We obviously won't implicate you, but we'd better be on the safe side—so cut out the metal round the bullet holes when you get back, and weld new bits in. That way there won't be any evidence at all, whatever happens. Jedrow and I won't mention Lubec, or this place, either—we'll have to work out some story about going off touring or something."

John still had thought written all over his face.

"What'll you do," he said slowly, "if the cops *don't* broadcast the fact that they want you? They might just start looking for you without telling the press and TV: they might figure that'd drive you underground. You can't very well give yourselves up if they haven't said they're looking for you, can you?"

"I doubt if that'll arise. If they don't find us after a few hours they'll ask for the assistance of the public. They couldn't hide a large manhunt for long, anyway. But even if they don't announce it, it doesn't make any difference. Jedrow and I'll just amble up to the Stampe at Lyon Airport and let them pick us up. They're bound to be watching that."

Rick and John suddenly looked as though I'd slapped their faces. Rick swallowed hard.

"They weren't watching it this evening," he said shakily. "We just went out there, a couple of hours ago, to pick up your Simca. If they'd been waiting for you they'd have grabbed us."

I got a whisky lock in my throat for the second time in five minutes.

"Christ, I'll say they would!" The thought sent a cold swamp of shock right through me. If Rick and John had been roped in when they weren't expecting it they'd probably have talked us all straight to the guillotine. Why the cops hadn't been there I couldn't imagine: if the carnage at the barn had been found in the morning, it shouldn't have taken them all day

to trace the Auster from its airframe and engine numbers and contact M. Sante, who'd have told them about me. Then they'd only have had to ask Customs and Immigration about us—and *bingo*, they'd have been all over Lyon Airport in minutes. Jesus, they *should* have been there hours ago. Rick and John must just have beaten them to it.

Then something else occurred to me: by now the cops must have talked to the air-show people and M. Merlin would have told them about the Simca—so at this very moment they'd be looking for that car like it was carrying the French gold reserves. . . .

Trying to stay calm, I said, "Where did you put the Simca?"

"In the drive behind the Cit . . ." John's voice trailed off and his eyes opened wide as the implication hit him.

"Exactly," I said. "With its number plate pointing straight out of the gateway for the first passing gendarme to see. Perhaps you wouldn't mind going and putting it in the garage? After that, you'd better go and get packed up and ready to leave."

John and Rick whizzed out of the room.

Jedrow and I looked at each other.

"Who set fire to that barn last night?" he asked. "You?"

I had my usual difficulty changing course, then said: "Christ, no! If it'd happened a few minutes earlier I'd've been trapped in the bloody thing. I haven't a clue who did that—but I guess whoever it was was the shotgun artist too. That's the biggest mystery of the whole thing: we seem to've got a third party joining in now."

That cheered him up. He and Lubec had already arrived at much the same conclusion anyway, but we had a few minutes of communal gloom while we both thought about it some more. We were still chewing it over when Rick and John came back.

"Ready to go?" I asked.

They were. They reckoned on driving all night and catching a Channel ferry from Boulogne in the morning. They seemed anxious to get going. I didn't blame them. I wished I could go too.

"Sort yourselves out a story to account for your time since Saturday evening," I told them. "Say you motored slowly up France, sight-seeing. Pick out a couple of places on your way back tonight where you can say you camped.''

They nodded. They both looked white and nervous. Making up alibis didn't seem to agree with them. Well, it didn't agree with me much either —but if the cops *did* get on to them, we didn't want the whole deal blown by some stupid discrepancy. All four of us went carefully through their mythical parting from Jedrow and me at Lyon Airport after the show.

At the end of it, when they were about to go, John said: "About the XK, Ken—d'you think we should change the tires? Those dirt roads leading to the barn were pretty soft: we may have left some tracks.''

I remembered seeing them. They weren't a big thing in themselves— plenty of cars run on Pirelli Cinturatos—but there was no point in giving out even slender clues when we didn't have to. The memory of the tracks nudged something in the back of my mind. I had the feeling it might be important—but then it was gone.

"Yeah, change 'em," I said wearily. "Get some secondhand tires, pay cash for 'em, and change them yourselves. Don't go to a garage to have it done.''

We said our good-byes, and a few minutes later the XK *whoomph*ed into life and crunched out of the drive.

After it had gone, Jedrow and I listened to the late-night news. Our names weren't mentioned. Well, they would be soon. . . .

I lay on the sofa and stared at the ceiling. The single table lamp made a pool of light up there. Somewhere in the house a clock chimed once. One A.M. Time all good children were asleep. I wasn't a good children—and I wasn't asleep, either. The thought of the cops made a hollow pit of fear in my stomach. To take my mind off it I lit another Gitane and rolled the events of the last week round in my head for the fiftieth time. There was something—some little item, maybe important, maybe not—that kept tripping a chord, then skipping away again, just out of reach. . . .

I sat bolt upright as the door opened. It was Louise. She was wearing a dressing gown and a gently tousled, middle-of-the-night look. She was carrying a tray with a bowl of soup on it.

"I could not sleep," she said softly. "I saw your bedroom door was open an' you weren't there. I brought you this. It might 'elp you sleep.''

"Thank you," I said. "Thank you very much."

Suddenly I felt shy. I wasn't used to pretty girls getting up to make me soup at one in the morning. Especially when they'd already made me one meal late that night—and even especiallier when they were Louise, who had hitherto shown every symptom of regarding Holland as several stages more undesirable than a bad case of leprosy.

I swung my legs down to a sitting position, and she put the tray on my knees. I expected her to go then—but instead, she sat down beside me. There was an awkward little silence while I shoveled up the soup. When I'd finished, I put the tray on the floor.

Now she would go. But there was something I wanted to say first. I found I couldn't look at her.

"Louise, look: I'm terribly sorry about your father getting hurt. I . . . I . . . couldn't . . ." I ran down miserably. I'd about said it all, at that.

"I know, Ken," she said softly. I turned to her in amazement. Her level blue eyes looked straight into mine. "I know what is going on now. My father told me. You did all you could. I think, like my father says, it would have been much worse if you hadn't been there. What 'appened wasn't your fault."

I said, "Oh. . . ." Nothing else offered itself. Louise hesitated, looked at the floor, then went on in a small voice.

"I am sorry I was so . . . bad about you before. I thought you were a terrible person. But now I know what 'appened. How your friend was killed, an' how you were made to crash. Even so I cannot understand anyone tracking down men to kill them: but I think also my father may be right when he says I know little of the bad things of life. I have never been shot at or had friends killed, so I am not fitted to judge you." She turned her head and looked me in the face again. "So I mus' apologize, very much, for what I said before."

I nodded dumbly. Somehow, her saying that made a lot of difference. She knew everything I'd done—yet she still worried about hurting me. It made me feel almost part of the human race again.

"Thank you," I said slowly. "Thank you very much for that."

181

Our faces were very close—and suddenly I realized that I liked this girl a lot. I looked into her eyes and tried to read what was there. Compassion, yes—and something else, too. Fear? I didn't know.

"Look," I said awkwardly. "I wonder . . . I mean . . . Well, look, when this is over, do you think I could see you again? I'd . . . like to, very much."

Oh, bloody scintillating, Holland. The golden tongue strikes again. I opened my mouth to make some other brilliant contribution, couldn't think of anything, and shut it again.

Louise studied the carpet. For perhaps half a minute she didn't say anything. Then she looked up at me again—and now I could see what else was in her eyes. It was pity.

"I am sorry, Ken," she said gently. "I would have liked to see you again, perhaps; but it would not be any good. We are not . . . the same type. An' I have a boyfriend in Paris. He is a doctor. We are thinking we might get married at Christmastime."

A silly little moment of hope curled up and died.

The clock chimed again. Two thirty. I rolled over on my right side in the big, lonely bed and tried to stop my mind going through the sound barrier. It didn't work, of course. Every brain cell in my head jangled around with the feverish activity of determined insomnia.

The mystery of whoever-it-was with the shotgun . . . Why hadn't the cops broadcast my name and description yet? . . . Fifty quid for a set of tires for the XK . . . What was Janie doing now? . . . Louise saying she couldn't understand anyone tracking men down to kill them . . . tracking men down . . .

Tracking!

Suddenly I had it. The loose piece. The tiny, almost forgotten factor that connected everything up.

I sat up in bed and turned the light on. I had some hard thinking to do.

CHAPTER 22

At six o'clock the next morning I was alone in the kitchen. Just me, a cup of coffee, the radio, and the young sunshine streaming in the window.

The French news, reasonably enough, was broadcast in French—which meant that I only picked up about one word in twenty, being as my French consists of a dozen swearwords and enough left over to ask stupid questions about the pen of my aunt. But that didn't matter: I was only listening for four words—and I'd understand *them* all right if I heard them. Two of them were Kenneth Holland, and the other two were James Jedrow. I glued my ear to the speaker and listened.

At 6:20 the high-speed *français* finally fizzled out, giving way to light music. I switched the radio off and started breathing normally again.

Again there'd been no mention of Holland or Jedrow.

I scribbled a note to everyone while I finished my coffee, then slipped quietly out the back door and got the Simca out of the garage. The tires crunched on the gravel, but if it woke anybody up they were too slow in reacting to do anything about it.

Thirty-five minutes later I pulled up beside a five-bar gate in the eastern boundary fence of Lyon-Bron Airport. This gate had been the car-park entrance during the air show, but now it was closed and padlocked. The Stampe was picketed, along with a few other leftovers from the show, about a hundred yards inside the field.

I clambered awkwardly over the gate, trying not to bang my hand. My left leg, suffering from its usual early-morning stiffness, caught in a bar and overbalanced me on the way down the other side. I went sprawling. As I scraped myself up I reflected that *that* little performance wasn't much of an advert for my abilities as a wing-walker. Anyone watching would be more likely to mark me down as the fall-about clown.

I wondered if anyone *was* watching.

I limped over to the Stampe, hauled myself onto the catwalk on the starboard lower wing, and sat on the side of the fuselage while I smoked a cigarette. A La Postale DC4 slid down the bright morning sky, touched down with a ponderous *squip* on runway one seven, and rolled along with its Pratt and Whitneys making growly rustling noises. I got down again, trod the cigarette end carefully into the dew-soaked grass, and for want of anything better to do, carried out a thorough preflight inspection on the aeroplane. Apart from needing more fuel, she was ready to go.

Two blackbirds cawed at me as I climbed back over the gate to the car. And that was all. No people about.

No cops.

The Holland-Jedrow manhunt didn't seem to have much steam this morning.

In fact, it didn't seem to exist at all.

Mt.-Vivaral was having another of its beautiful crystal mornings as I swung the Simca round the village square. The same proprietor was sweeping the same little café, the same women were trotting into the *boulangerie* for fresh bread and milk, and the same plane trees were still leaning skywards in the steeply sloping *place*. Somehow, all this surprised me. How could the place remain unchanged over the thousand years since I'd last been here?

184

The big solid house that was number *vingt-huit* rue d'Avignon was certainly the same. Its white stucco walls, neat disciplined garden, and elegant climbing plants all looked as if they were there to stay for several centuries. The well-rubbed brass plaque on the gatepost that said M. PAUL SANTE, AVOCAT possessed the same air of solid respectability. So did the gleaming XJ6 in the drive.

I closed the gate behind me and glanced at the tires of the Jaguar as I walked towards the front door. They were the fat, low-profile ER70 SP Sports that Dunlop made specially for the XJs and E types. Their zigzag tread pattern was bisected by a deep slot down the center of the tire, an idea borrowed from wet-weather racing boots. The theory is that the tread pushes water into the slot, where it gets siphoned out harmlessly instead of creating a "wedge" in front of the tire and causing aquaplaning. Quite effective, too—and very distinctive.

In fact, the tracks this set had left in the dirt road leading to the barn at St.-Galmier had been *very* distinctive indeed. The rain had probably blurred them out later on—but I remembered seeing them quite clearly in the yellow lights of the Mercedes as I bounced down the track after Haydon.

It took two or three good long rings to get Sante to the door. Maybe I'd caught him in the bathroom. Finally there was a series of scraping and clicking noises from the other side of the oaken portal, and then it swung open.

M. Sante didn't look very pleased to see me. In fact, he didn't look as if he'd have been pleased to see anyone right then. His eyes were puffy, his hair tussled, and he was wearing a rich wine-colored dressing gown over a suit of lurid and tasteless pajamas. He tried to work up the querulous indignant look of an honest citizen disturbed before *cafe*, but it didn't come off too well because he wasn't dressed for it and his heart wasn't in it anyway. He must have been expecting me, or someone like me. A shadow of worry—or maybe fear—crossed the back of his eyes.

"Please enter, M'sieur," he said. His voice was thick and hungover. It sounded as if the wine had been red last night. Perhaps he'd had trouble getting to sleep.

I stepped inside, and Sante poked his head round the door, took a quick look round, then closed it and slipped a burglar chain into place. He didn't seem to want to be disturbed. That was fair enough. Neither did I.

He said, "We will go to my *bureau*" and waddled off down the hall. I followed him into his study and he shut the door behind us and made his way round the desk. He gestured for me to sit down, then plumped himself into the overstuffed leather swivel chair that was obviously his normal habitat.

Behind his own desk in his own office, he seemed to gain confidence. Some of the avuncular heartiness of four days ago was back as he said, "Now, then, M'sieur 'Olland, 'ow can I 'elp you?"

"I've come for two reasons, Monsieur Sante," I replied slowly. "One is to thank you for not telling the gendarmes about me—and the other is to buy some stamps from you."

He seemed to sag in his seat, as if he had a slow puncture. His face went a couple of shades paler. But his hands waved in floppy support of the puzzlement in his voice as he said: "M'sieur 'Olland, I am sorry. But I do not think I know what you are talking about. Perhaps you 'ave made some mistake . . .?"

"No. No mistake, Monsieur. You have some stamps which you found in the Auster Mr. Charlton and I bought. That's fair enough—I'm not blaming you for having them. But I want to make you an offer for them which, in the circumstances, I think you would be foolish to refuse."

Real *Godfather* stuff—but Sante was still flopping his hands about and trying to look bewildered.

"Mais non, M'sieur," he persisted. "I am afraid you must be misled. What tells you I 'ave these . . . these stamps you speak of?"

I leaned forward and rested my elbows on his desk.

"Well, first of all, someone set fire to that barn on Saturday night so as to destroy my Auster. He could only have had one reason for doing that —to make all the interested parties think the stamps had gone up in smoke. And the only person who would want us all to think that was the man who actually had them—and that has to be you. I saw the tire marks of your car on the farm track. XJ6s aren't exactly thick on the ground around here.''

''*My God, that is preposterous!*'' Sante was halfway out of his seat, his voice shaking with indignation. ''You 'ave a big nerve, coming 'ere an' accusing me of all this because of a tire track. . . .''

''*Shut up!*''

My Chief Instructor's bark caught him right in the midriff. He folded back into the chair with an almost audible whistle of escaping air, wide eyes staring at my face. Perhaps my recent record of homicide had something to do with it: if I'd reached into my flying jacket with my right hand he'd probably have died of fright.

''You're right. I didn't come here with only a tire track to go on.'' He kept staring at me, seeming to shrink into the wine-colored dressing gown. ''There's also the matter of what you told the gendarmes—or rather, what you *didn't* tell them. When they traced the Auster back to you, you had to tell them about the man who bought it—and while you were doing that, one would have thought you'd also have told them about my·coming to you to dispute the ownership, wouldn't one? Very important piece of evidence, that: important enough to have every gendarme in the country looking for Holland by now.

''*But they're not looking for Holland, are they?* There's been nothing on the radio or in the press, and this morning I strolled round my aircraft at Lyon and then drove over here—and no one stopped me. No sign of a copper anywhere.

''And the reason they're not looking for me is that you didn't tell them about me—because you figured that if I got caught I might spill everything I know. You didn't know just *what* I might know—but you figured that it *might* implicate you, and you didn't want to take the chance. Even if it didn't get you into trouble directly, those stamps would become completely unsalable if I started bleating all about them to the coppers.''

Sante just sat and watched me, still looking as if I'd kicked him in the guts. He seemed to have run out of indignance. I took a deep breath and carried on.

187

"Your trouble all along was that you didn't know enough about the stamps. You probably found them quite a long time ago—during the first Révision Générale on the aircraft, at a guess. It would be pretty difficult to hide a load of stamps quickly in an Auster somewhere where they wouldn't be found during a major overhaul. So you found them—but then you were frightened of them, and quite rightly. They were enormously valuable. Had they been stolen? You didn't know. The most important ones were recorded as having last been heard of before the war—but there had to be more to it than that. How did they come to be hidden in the Auster? Was there someone, somewhere, with a claim of ownership? You didn't know—you couldn't know. So you decided to keep them for a good long time: prewar claims of ownership would tend to get thinner with time.

"You may even have anticipated what actually happened, though I imagine you stopped worrying about illegal-type owners showing up a long time ago. So it must have been a hell of a shock when three or four people suddenly wanted this particular old Auster. You obviously realized they couldn't all be after it for its own sake—and I must have confirmed it for you by telling you there was a dispute over it and then not going to the cops the way I said I was going to.

"So now you were in a right old jam. Haydon—sorry, you knew him as Hunt—was going to take the kite apart piece by piece. And when he didn't find the stamps there he was going to start working back—and you were going to be one of the things he worked back to. So you figured that if the aircraft was destroyed, Hunt—and I—would think the stamps had gone up with it and pack up and go home. How you proposed to get rid of the stamps after that without alerting everybody, I don't know; but I suppose it seemed that the only thing you *could* do was get rid of us first and worry about that later. So you followed Hunt, or maybe the guys who picked me up at Lyon Airfield, and when you found where the aircraft was you just sat around with a tin of petrol and a box of matches waiting for the right moment. The fight I started provided it: with everybody busy shooting at each other, nobody'd ever know just how the fire started.

What made you risk everything by joining into the fight with that shotgun I can't imagine. Probably you just aren't very good at this sort of thing.''

I seemed to be right so far, at least. Sante was staring at me with the sort of sick fascination I imagine a rabbit must watch a snake with. His face had gone the color of old parchment.

''What you had no way of knowing,'' I went on, ''was that Hunt and all his mob would get killed that night. Jesus, I wouldn't have put tuppence-halfpenny on me myself. But when they were, you were caught again by that same old lack of knowledge about the stamps. If you told the cops about me you'd probably get me out of the way—but at the same time I might squeal something about the stamps that would prevent you from ever selling them. Maybe they'd been stolen by Roberto Miere and maybe I knew who from or who by, or something—you simply had no way of knowing. You only knew I had to know *something* about them or I wouldn't have come here. So in the end you decided not to tell the gendarmes about me—for which I am profoundly grateful. I'll take that as balancing out the potshot you took at me by the barn. That makes us even.

''Now, if you're interested, I'll tell you how you can stop yourself getting killed over them.''

I opened up an inlaid wooden box on his desk and lo, there were cigarettes in it. I helped myself to one, and lit it with his big table lighter.

''Are we together so far?'' I gave him my best Get-those-bloody-wings-level glare. ''If you're going to be stupid and start denying everything then we'd better have it out before we go any further.''

He wasn't denying anything. He was looking as though he'd just caught a departing Mystère between the shoulder blades. After a few moments of silence he opened his mouth to say something, changed his mind, cleared his throat, and finally mumbled, ''Go on, M'sieur.'' His hands flopped in a small gesture of defeat.

''Okay, then. You've heard of the Mafia and the Cosa Nostra?'' He nodded, jowls shaking weakly. I told him the story of the stamps, keeping it brief. He sat very still, staring at my face as I went through it all. He didn't interrupt.

At the end of it I said, "Where were the stamps, incidentally?"

He stirred, like a man coming out of a bad dream.

"In the control sticks," he croaked slowly. "They were in envelopes rolled up in the control sticks. I find them one day after we get the aircraft. I am sitting in it, waiting to tow up some gliders, and I am fiddling with the stick. I am bored, you know? I pull the rubber handgrip off—and there is the first packet of stamps. There is another packet in the other stick."

I nodded. "Yeah, it had to be something like that. Anyway—let's talk about what's going to happen now. As you've probably realized, Haydon —or Hunt, if you like—could only've come from one outfit. And that's the family the stamps were pinched from in the first place. I don't know where that family is or who it is or where it got its information from—but I do know that not only do they have the whole story, they also have a list of the stamps."

This was a slight exaggeration, since all I knew for sure was that Haydon had said, "We'd know if they'd been sold," and that later he'd recognized the name of the Mauritius. But if he knew that, it seemed a safe bet that the family would know what the rest were.

"So now," I went on, "you're stuck with the bloody things. If you sell them the family will see them come on the market, find out who sold them —and come knocking on your door. And as you saw on Saturday night, they don't knock gently. And you won't be able to sell them in secret, either. They need to be verified by experts after being out of circulation for so long, and once that's all been done and they've been offered for sale, you could never hope to cover your tracks enough to keep your identity hidden from anyone who really wanted to find out. It just couldn't be done. If you sold them in someone else's name the family'd go and see the party concerned—and the party would bloody soon tell them about you once that lot started to lean on him. And you'd never get away with using a false name and selling them yourself: apart from anything else, the government would be on to you for attempted tax evasion. No— these stamps are too valuable, too conspicuous. You'll never get away with selling them now."

I paused for a moment to let all that sink in. It sunk, all right. When it had, I let him have the final broadside.

"Your only chance is to sell them to me," I said. "I'll give you fifty thousand pounds for them—that's over half a million francs. I can't give you the money until after I've sold them myself—but at least you'll get it and keep a whole skin."

Sante looked as if I'd clubbed him. A grandfather clock in the corner of the room ticked loudly into the silence as he tried to catch up with it all. After about a minute, a small shudder seemed to run through him. He said, "Excuse me—my pills," and opened a drawer in his desk.

And came up with a massive, ancient revolver.

He rested the butt on the desk top, and I got a long look down the barrel. I suppose it was only a .45—but from where I sat, it looked like a young torpedo tube. I kept very still. I am very frightened of guns viewed from that position.

"M'sieur 'Olland." His voice was surprisingly firm now. "Some of what you say has interested me—but I do not think you are altogether telling me the truth. You see, I have already started selling these stamps. I start five years ago or more—and no person has said anything. None of your so-called Mafia family has come to see me. So I think you are bluffing, telling me this story in order to frighten me into selling you these stamps cheaply. So now I want to know the real background to your coming here. And no more lies, please."

Now it was my turn to look clubbed. That he'd already have sold some of the stamps was a possibility that simply hadn't occurred to me. Because Haydon had recognized the name of the Mauritius and said he'd have known if they'd been sold I'd made the natural assumption that the family knew what all the stamps were. Now it seemed that they didn't. For a moment my brain staggered around weakly between my ears.

Then I had it.

Not all of it: there was more, just around the corner in the subconscious. But I had enough.

I leaned forward—slowly, so as not to excite the man—and helped myself to another cigarette out of the box. I maneuvered the big table lighter awkwardly with my left hand and made a small gesture with my right.

"The first thing I have to say is that you were bloody lucky. I told you the Mafia family had a list of the stamps—and that they certainly do. I didn't realize their list might be incomplete, but from what you say it seems it must be. It doesn't surprise me all that much, though, because my own list is incomplete as well. Old Man Miere could only remember the hundred or so most valuable stamps when he made it. After all, the last time he saw them was over thirty years ago.

"But these lists being incomplete doesn't alter the basic facts: so far you've been lucky because you must've started selling the stamps in the order of cheapest first, to test the reaction without risking the really valuable ones. It just so happens that you haven't yet got round to selling any of those the family can identify. But you will if you keep it up. If you've been pushing them out for five years, you're probably quite near that point now. And when you *do* let one go that they recognize, then they'll be coming to see you. And they won't be making you the sort of offer I am, that's for sure."

I dropped the lighter into my right hand and held up the left. "Look what they did to me during a friendly chat."

He looked. I brought my right hand casually back—and then threw the lighter at him with all the force I could muster.

It bounced off his skull with a dull *thud* as I followed through with my right hand and launched myself across the desk top. I got hold of the gun barrel, pulled the muzzle down on the desk to get him heaving the other way—and then, still holding the barrel, whipped my right hand up and backhanded him across the face. I felt the foresight grate across his teeth and continued the swing. He gave a sudden sharp screech of agony—and then I had the pistol to myself.

I stepped back, retrieved my cigarette from where it lay smoldering on the carpet, and then perched my aching hip on the edge of the desk, keeping the gun pointing vaguely in his general direction.

Sante bent over the desk with his head down, swaying gently back and forth and cradling his right hand in his left. Blood from his mouth dripped on to the blotter in front of him—but it seemed to be his hand that was really upsetting him. I guessed he had a broken trigger finger from me wrenching the gun away. Well, I wasn't sorry: the .45'd been his bright idea, not mine.

"Christ," I said. "I hate to think what the Mafia boys'll do to you. There's only one of me, and you had the gun—and look at you. The Mafia'd eat you for *petit déjeuner*."

I blew smoke out of my nostrils. Sante flinched. "You think you'll be all right because they don't really have a list of the stamps at all, don't you? Well, I'm sure you'll accept that if *I* really have a list, so do they. And if they don't, I'll give them one.

"I'll tell them about the two Post Office Mauritius, the five-franc gray *tête-bêche*, the Ceylonese fourpenny dull rose, the British plate eleven and all the rest. So they'll know, all right, Monsieur. Understand?"

As I spoke I dug Jedrow's list out of my back pocket. He took it with a shaking, bloodstained left hand and looked at it as if it was a grenade with the pin pulled out. He went an even whiter shade of pale as his eyes ran down it. I gave him a couple of minutes to absorb it.

"Or alternatively," I went on, "I'll give you the fifty thousand pounds so long as you've still got the hundred-odd stamps I've got listed, which I'm sure you must have or the family would have been down on you before this. With that and what you've already made on them you won't have done badly for a bloke who simply happened to find some stamps. You were just lucky—but I've had a friend killed, two aircraft crashed, bones broken, and become a killer myself over them. So what are you going to do?"

Sante was sagging in his chair, his eyes still on the list. There was a long silence. I blew more smoke, then crushed the cigarette out in the piston.

After a couple of minutes, which seemed hours, he slowly raised his shocked eyes to look at me.

"Okay," he whispered. "I will sell them to you."

I just nodded.

"Do you want to draw up some sort of legal agreement? That I'll pay you fifty thousand pounds or give you the stamps back within a year? You're a lawyer—you draw it up and I'll sign it, if you like." It didn't matter to me. Dead or alive I'd have got rid of the stamps before the year was out, and so long as I was alive I had no intention of welshing on the deal.

Sante shook his head. He looked tired and old and defeated.

"*Non*. It would not mean anything, with the background that could not be mentioned. Anyway, I think you will pay if you are successful. These stamps are worth nearly ten million francs; if you get even half their value you would be very foolish to risk everything by not paying me."

He climbed slowly to his feet, a man moving in a bad dream. "I will get them for you."

He walked over to a heavy framed picture of two gliders in formation, unhooked it, and fiddled with the knobs of a small wall safe underneath.

He opened the safe; took out a flat metal case covered with red leather, the size of a box of fifty cigarettes; and handed it to me.

Trying to stop my hands trembling, I opened it.

And looked at a million pounds.

It didn't look very impressive. The stamps, most of them dull-looking little squares, were all in individual little cellophane pochettes. I poked them around gently, trying to look as if I knew what I was looking for.

There seemed to be about two hundred of them. I recognized the pair of Mauritius from Miere's brief description, but that was about all. I picked them up in their little envelope and turned them over, trying to see what they had that would make someone pay £120,000 for them. I couldn't find anything.

I quit raking around. If I turned them over any more I'd find myself picking up the prettier ones, and since they probably weren't anywhere near the most valuable, such an action would mark me irretrievably as an unbeliever and a charlatan. I closed the case, snapped home the businesslike little hasp, and picked up Jedrow's list from the desk.

"Everything on the list is in here?" I hefted the case and Sante nodded. He was watching it as if I was about to snap my fingers and make it disappear. Well, I suppose I was, at that. I took his word for it: I was in no position to check anyway. It would take a team of the world's best stamp experts to do that. And if he'd tried keeping some back or giving me imitations, I could always come and see him again.

"Okay then, Monsieur," I said. "I will wish you *bonjour*. You will be hearing from me quite soon."

Sante just nodded again.

I broke open the .45, shoveled the shells into my pocket, and dropped the gun on the desk. Then I walked out.

I left him standing there wearing the numbed, unbelieving expression of a man who has just lost a loved one. The stamps must have been frightening him for ten years—but at the same time he'd had a lot of dreams in that little red box.

CHAPTER 23

The drive back to Lubec's place was full of ghosts and imaginary dangers. I drove slowly, taking lines round the bends that would give me maximum vision, and kept myself keyed up ready to give the Simca everything it had. Which wasn't much.

I tried to pull myself together—but the little red box on the seat beside me bred bad dreams. There was too much blood on it. Haydon's. Rico's. Harvey's, Pete's, Toni's, and the other man whose name I hadn't known. And Roberto Miere. And the little boy buried in an unmarked grave by his father somewhere between here and Paris on a night of death in 1939. And . . . Bill.

There was something chilling about the very smallness of that little red box, the size of fifty Players cigarettes, that held such enormous value and had caused so many deaths. For a while I felt something that could almost have been an echo of the feelings old Miere must have had when he was running for his life with his little boy dead behind him. Such a small box containing such immense power was a very frightening thing.

I squirted past St.-Jean Airfield without daring to look at it and hurtled into the village going way over the limit.

A 2CV ambled uncaringly out of a road to my right and I stood on everything to keep from flattening it. His right-of-way out here in the sticks. The howl of tires turned every head in the street, and a few people shouted things in French that I didn't understand. The little Citroën pobbled on uncaringly after the driver turned to survey me contemptuously through the dirty rear window.

It broke the spell. When I leaned down and picked up the box from where it had been thrown on the floor, it was just a little red box. It might contain something which could be turned to immense wealth, but that was in the future. For the moment, the chill had gone. It was just a box, no longer shrieking its secret to everyone I passed.

Just a box.

Almost, anyway.

It wasn't until the Simca crunched on the gravel of Lubec's drive that I realized I was hungry, hurting, and shaking from reaction. Again. I never seemed to arrive there in any other state.

Once again the front door opened as I dragged myself up the steps. And once again the sea of faces in the hall. I singled out Louise as I lurched over the last step. She met my eyes and gave me a tiny, nervous smile. Everyone—including Lubec, who was sporting a big sling with a plaster cast sticking out of each end—looked a little anxious. Probably wondering how many people I'd killed this time.

I said, "Morning, all" in the chirpiest voice I could muster.

"Ah, morning, Ken." Jedrow's gravel-truck tones were hesitant. "Er . . . we got your note. Are . . . are you okay?"

"Sure, why not?"

"Well, your hand . . ." He was looking at my left hand. It was dripping blood through the sodden bandages like a freshly cut sirloin steak. A trail of red spots led from the car up the steps into the hall, ending in a little pool by my feet on the parquet floor.

I'd got so used to keeping that hand in the background of things that I simply hadn't noticed it. It must have started bleeding when I grabbed the revolver, and been at it ever since. I'd kept it in my lap while I was driving, and the front of my jeans was wet with blood.

"Oh, Christ," I said intelligently. "It's bleeding again."

We trooped into the kitchen, and I sat at the table while Jedrow pulled back the sleeve of my flying jacket and Louise produced warm water and started stripping off the bloody bandage. Lubec poured coffee from a percolator, and then won a special place in my heart by giving me a glass of fine old cognac.

"How's the arm?" I asked him.

"Not too bad," he said, with his thin smile. "It hurts a little, but I do not keep going out and breaking it again, so I think it will be all right." His eyes dropped to the red box under my right hand on the table. "What is this?"

"The stamps. I bought them for fifty thousand pounds."

There was immediate and complete silence. Everyone stared at the box.

Having got over it myself, I'd forgotten the mesmerizing effect of £1 million in a box six inches square by an inch deep. I fumbled with the catch and opened the lid. Everyone stopped breathing, even Louise. I shuffled the stamps around and picked out the Mauritius Post Office in its little pochette.

"I imagine this must be the Mauritius," I said. "I can't recognize the rest offhand, but I think all the important ones are here."

The silence deepened. Jedrow and Lubec were staring, frozen where they were. Louise was white-faced, stopped in the act of unwinding the bandage.

Jedrow was the first to recover. He sank into a chair beside me and reached out a shaking hand towards the box.

"Where . . . where did you get them?" he asked in a hoarse whisper.

"I bought them from Paul Sante, the secretary of the Aéro Club de Mt.-Vivaral," I said. "I promised we'd give him fifty thousand pounds for them after we've sold them."

"Fifty . . . . thousand?" he whispered. "But . . . but they're worth somewhere around a million. How . . . how did you get him to sell for fifty thousand?"

Everyone's eyes switched to me, suddenly alarmed again.

"It's all right," I said wearily. "I didn't knock anybody off."

I hoped I wasn't going to have to go through the rest of my life constantly reassuring people on this point. The way everyone seemed willing to jump to the instant conclusion that I'd been blowing people's heads off was becoming tedious.

"Sit down and I'll tell you all about it."

They sat down. Louise recovered and went on with the medical treatment, though her eyes kept wandering back to the stamps.

The explanation took ten minutes of solid talking, during which things started to get fuzzy round the edges and a dull ringing cranked itself up between my ears. At the end of it I took another gulp of cognac and looked at my hand again. Louise had a pad over the hole and was trying to pull the edges together by binding it tightly with sticking plaster.

Jedrow seemed to be talking. I tore my eyes away from the Battle of the Hole and tried to concentrate.

" . . . bloody good show," he was saying. Just the sort of remark he would make. "Now we'll sell them and— "

"I think not." The quiet interruption came from Lubec. He was looking at me as he spoke. "I think Ken has thought of this too. If you sell the stamps in London your Mafia family will know who had them, just as they would have known if Sante had sold them. It seems to me, Ken, that we have bought Sante's problem. Is that not so?"

I nodded tiredly. There was a bit of general gloom as everybody thought things out to the same conclusion. Jedrow, looking very deflated, picked over the stamps halfheartedly.

"Act . . . act'lly, it's rather worse than that," I said. My tongue seemed to have grown too big for my mouth. I assembled the words, then plowed on.

"The family must already know our identity. Jedrow and me, anyway.

199

Haydon knew about Jedrow and me, or something about us, in England, and he was bound to have contacted his family to report back while we were messing about before we came out here. So when the news filters back that he an' his mob are dead, the first people they're going to come and see are us. Whether they think we've got the stamps or not. An' if Haydon got any messages off while he was in France, which he probably did, then he'll have tol' them he suspected us of havin' them anyway. *So whatever happens, we're going to cop it.*"

That really cheered everyone up. Jedrow sagged in his chair like a pricked balloon, staring at me.

"Yes," said Lubec softly. His voice was a hundred miles away. He nodded slowly, his image shimmering behind Jedrow. "Yes, I think you are right. Do you have any idea what you are going to do, Ken?"

I nodded gently. My head was heavy, and I didn't want it falling off.

"Yeah. Only one answer: *we've gotta sell the stamps to the family.* Doin' a deal with them's the only thing that might keep them off us."

There was a stunned silence.

"That's no good," snapped Jedrow. He was coming out from under. His voice was a dry rasp. "Quite apart from the fact that we'll get a rotten price from them, what's to stop them from having a go at us whether we sell them the stamps or not? And anyway, we don't know who they are or where they are. No good at all." He shook his head. He didn't think it was any good.

"I agree that we'll get a rotten price for them," I mumbled. "But if we only get half their value, that's half a million. Jesus, how much do you want? You plannin' to build a new Eiffel Tower or something? Or perhaps you'd rather have the full value and be dead with it. I also agree they might have a go at us anyway, even if we do sell them the stamps—but I still say that a deal is our only chance of keeping them off. As it is they're almost certain to want us dead in revenge for Haydon an' Co. If I can get to 'em with some sort of deal over the stamps I might be able to head 'em off that, at least."

Might. I wasn't too convinced myself, but as a plan of action it did

200

have one big thing going for it: namely, that it was the only one I could think of.

Jedrow certainly didn't like it—but he couldn't think of anything else either. He opened his mouth to speak, then changed his mind and shut it again. He appeared to be thinking hard.

Lubec was smiling his small sad smile again. "You certainly have a point. But you still haven't said how you're going to find the family. It seems to me you must go home and wait for them to come to you, yes?"

"No. Not bloody likely. If I wait for them to come to me, I'll probably get the rest of my fingers chopped off an' my brains blown out. I'm going to them. Catch them first. Start with th' advantage. Might work. An' I know where to start looking, even if I don't know where they are.

"*Y' see, they murdered old Stefan Miere.* They must have found him somehow. So I'm goin' to start lookin' in St. Kitts, wherever that is."

Now Jedrow was staring again.

"*Murdered* Stefan, you said?" He stuttered with disbelief. "But . . . but . . . Stefan was killed in a road accident. How do you . . . What makes you think . . .?" The old boy's face was white, and the slugged-on-the-back-of-the-head note was back in his voice. He had my sympathy. It was his big morning for bad news.

"Yeah, tha's right. Murdered." I collected my thoughts and trudged on. "You remember that I said Sante'd already sold some of the stamps? Well, if the family'd had a full list of them, they'd have been on to him long ago. But they weren't. So they can't have a full list. That's the first thing. But we know they know what some of them are—or *I* know, anyway, 'cause Haydon recognized the name of the Mauritius when I said it the other night. So if they've got an incomplete list, it's a reasonable guess that it's the same incomplete list we've got—an' doesn't that seem peculiar to you?"

It obviously did—but equally obviously it was just one more peculiar thing on top of a whole lot of peculiar things. Everyone looked bemused. Only Lubec was nodding slowly as if he was staying up with it all.

"You remember we wondered how all this happened at once? How

201

you got the letter Miere left you, and how Haydon was on to the same thing at exactly the same time? It always was rather a big coincidence, wasn't it?

"Only it wasn't a coincidence at all. My bet is that the family somehow got on to old Miere in St. Kitts and tortured him or drugged him—they're pretty good at that—until he told them what happened to the stamps. The same story he told you—and with much the same incomplete list, 'cause the ones on the list were the only ones he could remember. An' after he'd talked they killed him, making it look like an accident. As a result of that you got the letter he left you. It mus' have been like that. It's the only answer that fits everything—the lists, an' the fact that you all started looking for the stamps at once."

Now they were both nodding. I was right, all right—it was the only explanation that made sense of everything. It *must* have happened like that. There was another one of those stunned silences as they thought about it.

Louise unrolled a long length of sticking plaster with a hollow *zzwip*, and used it to top off the young turban on my hand. I watched the operation unseeingly: I was thinking about the West Indian island of St. Kitts. And what I might find there.

I didn't like the prospect at all. In fact, I was bloody terrified of it.

But it was the only idea I could think of.

BOOK THREE

CHAPTER 24

Three days later, as I looked out of the window of a VC10 at London dwindling away below, it was *still* the only plan I had. I still didn't like it, either—but no one had come up with any alternatives, so here I was. Speedbird 695 shuddered genteelly as the last stage of flap came up. I wondered, vaguely, if I'd ever see England again.

As we leveled off at cruising altitude, I pressed the buzzer for the stewardess. I got a mildly disapproving BOAC look for demanding *two* large Scotches at nine in the morning—but I knew what I was doing. One fair-sized belt of alcohol in a cabin pressure-altitude of about 5,000 feet produces instant sleepiness in Holland. I cranked my seat back down a bit and left the flying to the World's Most Arrogant Airline. I came to four hours later to eat their plastic lunch, had another Johnnie Walker, and then went back to sleep until halfway down the descent into Antigua.

I stepped out of the air-conditioned VC10-derness into a wall of West Indian heat.

The shock of walking through a doorway and going from 60 degrees in the aircraft to 90 degrees outside was total, as if one had just walked into an enormous oven. The brassy sun, hanging white-hot and malevolent in the sapphire blue sky, slammed heat and light into the white dusty airport like a vast cosmic welding torch. In that moment I completely understood the lassitude of the tropics: major exertion in this heat must be impossible, whether you were white or black. By the time I'd staggered across the apron to Customs and Immigration, sweat was forming stickily under my chin and dampening the armpits of my light cotton shirt. The other passengers getting off in Antigua were looking equally bludgeoned.

It was a scruffy, unkempt airport. There were no blast fences. The whine of jet engines as a Pan Am 707 started up cut through my head, thick and muzzy after eight hours in the same seat, like a knife. White coral dust swirled into the luggage bays and the restaurant as he fired up numbers three and four. The broken sign on the control tower said COOLIDGE INTERNATIONAL AIRPORT, and beneath it parts of the corrugated-iron roof of the customs building were wrinkled and bent, probably lifted by the jet blast of taxiing aircraft. There was a line of aluminium flagpoles on a wizened scrap of grass outside the buildings. The ropes slapped against them constantly with a mournful *tong . . . tong . . . tong* as the flags above fluttered in the hot trade wind.

Inside the tiny Customs and Immigration hall things weren't much better. It was a relief to get away from the white glare outside, but the heat was much the same. Immigration sifted slowly through the dozen or so disembarking BOAC passengers, squinting suspiciously at our passports as if they weren't sure what they were. Eventually, after producing my return ticket, I got a reluctant three-week stamp on one of the clean pages.

Immigration funneled us into customs, where the two officials sat uninterested and unmoving while we milled around watching the porters slinging our luggage off a trolley on to the low formica-covered counter that faced out to the apron. My battered holdall was treated relatively gently, while a couple of expensive Antler suitcases were slammed down on their corners and allowed to topple off the counter on to the cement floor. Definitely a big tourist drive going on here. If I'd been a legitimate holidaymaker with decent luggage, I'd have been sitting on a porter's head beating his brains out by now. My fellow passengers just stood around dumbly. Maybe it was the heat.

I picked up my holdall and put it on the exit counter. One of the customs men reluctantly turned down a tiny transistor radio that was belting out steel-band music, pasted a professional scowl on his face, and waved an arrogant hand in the direction of my worldly goods. If I hadn't been hiding something we'd have had a bloody good argument about that—I've got a thing about petty officials with a Hitler complex. As it was I opened the zipper of the holdall and tried to look bored and humble at the same time. He dipped his hands into it and raked over my few clothes.

And came up with the red leather case.

After a few moments' fumbling he got the lid open and peered inside. Thirty Players rolled around. He took one out, peered at the ends of it closely, and held it up to his nose and sniffed it. Looking for marijuana, probably. He seemed disappointed to find it was an obviously original Players Player. He picked out a couple more and checked them, then lost interest and closed the red case, dropped it back in the holdall, and waved me out.

I walked to the door, still trying to look bored. I was glad no one had ever told Antiguan customs men that cigarette cases are usually cigarette-sized: if you put two rows of cigarettes in my natty red case the ends overlapped.

I found a toilet, locked the door carefully, and checked the two long envelopes that were stuck firmly to my shins with sticking plaster. They looked safe enough, so I left them there. I unplastered Jedrow's .38 Smith & Wesson from the inside of my thigh, though, and put it in my pocket.

Next stop was the Leeward Islands Air Transport desk, where I found that the first scheduled flight to St. Kitts was an Avro 748 leaving the next morning at seven o'clock. I could probably have chartered a light twin and gone on that afternoon, but I didn't want to give people any reason to remember me. So I bought a ticket on the Avro and drifted off to have a look round. I'd never seen a tropical island before.

An hour later I was beginning to feel I wouldn't mind if I never saw one again, either.

I got a big American taxi at the airport and allowed the driver to talk me into a tour of the island for 30 Eastern Caribbean dollars. That was about £6. I didn't mind the outlay—I'd cleaned out my bank account before leaving Heathrow—but we hadn't gone 50 yards before I started to mind the heat. Experienced tourists don't go to the Caribbean in August: the temperature sits in the high 80s all day, and the trade winds drop to a useless sigh for weeks on end. The rush of air coming in through the car window as we left the airport and headed south didn't help a bit: it was like the hot blast you get 50 yards behind an idling jet engine.

The taxi driver was big, black, and garrulous. He insisted on reeling off a potted history of the island as we ambled along at a steady 25 mph between cane fields, palm trees, and scruffily colorful wooden villages. Since he talked with a broad West Indian accent I only understood about one word in six, but that didn't seem to deter him. When I said I was thirsty he said, "Oh. Oh. Oh. Righ', man, right" and jerked to a stop at a pink-painted, tumbledown wooden bar in one of the villages. That cost me three Heinekens for each of us—but I was never so glad to buy beer.

Over the third one, I asked him casually if there was any Mafia on the island.

"Oh, yeah, man, sho' dey is," he said. "Ev'yone know dat. Dey run de casino at de Vacation Inn, down to Willoughby Bay. Dey don' make no hassle."

"Don't they? I thought they were supposed to be a real bad bunch, the Mafia." I tried to sound slightly disappointed. Holland the sensation-seeking tourist.

It worked, too. The taxi driver instantly changed his tune. If I wanted lurid Mafia, I could have it: especially if it meant he could sit there drinking beer.

"Well, man, I don' call 'em *bad,*" he said, "but I sho' don' go lookin' for no bad time there. I reckon dey cut you pretty quick, you give 'em a hassle. De boss men, dey walk wi' guns all de time. Dey okay if you leave 'em alone—but nobody don' start trouble dere. No, man!" He shook his head.

"Who is the boss, then?" I asked.

"Dat's Scipio Challese. He a *raas*. He got a brother call Larry. Larry work in de casino, but he got a couple whorehouses as well. Scipio don' like dat. Then dere's Scipio's sons: Rico work here, though I don' see him of late, an' de other one, Alberto, he's over in St. Kitts most of de time at de new casino."

I found I was gripping the beer bottle fit to break it. I relaxed.

"They operate in St. Kitts too, then?" My voice sounded tense to me, but the driver didn't notice anything.

"Yeah, dey jus' open up a new casino dere. Scipio, he always going over dere. I see 'im at de airport. He got 'is own 'plane. Alberto fly it. You wanna see de casino? I take you dere dis evening, you wanna go."

I said no thanks and changed the subject, trying to get my voice back to normal. Every nerve end tingled with adrenaline.

As easy as that!

I'd expected a long search. I hadn't reckoned on the fact that everyone on a small island like Antigua would get a vicarious thrill out of knowing all they could about the local Mafia family. And it all fitted: the new casino in St. Kitts . . . Miere being killed there . . . and the name Scipio, too.

Haydon dying in a French wood and mumbling "Ship'll get you"—only it hadn't been "Ship" he'd said: it must have been "Scip." Death had blurred his voice.

I got myself driven back to the Sugar Mill Hotel, near the airport, and paid the man his 30 bucks plus a 5-dollar tip. It must have been the first tip he'd ever earned by drinking a customer's beer.

After dinner I phoned the Vacation Inn casino. A suspicious-sounding New York accent said Mr. Challese wasn't there, and who's this speaking? I rang off.

Then I walked down to the airport and ambled into the control tower. I learned that Challese had a Beechcraft Twin Bonanza—and that it had gone off that morning to St. Kitts.

I stumped slowly back to the hotel, listening to the crickets and tree frogs zinging and chirruping in the hot night. It took me a long time to get to sleep.

CHAPTER 25

Even at eight o'clock in the morning the airport of Golden Rock, St. Christopher, is a hot, dusty place. They were building a new runway alongside the old one that year, and the dust from the workings drifted across to the terminal building along with the constant ululating growl of machinery. Even the two-tone green Avro 748 that brought us seemed in a hurry to get out of there. It whined off the bumpy little strip and was away between the two hills to the east while I and the half-dozen other St. Kitts arrivals were still going through Customs and Immigration.

In the tiny parking space beside the customs hall stood a blue-and-white Twin Bonanza. It was American-registered.

Challese's aircraft.

The immigration man asked me what I was going to be doing in St. Kitts. I could feel the plaster holding the envelopes to my shins and the weight of the Smith & Wesson taped to the inside of my left thigh.

"Holiday," I said.

He wished me a pleasant stay, customs gave my holdall a cursory mauling, and I stumped out of the terminal, picking up a map of the island on my way out. A dozen taxi drivers materialized out of thin air as I came down the steps from customs, and I picked the dullest-looking one on the principle that he'd probably forget me the quickest. I asked him to take me somewhere I could hire a self-drive car, and he drove me through the town of Basseterre to a tumbledown service station on the far side. I didn't complain: even that short drive had been enough to show me that all the service stations around here were tumbledown. I hired a battered Avenger for a week, paying the hire charge of 125 Eastern Caribbean dollars in advance. Surprised at getting that much cash in hand, the proprietor took no more than a casual glance at my International Licence. He told me I ought to get a Kittitian Visitor's Licence and I said I'd see to it right away. Like hell I would: I wanted my name on record in as few places as possible in St. Kitts.

Next, I drove round looking for somewhere quiet. I ended up at a place called Frigate Bay, a small level area at the base of the southern peninsula of the island. Frigate Bay was crossed by two new roads in good condition with a real live roundabout at their intersection—and that was all. No buildings, no nothing. The first road got you there and then continued southwards to the distant tip of the peninsula. The second road took you across the flat patch, halfway up a hill to the north, and then stopped in the middle of nowhere. There was sea to the east and west, and hills north and south. A sign as you entered the level area announced that this was to be the site of FRIGATE BAY DEVELOPMENT, and included a colorful map to illustrate where all the buildings were going to be. I didn't bother to study the map: the developer, whoever he was, had obviously had a cash failure or run foul of the government. The deserted aspect of the place was the only thing that interested me.

I drove the Avenger up the hill to the end of the road, sat there for an hour watching for any trace of movement anywhere around, and at the end of that time untaped the envelopes from my shins. Quite a lot of hair came off with them. I selected a Western Australia One-shilling Brown and put that in my pocket in its little pochette. The rest went into the red box. I went to the back of the car and found a screwdriver, scraped away a small hole underneath the concrete at the side of the road, and pushed the box into it. Then I covered the hole up carefully, scattered the few crumbs of loose earth that were left over, and spent another ten minutes staring around. I suppose I could have put the box in a bank safe-deposit, but I didn't know whether you had to declare the contents of such objects when you did that in this part of the world—and anyway, I didn't want to leave my name lying about, particularly associated with mysterious boxes.

Reflecting that burying these stamps seemed to be a popular pastime among their fleeting owners, I drove off in search of a cold beer.

And Mr. Challese.

Ninety minutes and two beers later I'd managed to find the new casino without actually asking anyone where it was. It turned out to be perched on a high point on the west coast, with the town of Basseterre to the south and the towering lush green slopes of the island's mountainous interior hoisting themselves into standing cloudcaps to the north and east. Pausing on the entrance steps to the place, I looked north along the coast. A colorful wooden shantytown straggled untidily along the seashore, and beyond that, about five miles away, I could see the ancient ramparts of the fort on Brimstone Hill. The English had been trounced there by the French in 1780 something. I hoped it wasn't an omen.

I finished climbing the steps and stumped slowly into the lobby. The cool and shade were a relief after the brassy pounding of the midday sun outside. A tough-looking Negro in a very white shirt and a black tie sat behind a counter marked RECEPTION. There weren't many guests around: to the gambling-junket crowd, 11:30 was probably the crack of dawn.

I walked over and said, "I'd like to speak to Mr. Scipio Challese, please."

The man looked me slowly up and down. My accent and the "please" seemed to convince him I was not one of the boys.

"I don' think Mistuh Challese in," he said finally.

A tiny insolent smile twitched the corners of his mouth. Working for this lot he probably didn't get much chance to sneer at small and harmless white men.

I took the Shilling Brown out of my pocket and leaned my elbows on the counter. The Smith & Wesson in my hip pocket *clunk*ed against the wooden wall. I dropped the stamp in front of him.

"Why don't you go see him right now and give him that with my compliments?" I said quietly. "Tell him I'll wait here for the next sixty seconds, then leave."

I'm afraid snotty receptionists affect me in the same way that bloody-minded customs men do. And this time I didn't have to take it. He rose to his feet, uncertainty and anger marching into his big black face like a Jaeger battalion. He towered over me, so that I had to tip up on one elbow in order to keep my scowl on target. After a moment's hesitation, he said, "Wait" and disappeared through a door in the back of his cubicle.

I waited for perhaps half a minute; then a door opened alongside the reception desk and a short fat man with thin gray hair and a pasty white face came out. He was wearing a colorful open-necked shirt outside a pair of trousers in a loud check. He looked about as tough as an overfed rabbit.

We looked at each other for a moment; then he growled, "Come in."

I passed him and went through the doorway. He followed and shut the door behind him.

The room was a small office, furnished with more money than taste. There were two other men in it. The youngest was about my age, heavily built, with a shock of curly dark-brown hair. He was leaning, relaxed, against the far door of the office. Even in repose, his muscular torso rippled the purple tee shirt he was wearing. He looked like a younger edition of the late lamented Rico.

The other man was sitting in a big comfortable chair behind a paper-strewn desk. He was leaning forward with his forearms on the desk and the stamp in his hands.

This was the man I'd come to see.

I was slightly surprised to find that at close range Scipio Challese looked not unlike how I'd imagined him. One visualizes the head of a Mafia family as being a strong, swarthy man with tight black hair and hard features—but common sense tells you such type-casting will probably be way off the beam. So I was surprised to find that Don Scipio conformed almost completely: he was big-boned, had crinkly black hair *en brosse* with a touch of gray at the temples, and the planes of his deeply tanned face were hard and determined. He must have been over 60, but the passing of the years had done little more than etch purposeful lines round his eyes and mouth. He had thick, slightly damp lips, and his expressionless black eyes watched me from under heavy brows. He was wearing an expensive dark blue lightweight suit, white shirt, and silk tie.

Behind me, Fatso said, "Sit down."

I sat down across the desk from Challese and crossed my legs. Now I'd got here, my palms were sweating and tension balled up in my stomach.

Challese let the silence build up for a while, then glanced down at the stamp and back up to my face.

"Where did you get it?" he asked. He had a deep, bass voice, with Europe underlying the slight American accent. He spoke with almost no inflection. A voice accustomed to command.

"It's one of a collection I have been asked to sell," I said. "The owners have instructed me to offer them to you at well below market price. I have a list of the most important stamps of the collection, and there are a hundred and twenty-eight additional, largely unidentified stamps which are not on the list."

"Show me the list."

I dug a copy of Jedrow's list out of my back pocket and passed it across. Challese checked it carefully. A loud American voice floated through the door as its owner passed through the lobby; then there was silence again until Challese finished reading and looked up again.

"You're Holland, aren't you?"

"Yes." No point in denying it: Haydon must have passed back my description or he wouldn't have recognized me in the first place.

The character in the purple tee shirt stirred slightly. The name seemed to mean something to him. Challese turned and looked at him and he

214

subsided again. There was something infinitely chilling about the Don's obvious absolute authority. He turned his black eyes back to me.

"Holland. You killed my son and some of my employees. Why have you come to see me?"

I looked steadily back at him for a few seconds to give the lump in my throat time to subside. The plain truth was that I was terrified. Perhaps Challese in his own environment had something to do with it—but even knowing Haydon and Rico and the others hadn't prepared me for the utter menace of the man. His lack of emotion was a thousand times more frightening than any ranting and raving would ever have been. It seemed an age before I got myself collected enough to speak.

"I've come because I knew that if I didn't you'd send someone to me," I said. Challese watched me expressionlessly. "You've lost a son, and I've lost a friend who was a brother to me; if there is more fighting there are going to be more deaths. If your man Haydon had negotiated with us instead of trying to kill us, none of this would have happened. These stamps represent enough money for us all. I have them, and I have hidden them. No one else knows where they are—not even my friends; so if anything happens to me no one will ever find them. If you want them I will sell them to you at a price that will enable you to make a profit of over one hundred percent, even after the taxes that you'll have to pay on an open sale. As part of this deal, I want no more killing."

Challese frowned. His black eyes burned into mine.

"I think you are forgetting something, Holland," he said. He spoke very softly, like the silence before death. "As you said, I lost a son. I also lost a *consigliere*—you know what that is?"

I nodded. That must have been Haydon. He leaned forward, his face darkening.

"And why? Because I was searching for something *that was mine*—that's why! Not something that I wanted to steal from you: *something that had been stolen from me*! Fiore took those stamps from me over thirty years ago. Since they were stolen before they were ever put in that plane, you don't even have a *legal* right to them. But you kill my son and five—*five*!—of my men and then come here and offer to sell *my* stamps to *me*!"

215

His voice had gone axe-hard round the edges as he talked, and the black eyes seemed to bore through my skull. My skin crawled with fear. I couldn't move. I had to swallow dryly a couple of times before I could speak again.

"I didn't come here to talk moral issues with you, Challese—but since you brought them up, how about old Fiore? You killed his little son and drove him into a hermit's life—and then when you caught up with him, an old man, you weren't satisfied with just getting information out of him. Oh, no—you had to kill him afterwards, too. And then you send your thugs round to us. If you'd put it to us and offered us a few thousand it might have been different—but no, your bloody people went ahead and murdered Bill Charlton. And then tried to kill me—not once, but several times. They wrecked our aircraft, broke my hand up, tortured me, threatened us, and shot at us—and then *you* suggest that *I'm* in the wrong!"

In spite of being terrified, I found I was trembling with fury.

"Jesus, man: we didn't go gunning for your mob—they came at us. If they hadn't done that they'd still be alive. I wasn't chasing after your bloody stamps—I never fired a shot that wasn't self-defense. If you think *you've* got a legal right to them after all that, then try going for your bloody lawyer! But if you want them from me then you'll pay for them— and the price is one million two hundred thousand dollars U.S.!"

There was a brittle, electric silence. The black eyes never left me. In the stillness I actually felt the short hairs on the back of my neck begin to prickle.

"One . . . million . . . two . . . hundred . . . thousand?" Challese's voice was a hoarse whisper, unutterably menacing. "You want to sell my stamps to me for one million two hundred thousand dollars?"

"Right. And you've got no choice, either. You can knock me off here and now, but you'll never ever find the stamps if you do."

The silence deepened. Challese's eyes were hot with venom. His jaw muscles worked as he stared steadily at me.

After an age he seemed to come to a decision. His body relaxed slightly, and the jaw muscles stopped moving. His control was almost as frightening as his rage had been—more so, in fact. Now he was thinking again.

"How do I know these stamps are genuine?" His voice was back to a bass growl.

"You don't. Neither do I, come to that. But I'm betting on them. There'd be no point in me deliberately trying to pass you duds. If you find they're not genuine then you'll come after me, won't you? And that's what I'm trying to avoid in the first place."

Way down in the back of Challese's eyes something seemed to strike a chord of humor. It was there for an instant and then gone. He nodded slowly.

"Yes, that's right. We'd come after you."

He paused. Then: "How do you want this money?"

The young man stopped leaning against the door and tensed on the balls of his feet as if he was about to jump on someone. There was another small noise behind me. Challese looked unhurriedly round the room at them both. There was no more movement, but the young man didn't relax. His eyes stayed ranged on me like gun barrels. I ignored him. After Challese's burning gaze, I was tempered—or maybe I just didn't have any fright left.

"I'd like you to telegraph the funds to a bank I shall name," I said. "I'll give you the stamps when the bank has confirmed the transfer."

He frowned.

"No. I've no way of knowing you'll hand over the stamps once the money's in your bank. I'll get a million dollars in cash and give it to you when you bring me the stamps."

That shook me. I wasn't sure what the restrictions were on taking dollars out of the States, but I knew enough to realize that you don't just walk out with a million in a suitcase. Unless you're Scipio Challese.

But by the same token, you don't amble through the customs at Heathrow with that sort of money wrapped up in your dirty shirts. Or I don't, anyway: I'd look so nervous they'd take the fillings out of my teeth to see what I was hiding.

"No, that's no good. I don't want cash. It's too bulky, too easily traced, and too difficult to move. And it's not a million. It's one million two hundred thousand. If you like I'll lodge the stamps with a bank, and we can explain to the manager that they are being sold to you for that amount, and are to pass to you when the transfer is complete.''

He didn't like that: it would mean producing the stamps in the West Indies, which would create enormous tax complications. I didn't like it much myself, since I'd have to tell some story about how I got hold of the stamps and then I'd probably get roped in myself for capital-gains tax, or whatever they had in these parts. But I wasn't taking cash. There was another silence while we both thought about it. My nerves twanged like guitar strings in my guts.

''All right, Holland.'' He leaned back in his chair. ''I'll get you a certified check—you know what that is?—and hand it over to you in exchange for the stamps. Tell me who your bank is and where I can get in touch with you when the check comes through.''

A certified check is one that can't be stopped after the bank has issued it. It wasn't what I wanted, but it was obviously the best I was going to get. And since I could have it paid into any bank in the world, it was a damn sight better than declaring income in the West Indies or carting a little black bag of money halfway round the globe.

''Okay. You get the check. I'll stay in touch with you. Leave the payee's line blank—I'll fill that in myself. Have the bank certify it and send it back to you, and I'll phone you every day until you've got it. Then I'll want a photostat copy so I can have it confirmed through my bank. When that's been done I'll contact you again and tell you where the exchange will take place. I'm not handing over anything in here.''

He nodded slowly, surprise flickering across his eyes. He probably hadn't expected me to know so much about banking. A certified check is almost like a bearer bond. You send your normal check to your bank and they certify it by withdrawing the money from your account then and there and stamping the check to that effect. Then they'll forward it to the payee or to his bank or back to you or wherever you want. Challese would never let it come straight to me; but by insisting on a photostat I'd be able to have any bank verify by Mufax—pictorial telegraphing—that this check, when presented, would be honored. In other words, that there was no forging going on anywhere. Filling in the payee section myself meant that Challese would have no knowledge of the whereabouts of my account, so he wouldn't be able to tip off any tax authorities or make life awkward for me in any other way. Elaborate lengths that people don't normally go to—but then, people don't normally extract over a million dollars from characters like Scipio Challese, either.

He was probably thinking along the same lines. The black eyes bored into me for a few moments more. But when he spoke, his voice was normal.

"Very well," he said simply. "If that's the way you want it."

My heart sank.

I stood up slowly and deliberately.

"All right, Challese, I'll be in touch."

I walked to the door. The fat man shifted nervously as I got near him, as if he wasn't sure whether to try and stop me or not. At the last moment he decided not, and scuttled sideways out of my way. He was sweating.

I opened the door, then turned round and took a last look at the three of them.

"One more thing," I said. "I don't want to find Alberto or Larry here following me around in the next few days. I'm not going anywhere near the stamps anyway, and I don't like people underfoot. Okay?"

Alberto tensed on the balls of his feet, fists clenched and face suffused with anger. Larry licked his lips, and his eyes darted nervously round the room.

Challese just looked at me expressionlessly.

I closed the door on them and limped out.

I made it to the car and dropped into the driving seat like a wet bag of cement. It took an age for my shaking hand to get the ignition key into the keyhole. When I finally got the car started I drove down the short road

219

from the casino, turned north, then threw the car along the winding coast road for a couple of miles until I came to a deserted spot where I could pull off in the brush.

There I switched the engine off, put my head in my hands, and let myself go in a storm of shivering. My whole body quivered with reaction, every muscle screwed up tight and jumping. It lasted for perhaps two minutes. When it was over I was limp as a shot rabbit, drenched in sweat, and feeling thoroughly sick.

I had never been so frightened in all my life.

I was frightened partly because that interview with Challese would have frightened anybody: but far more than that, I was frightened because it looked as if I'd miscalculated badly.

Probably fatally, in fact.

I'd banked on Challese being willing to cut his losses and buy the stamps at half price to avoid any more bloodshed. Back in France, when I'd first thought of it, the idea had sounded plausible—but now I'd actually met the man, it seemed totally ridiculous. I simply hadn't anticipated the animal ferocity of the bastard: he wasn't about to pay 12 cents to avoid trouble, never mind $1,200,000. Christ, he probably didn't even regard me as trouble at all, here on his home ground. I'd been lucky in France and England—but here in St. Kitts, in Challese's backyard, his organization was capable of hammering me into the ground like a reversing locomotive and never even feeling the bump.

You, Holland, have bitten off a bloody sight more than you can chew.

The facts were still the same as they always were, of course: I'd still had no other choice but to try for a deal. And I'd got one, too—except that Challese was planning to kill me as soon as it was through. I'd seen it in his eyes. The only thing that was keeping me alive right now was the fact that I was the only one who knew where the stamps were; but as soon as I'd handed them over, he was going to blow my brains out and retrieve his check from the corpse. That was why he'd insisted on a certified check: it could be paid right back into his own account, and no questions asked.

So what could I do about it? I sat and thought for nearly an hour, while the West Indian sun hammered down and turned the car into a furnace.

And the only thing I came up with was that I'd have to make a very slick job of the hand-over arrangements, so as to get that check into a bank and myself away before Challese could stop me. Once it was paid in, he wouldn't get his money back whatever happened—so there'd be no practical advantage to killing me.

So maybe, if I then got off the island real pronto, he'd decide that it wasn't worth sending people after me for motives of pure revenge.

It was one hell of a big *maybe*.

CHAPTER 26

I sat there until I ran clear out of worry.

Then I started the car up, drove back to Basseterre, and threaded my way to the central square near the sugar wharf—a place curiously named The Circus. Like most major West Indian towns, Basseterre is a lurid hodgepodge of ancient and modern, riches and poverty. Ramshackle wooden shanty shops, run by gnarled old Negroes, slouch alongside glass-and-concrete supermarkets owned by Syrian-Kittitians, whose trading forefathers settled in the islands in the last century. By the waterfront the centuries-old fish and fruit market trades daily over sun-bleached wooden barrows, old prams, or scraps of filthy tattered canvas spread out on the sand of the beach or the pavement alongside. Brightly dressed blacks mill around the market, bargaining at lightning pace in their shrill singsong accents, until just before nightfall, when the whole colorful pageant dissolves in minutes as the traders pack up their wares and go home.

The Circus itself is a typical mixture. The small clock tower in the middle of it was there when Admiral Hood shouldered the French fleet out of

Basseterre Harbour in 1780—and nowadays it is surrounded by the battered Hillman Hunters and the vast multicolored American cars of the town's taxi drivers. On the seaward side, the old stone archway leading to the wharf once stood over the passage of fortunes in rum, cotton, sugar, and munitions in the Spanish Main days of the eighteenth century. Now it, and the other ancient buildings, sit shoulder-to-shoulder alongside the trim modern banks that cluster round the square.

It was the banks I was interested in. I parked the car, pushed my bandaged hand carefully out of sight in my left hip pocket, and tried to hide my limp as I swung open the glass door of Barclays DCO.

The air-conditioned interior was like stepping out of an oven into sweet reason. The white manager was helpful but obviously curious when I told him I wanted to open a numbered account in their branch on Grand Cayman Island. He probably didn't get many requests like that in St. Kitts. The tax-free Caymans are rapidly taking over from Switzerland and Liechtenstein as a haven for tax avoidance and undeclared capital—but St. Kitts isn't exactly one of the world's great money markets, so there wouldn't be much of that sort of business going through his little branch. He told me it would take a day or two to get my account number through, unless I was in a big hurry, and asked me what I was going to use to open the account. I told him it would be a certified check for a very large sum deposited through his branch, and that I'd want to have a photostat of the check verified before I presented it. His eyebrows climbed into his hairline at that, but he said yes, it was possible, and yes, they had a Mufax.

I left him staring after me with a suspicious expression on his face, and went back out into the heat.

When I got to where I'd parked the car, I picked up a tail.

He was a big Negro with a battered blue Chevrolet who looked about as inconspicuous as an alligator in a bath. He gave me a long hard look as I got into the Avenger, and had the Chev fired up before I'd even decided where I was going to go. I led him on a pointless amble round town for a while to make sure he was following me, then started to look for a hotel. Black Power was never more than 100 yards behind. Either Challese wanted me to know I was being followed in the hope of unnerving me, or the blue Chev was merely a decoy to make me think I was ahead of the game while a really skilled watcher kept a second eye on me from the background. I couldn't see anyone else, but that didn't mean a thing: I wasn't fooling myself that I was good enough to spot a really clever shadow, especially since all he'd have to do for the moment was keep the Chev in sight.

I decided to ignore it. All I was going to do for the rest of the day was find a hotel and loaf anyway, so there was no point in looking twitchy by trying to shake everyone off. Whatever I did I couldn't expect them not to find out where I was staying: on a small island like St. Kitts, Challese could track me down in minutes whenever he felt like it.

In the end I opted for a place called the Ocean Terrace Inn, not far from the casino itself. It seemed to be the best and most popular place on the island. The quality didn't concern me, but the popularity did. I figured that the more people there were about, the less the likelihood of my being blown apart in my hotel room.

Black Power watched me carry my bag into the hotel, stuck around outside for twenty minutes to satisfy himself I wasn't going to lam out of there after one rum punch, then ground the Chev into life and disappeared to make his report. From the window in my hotel room I watched the car snort off in a trail of dust and blue smoke, and looked for his successor.

I couldn't see anyone, so I did the intelligent thing and had a shower, then lay on my bed smoking Lucky Strikes and staring at the ceiling until it was time for dinner.

For the next three days I stayed in the hotel, getting up late, going to bed early, and disappearing for most of the day so that people wouldn't remember me too much. On Friday, the day after I'd seen Challese, I went into town and bought two rolls of bandage, antiseptic pads, and another roll of sticking plaster. Then I drove the Avenger up to the deserted fortress of Brimstone Hill, found myself a quiet shady room with hundreds of tourists' signatures on the thick stone walls, and spent a painful hour carefully changing the dressing on my left hand. The stitches looked as if they were ready to come out, but I left them anyway. I didn't want the hole opening up again and leaving a trail of blood all round St. Kitts if I happened to knock it. At the end of the hour my hand was pounding and I was sweating with pain, but I had everything taped up tight and there didn't seem to be any signs of infection. I took the old bandages with me back to the car and used the driving mirror while I stripped the dressing off my head and put on a smaller one. That cut didn't look too healthy, but there was nothing else I could do with it. I buried the bloody remains in the loose earth by one of the massive stone walls of the fort and was glad that August isn't a good month for tourists in the West Indies. Brimstone Hill was completely deserted, a ghost fort baking in the sun.

When I got back to the Ocean Terrace that evening, someone had searched my room. They'd put everything back in place, but they'd done a real thorough job. I'd made a careful note of the way everything was when I'd left, and they'd been through every nook and cranny. They'd even taken the front off the air conditioner.

I rang Challese from a roadside pay phone on Friday evening. He was expecting the check first thing on Monday morning, he said. I came away from the phone with my nerves twanging, facing the prospect of a weekend of suspense.

On Saturday, strolling down a street in town called Liverpool Row, I picked up another tail. He was as obvious as Black Power had been, but a lot more frightening.

This time it was Alberto.

He kept about 50 yards behind me, staring at me unwinkingly with his gun-barrel eyes whenever I looked at him. His presence was obviously a deliberate attempt to play on my nerves—and it was working. I was jumpy as a cat. For a while I thought about luring him into a deserted alley and bouncing the Smith & Wesson off his head, but gave the idea up because in the first place there aren't any deserted alleys in Basseterre on a Saturday morning, and secondly, and more importantly, Alberto didn't look the sort who would hold still for a one-handed lightweight bouncing him with anything anywhere. In fact, he was probably hoping I'd try something like that so he'd have an excuse for redesigning my face quite extensively. I wondered if Don Scipio knew what he was up to.

After about half an hour of leading Alberto around I came across the Norton Commando. It looked so out of place sitting on its center stand between an American taxi and a wooden handcart that I stopped for a moment to look at it. The owner, a young Portuguese West Indian, came out of a shop and we started talking the way motorcyclists will the world over. It was the only one in the Leeward Islands, he said, and yes, he did have a lot of trouble getting spares for it. While we were talking I glanced up the street and saw Alberto leaning against a shop window watching me — and that was when I got the idea. A time might just arrive when it could be very useful to have the fastest transport on the island.

When I first suggested that the West Indian might like to rent out his Commando for a few days he was dead against the idea: but the production of 400 E.C. dollars for a three-day hire soon changed his mind. He pocketed the money and asked me when I wanted to take it. I glanced at Alberto and said right now, so we ended up with me giving him a lift home on it then and there. I arranged to leave it at the airport if I didn't see him before I went. Alberto watched as we accelerated past him.

I dropped the owner off and took the bike for an airing round the island. St. Kitts is basically an extinct volcano rising steeply out of the sea, and a lot of the coast road winds sharply round the shoulders of volcanic ridges. The Commando was rather a lot of motorbike for these sharp bends and bad surfaces, but I wasn't in a hurry. I just tooled along enjoying the self-made wind and the feel of a powerful bike under me again. I had to operate the clutch with forefinger only, which was a bit of a strain, so I only used it for starting and stopping, making all the gear changes clutchless. On one or two straight stretches I wound it up to about 90 mph before chickening out. As Commandos go it was a bit on the flat side and the rear suspension needed reshimming, but even so I had no doubt it would leave any other vehicle on the island standing. I couldn't imagine *why* I might want to leave anything standing, since there is nowhere to run to on an island the size of St. Kitts anyway, but I still found the feeling comforting.

On Sunday I left the bike at the Ocean Terrace and walked into town to pick up the Avenger. I drove it back in time for lunch, then spent the after-noon sunbathing on the lawn outside the bar. I kept my money and the Smith & Wesson wrapped up in a towel beside me. Challese's henchmen were welcome to turn my room over as often as they liked: if they wanted to spend a few hours staring suspiciously at my razor, that was fine with me.

As it turned out, Alberto and Larry preferred to spend their time staring suspiciously at me. Or at least, Alberto did: Larry looked unhappy and sweated like a pig. I suspected he could think of other things he'd prefer to be doing, but had been dragged along by Alberto or ordered to go by Challese. The two of them walked up to the bar, which was an ornate bamboo effort with a thatched palm-frond roof and no sides, and sat on a couple of stools drinking beers and looking at me. When they first arrived my guts did a flick roll and every nerve in my body quivered; but strange-ly, after a few minutes I got used to them. They were obviously here to unnerve me, but I'd been so frightened anyway in the last couple of days that a little bit more now didn't make any real difference.

After they'd been there for half an hour or so I got up and went to the bar for a drink, favoring them with my very best scowl en route. Alberto looked as if he was about to explode, but Larry started as I stared straight at him. I leaned on the bar near him and he carefully looked past me. I could see his temple glistening with sweat. This side of Mafia life was ob-viously not his forte. I took my drink into the sun and lay down again, keeping my hand on my towel.

A few minutes later they got up and left. As soon as they were gone I slipped quickly up to my room and watched them from the window. They walked past the Avenger, paused by the Norton, then got into a big black Buick and swished away. I breathed out: I'd half expected them to back over the Commando so that I'd no longer have rapid transport, but maybe they wanted to avoid the publicity right then.

I didn't have to phone Challese the next morning. When I came down to breakfast the receptionist handed me an envelope sealed with wax, with my name on it.

Inside was a photostat copy of a certified check for $1,200,000.

CHAPTER 27

The bank manager had been suspicious of me all along. Now he sat with the photostat in front of him looking as if I'd just dropped a grenade on his desk. His eyebrows disappeared into his distinguished gray hairline, his suntanned face paled, and he had to work his mouth several times before he could get the words to come out.

"You . . . you're going to open your account with *this*?"

I nodded.

He swallowed hard again, eyes sliding around his office as if he was looking for a hole to bolt through. In a sense I could sympathize with him: it didn't take a lot of imagination to work out that there was something very fishy indeed about a man opening a numbered account with such an enormous check—especially when the check came from another numbered account. It was pure coincidence—yet hardly surprising, when one thought about it—that Challese was also using a Cayman bank and a numbered account. The significance was certainly not lost on our friendly Barclays manager, who was currently floundering in a sea of uncertainty, obviously wondering if there was anything he should do, or anyone he should contact, before dealing with the check on behalf of the Cayman Branch.

In the end he seemed to come to the conclusion that the only thing he *could* do was pass it on in the normal way. He was quite right: just because I was putting it through his branch didn't mean he actually had anything to do with the transaction. That was purely Cayman Island Branch business. I could see his face clear slightly as he finished thinking it through. He still regarded me as a gangster who was quite likely to haul a bleeding corpse into his office at any time, but he felt better for knowing he was professionally in the clear.

Yes, he said, he could have the photostat checked for authenticity by early afternoon. And when he had the check he would send it on immediately with instructions that the dollars were to be converted into sterling, and that my checkbook would be forwarded to the Barclays Head Office in Lombard Street, London, for me to pick up at my convenience. Here was my Cayman account number, and no, we don't keep any records of it here.

I thanked him and left. He didn't shake hands with me. Frightened of contamination, probably.

In the main vestibule of the bank I begged an envelope and a sheet of paper, and scribbled a brief note to Jedrow giving him the account number. I found a 35-cent stamp in my wallet, stuck it on, then put the envelope in my back pocket for posting.

I picked up a double tail as I walked out of the bank.

The first section was Alberto, sitting in his black Buick on the other side of the Circus. I knew he couldn't be serious about that, so I looked up and down the street for the real shadow. After standing there for five minutes, I thought I had him tagged—though I wasn't sure, by any means. The suspect was a very touristy-looking gent in loud Bermuda shorts and a short-sleeved cotton shirt, staring industriously into a shoe-shop window. A green MGB was parked at the curb near him.

I kicked the Norton into life, tooled gently round the Circus, and looked back to make sure the Buick was following me as I rode slowly up Fort Street, the main drag in Basseterre. There was no sign of the MGB. I waited until Alberto had reached the narrowest point of the street, then wheeled the Commando round in a brisk U-turn and accelerated smartly past him in the opposite direction. I got a glimpse of his contorted face behind the wheel before I dived off down a side road, took a couple more turns, and ended up in front of the Post Office. No more sign of Alberto or the MG. Maybe I was wrong about the touristy character. I left the bike ticking over lumpily on its side stand, dropped the letter to Jedrow into the airmail slot, and was off again within fifteen seconds.

Then I rode out to the airport and made a reservation on LIAT's afternoon flight to Antigua. It was due to take off at 1600 hours. By that time I'd be a rich man.

Or a dead one.

After that I just rode round the island, pushing the Norton hard as a panacea to my screaming nerves. I went up the eastern shore, round the north tip of the island, and back down the west coast. The distance was about 35 miles. Apart from the streets of Basseterre, that one great-circle route represented the only half-decent paved roads on St. Kitts.

At one o'clock I arrived back at the Ocean Terrace. I was far too strung up to contemplate lunch. I went to my room, dug my passport out of my holdall, and buttoned it down in a shirt pocket. The rest of the stuff in the bag was only clothes and a toothbrush, and I didn't mind sacrificing them on the altar of mobility. I paid my bill and dropped the bag in the Avenger, to be collected if I had the opportunity. As an afterthought I went back into the hotel and phoned the garage where I'd rented the car. The man said he'd be happy to pick it up from the Ocean Terrace in the morning.

So now I was clear out of excuses for wasting any more time.

I cranked the Norton up and headed into town. Alberto tagged on behind in his Buick immediately I turned on to the main road. I didn't try to shake him off, but I wondered where the serious tail would be. In town, I guessed. That was when they'd start getting really interested.

I felt the way I supposed a man must feel when he takes that last walk to the electric chair. My mouth was dry, my knees shaking, and nervous tension was swelling like a hard ball in my stomach. I was very aware of everything around me. The Norton snarled quietly, a dozing tiger ready to roar when I needed it. The Smith & Wesson rode heavily in my right hip pocket. The warm wind of my progress pressed my hair back and rippled my shirt. Even through my sunglasses Basseterre Harbour looked incredibly blue and bright in the hot sun as I eased down the hill into town.

The bank manager was even more nervous this time, as if he sensed the tension in me and the feeling of impending climax. Yes, he'd put the photocopy on the telegraph; and yes, the check would be honored when it was presented. I put the copy away carefully in my wallet to compare with the real thing when the time came, and told him I expected to be back before his three-o'clock closing time. That made him even more nervous. He seemed to get smaller in his chair. His worried gaze followed me as I walked out of his office.

Once again the heat was like an oven as I stepped out of the air-conditioned bank. Sweat collected at the bridge of my nose and trickled down the lenses of my sunglasses as I crossed the square to Alberto's Buick. I kept my right hand on the Smith & Wesson. Alberto's face was impassive, but I could see the hate deep in his eyes. A wave of nausea induced by pure fear welled up in my throat as I covered the last few yards.

It was 1:45 P.M.

"Tell your father I'll meet him outside Barclays over there at two thirty," I said to Alberto. "Tell him to bring the check, and I'll swap it for the stamps right there."

Alberto looked at me.

"He won't do it there," he growled. "He wants to examine the stamps before he hands over the check. He can't do that out in the street."

"Oh, yes, he can. We'll swap stamps and check at the same moment; then I'll wait while he sits in his car and checks them through. That's the only way he's going to get them. You can forget any ideas about getting me inside a building with them."

I didn't bother to say "Tell him to come alone." No point in wasting your breath in the tropical midday heat.

Alberto stared up at me for a long moment, the muscles of his shoulders moving under his shirt and hatred bubbling in his eyes. He was right that Challese wouldn't like the arrangement. They could hardly grab me and snatch the check back in the middle of town in broad daylight, and if they intended to knock me off before I got it into a bank they'd have to do something pretty drastic to prevent me walking three paces into Barclays once I had it in my hot little hand. And if they did try anything I could yell bloody murder and the scene would be knee-deep in cops from the police station round the corner in no seconds flat. Then, at the very least, Challese would have to do some explaining about what he was doing floating around with over a million pounds' worth of undeclared stamps in his pocket.

It was true that the Holland Method wouldn't give Challese a lot of protection if I was intending to slip him a load of cheap imitations. But I felt sure he wasn't seriously expecting me to try anything like that. It would be like handing a rubber bone to a starving wolf.

So I said to Alberto, "Get going and tell him," and turned and stumped away.

Sweat trickled down my spine where his eyes still bored into me, and I wondered if he could see my legs and hands shaking.

The Buick *woof*ed into life and tore off in a howl of spinning tires as I reached the Norton. I felt like sitting down on the curb and being mightily sick.

Instead, I kicked the bike into life and growled slowly up Fort Street, eyes searching frantically for the tail I knew had to be around somewhere.

I saw no one.

The Norton rumbled gently as I took the airport road out of town. Come on, damn you! Where the hell was that tail, for Chrissake? I ambled along in second at 20 mph, nerves zinging and twanging. They knew I'd be fetching the stamps now: there *had* to be a tail. . . .

The green MGB eased round the last corner out of town and poked its nose through the dallying traffic on the airport road.

I opened the throttle and the Norton took off with a bellow of power. The speedo clawed its way through 80 as I shot past the sugar factory and tramped into third. The tall cane fields on either side blurred into a rush

232

of sun-washed green. At 95 I banged it into top and hugged the crown of the road. This was a suicidal speed for a narrow road with high sugar cane on either side and West Indian drivers abroad — but I wasn't about to let the MG get too close.

I glanced back and saw the car getting smaller, so I eased off slightly. I didn't want him close — but I didn't want to lose him yet, either. I flashed past the turning to the airport at something over 80 and got a glimpse of a bright blue taxi dipping its nose heavily as it braked. For a moment I hoped he might pull out in true local fashion and clobber the MG. But he didn't, of course. I looked back again and saw the low green car shoot past the turning, rocking with speed. Catching up again.

I crouched down a bit, gripped the tank more firmly between my knees, and wound the twist grip open all the way. The engine thundered, and the slipstream rose to a keening roar. My eyes watered behind my sunglasses and I had to blink to steady my vision. The cane tumbled past like a mottled green tunnel and the bike pitched under me as we shot up a small hill. The suspension opened out and everything went light as I zipped over the top, praying there was nothing coming the other way. Down the other side, a bang and a heart-stopping weave as the Norton shot over a bad patch of road in the bottom of the dip. Then I was braking hard and cogging down as the T junction at the bottom of the next dip leaped up at me. Beyond the junction the blue sea gleamed and shimmered.

I'd crossed the neck of the island from west to east in less than three minutes.

I almost overdid that junction. The back tire howled as I braked as hard as I dared. At the last second I stopped braking and threw the bike left, nearly lost it on a patch of loose gravel, recovered way over on the wrong side of the road, and tore away in a soaring snarl of revs.

This speed was lethal. It was only a matter of time before I met someone lolloping along the other way in the middle of the road.

My only consolation was that it was worse for the driver of the MG. I *might* be able to squeeze the Commando through the gap when it happened; he certainly wouldn't get away with it in a car.

I snatched another backward glance as I started braking for the first bend round the volcanic shoulders. The B, heeled hard over, was just snaking out of the junction. The man could certainly drive.

I threw the Norton left, then right, sticking my toes out and down slightly to feel for the ground; yanked it upright; roared hollowly over the short wooden bridge spanning the rock-strewn gully between the hills; then banged it over to the right again and wound open the throttle. The bike shot down the bumpy road along the side of the shoulder, leaving the blare of exhaust slamming round the valley.

The road, carved out of the steep hillside, snapped sharply left round the bulge of the hill. The cliff rose steeply on my left-hand side, making the bend completely blind. I swung far out to the right, then decked the Norton down to the left until my shoe zipped on the roadway. At the last moment, when I was laid far over and should have been accelerating hard, some instinct made me leave the throttle shut for an instant longer to tighten my line. The bike weaved heavily in protest at being laid down so hard without power, but a Norton is a Norton, so I stayed aboard and hugged the cliffside.

A crawling Austin Cambridge appeared and was gone in an instant, flashing past inches away from my right foot.

For a second I heard the indignant *tee-et* of his horn; then I was gone and the noise lost in the blare of the Commando's acceleration. Reaction belted me in the guts as the adrenaline pump hitched itself belatedly into gear. That had to be the eighth of my nine lives.

I wondered how the MG would get on. All right, probably, damn him: he'd meet the Cambridge on the straight or the right-hand curve before it.

The Norton bellowed into the next valley, leaped and bucked round the bumpy right-hander at the end, then barked its way up through second and third as I dashed along the side of the spur. This time the left-hander round the shoulder was a little wider and curling steeply uphill. I threw a glance across the valley as I started braking for it. No sign of the MG — the Cambridge had probably slowed him up a bit.

Then I was round the shoulder. The road pulled steeply upwards for about a hundred yards, then flicked right again and dived down into an expanse of cane fields.

Just past the apex of the bend, a dirt road lined with coconut palms led off up the hill.

That was for me. I laid the Norton into the right-hander— then yanked it upright halfway round, stood on everything, and shot into the dirt road.

A bleached white board saying POVEY'S ESTATE zipped past as the bike started to slide on the loose gravel surface. A Commando ain't too handy on the rough—but fear was working for me and I got it tamed, then whizzed off the track in between a couple of coconut trees.

I killed the engine and tugged the Smith & Wesson out of my pocket. And waited.

There was a telltale cloud of dust hanging over the drive to testify to my slithering arrival. If the man in the MG saw it and turned up here he'd have to go slower than I had or he'd wrap the car round a tree.

And as he went past me he was going to get shot.

For a few seconds there was buzzing, fretful silence. I felt as if I had cotton wool in my ears, the way you do after a loud noise suddenly stops.

Then I heard the distinctive hollow rasp of an MGB accelerating hard.

I couldn't see the road from where I was, but I could follow him from the sounds. The engine died for an instant, then blipped smartly as he whipped down into second. I cocked the revolver, rested my left elbow on the tank, laid my gun wrist on my left hand to steady it, and sighted down the dirt road at driver's head height.

There was a hollow growl of acceleration, a momentary screech of tires; then the sound of the car was running away down the hill. It changed into third, then top, back to third, and rounded a distant bend in a screech of tires. Then finally there was the fading sound of acceleration again.

I let go of a very old breath. My gun hand sagged on to the tank and I let my head droop on to my chest for a moment as the taste of bile welled up in my throat. After a moment or two I stuck the revolver back in my pocket, paddled the Norton out on to the dirt driveway, and bump-started it as it rolled down the slope towards the road.

I was grateful for the slope. I didn't feel up to kick-starting right then.

CHAPTER 28

I glanced at my watch as I headed the Norton back the way we'd come. It was 2:05. I wound the twist grip and we were off and running again—fast, but not the suicidal headlong dash of a few minutes earlier. I kept glancing back as I accelerated the Commando along the short straights between the bends. No sign of the B.

By the time I'd passed the junction with the road leading to the airport and town I'd stopped worrying about it. Round about now Bermuda Shorts was probably coming to the conclusion I'd given him the slip. He'd almost certainly stop and ask someone, since any pedestrian would have to be blind and deaf not to have noticed my meteoric passage ahead of him. But finding out that I'd nipped off somewhere wouldn't be a great deal of help. I could have gone up any number of tracks leading up the mountain—or I could even have cut off across country in some places on a motorbike. He'd have no way of knowing, and bearing in mind the time factor he'd have no choice but to give it up.

But he'd certainly be back in town by 2:30. . . .

I arrived in Frigate Bay by going south down a dirt road leading along the east coast. The new roads which sat bare, waiting for the development that never came, were over a scrubby slope off to my right. From where I was I could see the point on the northern hill where *my* road ended, even though I couldn't see the road itself.

I stopped the Norton and sat astride it in silence for a couple of minutes, staring round.

No one about.

No sound of engines.

I cranked the bike into life, jounced off the road, and headed up the hillside, threading carefully between the scruffy cassia bushes. I met my road halfway up the hill, turned on to it, and stopped by the place I'd buried the stamps.

Still no sign of anyone.

I dug the stamps out, inevitably collecting a stab of panic before my scrabbling fingers touched the box. Moving quickly, I dug four heavy envelopes out of my back pocket, opened the box, salted the stamps away in them, and sealed them up. They made four bulky little packages. I stuffed them into the shirt pocket that wasn't full of passport, and buttoned the pocket carefully. Then I threw the box away into the scrub.

The time was 2:23.

I got back on the Norton, bump-started it down the hill, wheeled it round the roundabout in the middle of nowhere, and took the road to town.

My mouth was dry clear down to my throat, and my knees trembled against the tank. I felt cold in the white-hot West Indian sun.

The usual clump of taxi drivers were perched on the steps of the clock tower in the middle of The Circus. A few pedestrians sauntered past, lethargic in the heat. The glass doors of the bank were ten yards away—the crock of gold at the end of the rainbow.

The Commando stood by the curb on its center stand, ignition switch on and ready to go.

It was 2:32.

No one showed up.

Nerves screaming, I couldn't stop myself pacing up and down. One or two taxi drivers watched me curiously. I thought I got a glimpse of the worried face of the bank manager behind the glass doors of his air-conditioned haven.

No one.

Two thirty-five.

Sweat saturated my armpits and the inside of my elbows. It ran down my nose and my chin and made the shirt stick to my back. My left hand throbbed. The Smith & Wesson weighed like a field gun in my pocket.

Two forty.

The green MGB burbled slowly into the square and parked on the other side. Bermuda Shorts got out and half-sat casually on the front fender, watching me.

Fear wound up in my stomach like an air-raid siren. I wanted to retch.

Two forty-four.

Alberto drove up and parked directly opposite the Norton. He just sat there in the Buick. The black paintwork shone liquidly in the sun.

It reminded me of a hearse.

Two fifty-five.

My legs wouldn't walk anymore, so I sat on the Norton. My tongue tasted vile in my mouth. Bermuda Shorts got back into the MG.

Three o'clock. Scipio Challese wasn't coming. A distorted figure behind the glass doors of the bank slid the bolts to and turned a key in the lock.

I was out on the street with a million pounds making a flat bulge in my right shirt pocket.

I plunged down suddenly on the kick start, rocked the Commando forward off the stand, and kicked it into first as I wound open the trottle. The front wheel pawed the air, and the rear tire shrieked with wheelspin. The bike snaked viciously, I shut the throttle for a moment and caught it, and then the right footrest was scraping the ground as I threw it frantically round the bend leading to the market.

There were howls of protest from the milling blacks as I streaked past the stalls, but they were lost behind me in the thunder of the engine as I trod into second and kept the throttle hard open. I registered a movie-frame glimpse of people darting out of the way and others wheeling round at the noise—and then it was all gone.

Ahead of me the road dropped into a small gully with water in the bottom, one of several drainage channels from the town to the sea. You normally slow up and sidle in and out of these dips at walking pace. I took off from the downslope at about 50, hit the other side front wheel first, and fought a tank-slapping speed-wobble for the next 50 yards.

I was ready for the next gully. I approached at about 60, slammed open the throttle in second, then stood up on the footrests and yanked at the handlebars as the bike took off.

I glanced back. The front of the MGB was rearing up like a gaping crocodile mouth as it leaped out of the first dip.

I turned back to where I was going and flung the Norton to the right past a small monument on a fork in the road.

I'd been riding hard to outrun the MG before—but now I was going berserk. I hurled the Norton through the outskirts of town, taking the fastest lines with complete disregard for the possibility of anything coming the other way. My guardian angel put what little traffic there was on the short straights. I didn't want innocent people killed—but I prayed the B would meet something when it was committed to a bend.

It didn't.

I roared out of town with the green sports car about 300 yards behind.

I was beating the car hands down on acceleration, but he was pulling up on the braking for the bends.

We thundered north, past the turning to the casino, and into another set of those bloody hairpin bends. Into a valley and hard left—footrest grinding on the road, bike bucking on the bad surface, scrubby valley wall wheeling in front of me.

Blast down the short straight . . . hard into the left-hand side, then throw the bike over to the right . . . cut in on the apex . . . let her drift back out towards the sheer drop accelerating out of the hairpin . . . all the way open again . . . brake hard . . . into the left-hander, moment's panic as she wiggles on a patch of gravel . . . open up . . . brake . . . right again . . . chop in to the wrong side of the road on the apex . . .

And come face to face with a battered five-ton lorry.

It happened too fast for thought. I was on the right-hand side of the road laid over as far as I could go. The lorry was a couple of feet out from his edge. The massive front bumper and the high cab reared over me.

I kept going and shot through the gap on his nearside.

I had a momentary glimpse of huge wheels with heavy-shod tires inches from my left elbow. There was a vicious hiss of air-brakes alongside my ear as I flashed past the back and out into the daylight on the other side.

Then I was gone.

The bang of reaction made my eyes water and every nerve twang as I accelerated down the road towards the next bend. I blinked furiously, chucked the Commando round to the left, then automatically looked back at the lorry as I ripped up the straight. By then I was a quarter of a mile away.

It had stopped on the bend. A dozen workmen in the open back were disentangling themselves after the sudden braking.

Then as I looked, they all tumbled suddenly towards the cab again as the lorry jumped backwards. It seemed to leave the ground, move back several paces in the air, then stop. I slowed without thinking, watching incredulously.

With the deliberation of a slow-motion film the mangled remains of the MGB curled outwards from in front of the lorry and dropped out of sight down the shoulder of the hill.

The appalling double *crash* . .. . *crunch* drifted across, muted by distance, over the pobbling noises of the slowing Norton.

For a moment I was stunned. I swung the bike round the next bend, and the road opened out straight for a distance. I rode along automatically.

There was no point in my going back: the workmen in the back of the lorry would be unhurt, and the driver, way up above the level of MGB arrivals, should be all right unless he'd got unlucky with the steering wheel. Bermuda Shorts was probably dead, and I didn't give a damn about him, anyway.

I started thinking about what I was going to do.

Obviously, Challese had never meant to turn up with the check. He had it all right, or the bank would never have okayed the photostat—but he'd only got it to make me get the stamps out of hiding. Once I'd done that I'd become family target number one.

So much for my bright idea of a deal.

The only thing I could do now was get the hell *out*. Off the island on the four-o'clock flight. St. Kitts isn't a big place, and I didn't feel like sharing it with the Challeses anymore.

However, I couldn't turn back and head straight for the airport. Doing that would take me past the scene of the MGB's demise, and there would be people there who would like a word with me. I reckoned I'd probably be all right if I kept going: I'd been traveling far too fast for anyone to get a good look at me as I whipped past the lorry. There was a faint possibility someone might have recognized the only Commando on the island, but among a lorry-load of Negro laborers I didn't think it very likely.

I looked at my watch as the Norton rumbled through the straggling shanty village I'd seen from the steps of the casino. Three fifteen. Just thirteen minutes since I'd taken off from the square in Basseterre.

Okay—if I couldn't go back, I'd go forward. I just about had time to make it round the island and back to the airport before the four-o'clock flight.

If Challese wasn't covering the entrance to the airport road, that was.

I decided to worry about that when the time came.

I changed down and opened the throttle. The Commando's engine note changed from a low mumble to the harsh snarl of acceleration. I glanced over my shoulder as the speed built up.

Alberto's Buick was coming out of a bend, rolling heavily with speed, about 200 yards behind me.

241

Somehow the prospect of anyone still being behind hadn't occurred to me—but just because I couldn't go back hadn't, of course, meant that Alberto couldn't come forward. He'd probably had trouble getting the big Buick round the lorry, but apart from the sheer physical difficulties there was no reason why the crash should have held him up. He wasn't the type to have stopped to see what happened to his mate in the MG.

It didn't make any difference: so long as I kept the Commando moving fast I couldn't see it being caught by that great tank of a car, however well he drove it. He might even guess I was trying to get to the airport, but there was nothing he could do about it. As far as I knew there was no road over the top of the island that he could use to cut me off—and even if he tooled into the airport right behind me, which he wouldn't unless my faith in Norton Commandos was vastly misplaced, he could hardly walk up to a crowded departure gate and blow my head off in front of everybody.

I leaned into the wind and ripped past the straggling huts at over 80, praying that none of the inhabitants would choose this moment to go jay-walking. The Buick fell back a little.

Ahead, the road bent right past a church. I threw the Norton round it—and dropped straight into another of those bloody drainage gullies with a smash that rammed the suspension down to the bump stops and shook every tooth in my head. The bike popped out the other side like a ricocheting bullet and came down front wheel first and slightly askew. For an instant I thought I'd lost it; then with a stomach-wrenching effort I got it untwisted in time to stop myself hitting the native huts. A group of blacks who'd been paralyzed by my arrival shook their fists and shouted as I wound the power back and tore on.

I supposed Alberto knew about that gully. Pity. I'd like to have seen the Buick hit it at the speed I'd just done. He'd be nicked for low-level aerobatics.

A few seconds later I ran out of the village, shot along a fairly open stretch of coast road, then slowed down to about 70 for another shanty-town called Half Way Tree Village. There was no sign of the Buick be-

242

hind me as I blared down the straight main street scattering people and chickens. I collected the usual waves and shouts lost in the bellow of the engine.

Out of Half Way Tree was a long left-hander. I wound the throttle open, laying the Norton further over as the speed built up. Ninety—95 —100. The slipstream thundered in my ears and flattened my cheeks and whipped the roar of the engine away behind me. The bike chopped slightly over some ripples, then steadied. The ramparts of Brimstone Hill reared up on my right, and the sun-burnished sea glinted to the left and ahead.

About 100 yards in front of me, just visible round the bend, a long white car pulled slowly out of a side turning.

And stopped right across the road.

I yanked the Norton upright and hauled on the brakes.

The tires howled and the back end started to slide out. Everything moved in the terrible slow motion you get when you know the crash is inevitable.

Stop braking . . . sickening weave as the rear tire bites . . . chuck her down left to stay on the road . . . brake again as you pull her up . . . screaming of tires from miles away . . . front wheel going . . . pump brake . . . snaking . . . going to hit the car dead center . . . back wheel locked . . . sliding. . . .

Stopped.

Dust in the air.

The car 3 or 4 feet away.

The Norton was in the middle of the road at a slight angle. I didn't know how I was still aboard, but I was. My muscles quivered like jelly. There was a noise. It was the Commando, ticking away lumpily beneath me. I was still holding the clutch out, gripping the lever like a vise with the one finger of my left hand. I put my right foot back on the footrest and started tapping the gear lever down through the gears to find neutral. It was a pure reflex action.

The driver's door of the white car opened, and a Negro head appeared over the roof.

It was the man who had followed me before in the Chevrolet.

Then I saw the two other men several paces behind the car. They'd wanted to be out of the way when I plowed into it. One was Larry.

The other was Scipio Challese.

Seeing Challese brought me back to life. I looked round frantically. There was a howl of tires behind me—Alberto arriving in the Buick. The hillside? No go—there were ditches on both sides of the road. The only possibility was the tiny side road off to the right that the white car had pulled out of. There were a couple of feet between the ditch and the rear fender of the car.

I took it. I had no choice.

I wound the throttle open and dropped the clutch and wrenched the bike at the gap as the rear wheel spun and gripped in the explosion of power. The left footrest clipped the side of the car, the bike snatched over to the left, and I kicked the ground away frantically. It weaved right, nearly got away from me—and then I had it and we were thundering up the hill.

I got my feet up on the rests and trod into second. Snatching a glance back, I saw Alberto frozen halfway out of his car. Challese was standing still and pointing his arm at me. The arm jerked, and a puff of smoke came from his hand. I looked to the front and crouched down on the tank.

The narrow road pulled uphill and crossed the tracks of a tiny sugarcane railway—and suddenly I recognized it. It was the way up to Brimstone Hill Fort. I remembered a drainage gully just in time to stand up on the footrests and jump it — and then I was braking frantically for the first of the vicious little hairpin bends through which the road tacked up the steep hillside to the fort itself.

I think I grounded the footrests on every one of those bends. I don't know why I kept going—looking back on it, it would have made more sense to dive off into the bush at the bottom or take one of the dirt roads running into the cane fields on the way up. But by the time I'd thought of that I was high up the sheer side of the hill and well above all the possible turnoffs—and I wasn't about to turn back. I didn't know how far behind Challese was—and I needed to go pouring back down the road and run slap into Alberto's Buick like I needed a hole in the head.

244

So I kept going and roared past the hut selling souvenirs on one of the bends with my left foot scraping the ground. The place was closed up, of course. Nothing would have been more welcome at that moment than a large crowd of camera-toting tourists. But it was out of season.

I dived through the archway in the outer perimeter wall of the fort itself. The snarl of the exhaust thundered back at me off the stone walls. Down into first . . . one more very steep left-hander . . . a right through another arch . . . and I shot up the last straight stretch and on to a small grass car park. I threw the bike round the car park looking for an out. Apart from a useless little dirt track leading to a small grass knoll alongside the fortress, there was none.

So this was it. I skidded to a stop beside a wall, left the Norton leaning against it, and sprinted up a flight of stone steps leading to the main fortification. I tugged the Smith & Wesson out of my pocket as I ran.

CHAPTER 29

Brimstone Hill Fortress was built by the British in the early 1700s. It sits on a sheer 800-foot volcanic pimple rising suddenly out of the rolling foothills of Mounts Misery, St. Kitts's central mountain. The slave labor involved in dragging the enormous dark stone building blocks up the hill must have been incredible: those old-time soldiers didn't mess about when they built their forts. It even worked reasonably well, too — eight thousand French soldiers took a whole month to siege the hill into submission in the war of 1782.

The guts of the fortification is a five-sided edifice about 100 yards across called the Citadel, right on the peak of the hill. The outer perimeter wall runs round a much bigger area about 150 feet below the Citadel. I suppose you started off defending that, then fell back upwards for the last stand when things got tough. The Citadel is built along the usual fortress lines: just inside the walls are ramparts on which the cannons sat and poked their snouts out through the battlements. Beneath the ramparts are powder rooms and sleeping quarters and what have you, with little slit windows in them so you could help the cannon effort along by pooping off at the enemy with your rifle before turning in for the night. The rooms all open on to a central quadrangle. This is about 12 feet below the level of the ramparts, and open to the sky.

Access to the Citadel from inside the perimeter wall is by the last stretch of road, then the flight of stone steps I'd just run up. The view from the top is breathtaking. You can see the whole western seaboard of St. Kitts, and on a clear day you can also see the islands of St. Eustatius and Saba to the north and Nevis to the south.

But right now I wasn't looking at the scenery. The only view I was interested in was the road below. I reached the top of the steps with sweat pouring off me and ran to one of the battlements. Both the big white car and the Buick were making their way slowly up the hill. I froze and watched them, hoping my head looked like one of the restored cannons dotted along the ramparts.

For several long minutes nothing happened.

Then I saw Challese stride purposefully through the stone archway in the outer wall. Larry scuttled after him. The two of them vanished under the lee of the road, which doubled back above their level before reaching the grass car park and the stone stairway. They were much too far away for any fancywork with a .38 revolver. Even if I was any sort of shot, which I wasn't.

But they weren't too far for me to see the guns in their hands. Or the walkie-talkie that Challese carried.

Now I knew how come I'd been ambushed: Alberto had simply kept Pop informed on the radio. And the fact that Challese had parked himself on the northern road out of town in the first place meant that they must have at least one more crew out, to cover the airport road in case I went that way. And quite possibly a few more dotted around the island on top of that. Very cheering. Since the rest of the mob would now have undoubtedly been called here to help with the mopping up, it looked as though I might as well stick the muzzle of the Smith & Wesson in my mouth and save myself the suspense.

Furthermore, since Alberto and Black Power were not with Challese, the obvious conclusion was that they had some bright idea about out-flanking me.

I crouched in my battlement and tried desperately to think of something constructive. The sun hammered down and bounced off the stone of the fort. Sweat dripped off my chin. A green-and-yellow lizard ran across the top of the wall, puffed his dewlap at me indignantly, and vanished over the side.

I could think of nothing.

Unless I jumped over the wall after the lizard, there was no way out apart from the steps I'd come up. Jumping involved a 40-foot drop on to a steep scrubby slope; even if I survived that I could hardly expect to land quietly, and Challese would be on to me like an express train while I was trying to get my eyes uncrossed after the impact. There might well be an-other way down from the back of the Citadel—but with Alberto and Black Power on the loose I wasn't about to go looking for it.

The sound of footsteps drifted up to me.

I darted back to one of the walls near the entrance and slid an eye round a stone pillar at the top of the steps. Challese and Larry were just coming round a bend about 60 yards away. There was nothing wrong with Chal-lese's nerves: he must have realized I was up here with a gun, but his step never faltered. Larry was hanging back, clearly nervous about making the exposed climb.

I cocked the Smith & Wesson, reached round the pillar, took very care-ful aim, and squeezed the trigger. The gun went *boom,* the noise echoing round the Citadel. Challese jumped back as a puff of dust coughed up near his feet; then he vaulted over the low wall at the side of the steps and disappeared from sight.

Very smooth. He must have had that in mind as an escape clause before he even set foot on the stairway.

Larry froze, staring up towards me white-faced. I took aim again, fired, and kept firing as he turned and ran full pelt down the steps. The re-volver bucked in my hand and the gunfire rolled and thundered round the empty battlements. More puffs of dust sprouted from the stonework; then

248

he was gone, scuttling out of sight round the bend. The echoes died away, leaving a buzzing silence in their place.

I ran, crouching, back from my wall into the entrance to the Citadel quadrangle. No point in staying at the top of the steps now there was nothing to shoot at. People would know where I was.

I skidded to a stop in the cool shady archway of the entrance, wondering where the hell I was heading for. The quadrangle was in front of me, with all the rooms round the sides of it. That was no good: rat-in-a-trap stuff. A stone stairway in a passage on my left headed up to the ramparts. I took it, my hurrying footsteps echoing hollowly. At the top I burst out into the sunlight again, on the main rampart. No hiding place here either. Ahead of me a squat little watchtower rose out of the ramparts, narrow stone stairs leading up to it.

Not good. But there was nowhere else. I shot up the stairway.

The watchtower platform was dusty, sun-bleached stone. The crenellated walls rose up about 6 feet above the level of the floor. I crouched in a corner, where I couldn't be seen through the slits, and broke open the Smith & Wesson and emptied out the used cartridges.

I'd fired all five rounds. I dug the spare shells out of my pocket. There were ten of them. I'd have to be more careful. Using thirty-three percent of my firepower for frightening the pants off Larry hadn't exactly been Clausewitz strategy.

I closed the revolver, cocked it, and waited for something to happen.

Nothing did.

For a long time there was utter silence.

A hummingbird zipped up to the watchtower; hovered stationary over me for a moment, its wings a blur; then disappeared. A lizard ran across the stone floor with a small scurrying sound.

The white-hot afternoon sun hammered down.

The stonework I crouched against was hot. I had dust in my throat, and sweat collected at the ridge of my nose and ran down my sunglasses. I was hot and sticky all over, great damp patches showing on my shirt. I wondered if the stamps in my pocket would be affected by sweat. It didn't seem to matter very much. My left hand and the cut on my head throbbed nastily.

The silence hummed with tension. A couple of yellow birds *chirrup*ed in a flamboyant tree a little way down the hill.

And I slowly faced the fact that I was certainly going to die here on this small dusty stone floor under the tropical sun.

The realization didn't frighten me as much as I'd expected it would. In fact, it actually seemed to calm me a little.

In my job I'd faced the prospect of death more than most people probably do. I'm not brave, but it was the life I wanted and I was prepared to pay the price, in risk, for living it. The price hadn't seemed so high in recent months as it once had, anyway. I'd always known that every week, every year I kept it up reduced my chances of dying of old age by that much more. All air-show pilots and performers know this: they accept it or they get out.

I did know I hadn't expected to die like this, in the hot sun on a dusty stone floor. I'd imagined the instant's panic and the explosive *crunch* of a crash and then nothing; and I'd imagined slipping away into the darkness lying in a hospital bed. But not this.

Not that it made a lot of difference. I just wished it wasn't so hot. I held the gun carefully between my left thumb and forefinger and dried my sweating right palm on my trouser leg.

Still the silence.

I thought about Janie. It was five past four—five past nine in the evening, back in England. If things had been different—if I'd been different —we might just have been finishing dinner at home now. Or maybe taking a walk along some riverbank in the twilight of the summer evening before going to a restaurant.

If things had been different.

If . . . if.

But ifs don't change anything. I was 4,000 miles away from England, hot, dusty, sweating, very lonely, and resigned to dying in the tropical sunshine. I vowed to myself that I'd take Scipio Challese with me before it was all over.

The sound of a car drawing up brought me back to paying attention. I crawled quietly across the floor of the watchtower and looked over. An MGB, a blue one this time, drew up alongside the white saloon. Two men got out and disappeared under the wall. A few minutes later one of them came through the perimeter-wall archway, following the same path that Challese and Larry had done.

The other man was probably making his way round the hill somewhere to contribute to the flanking force. They both seemed quite superfluous to me.

Slow footsteps echoed round the hollow walls of the Citadel. I crawled back to the wall facing the quadrangle and peered through the slit there.

Alberto, holding an automatic the size of a young field gun, was walking across the quadrangle from the far end towards the watchtower. He was looking round as he walked, swiveling his head to make sure I wasn't crouching in one of the doorways drawing a bead on him. Every now and then his eyes ran along the ramparts. He wouldn't spot me for the moment —he'd need more than good eyes to see me through the tiny slit in the watchtower wall.

I brought up the revolver and got him square in the sights, resting my hand on the bottom of the slit to steady it. He was too far away yet, though. This gun was about as accurate as my shooting, and I knew that once I squeezed the trigger I wouldn't get a second chance: if I missed he'd be in one of the rooms and out of line with my slit before I'd even got the hammer back again. Then I'd have given away my position for nothing.

So I waited, watching him over the sights.

He stopped in the middle of the quadrangle, still looking round, automatic at the ready. Still too far away to be sure. Or maybe I was just frightened of breaking the silence.

The sun beat down like a welding torch.

Suddenly there were more footsteps, ringing hollowly in the entrance

251

passage beneath me. Scipio Challese came into view from underneath the tower. He walked over to Alberto in the center of the quadrangle. I shifted the attention of the Smith & Wesson to him.

The two of them stood there talking for a while, looking round as they did so. My sunglasses were fogging with sweat. I pushed them up into my hair.

Come on, Challese: take a few steps this way. . . .

He walked off towards the far end of the quadrangle.

Alberto came towards me, then turned left out of my line of sight.

I craned round, trying to see where he was going. I couldn't, so I looked back at Challese. He was climbing a flight of steps on to the battlement platform on the far side of the quadrangle. When he reached the top he strolled slowly round the wide ledge to my left. After about ten paces he stopped and leaned against a cannon. He was holding something that looked suspiciously like a Schmeisser machine pistol. This mob certainly didn't skimp on their weapons: those Schmeissers are lethal. He still had the walkie-talkie in his other hand.

I could hear footsteps echoing below—and suddenly I realized what was going on. Alberto must be searching the rooms around the quadrangle while Challese covered him from above.

They were being thorough. When they'd finished going through the rooms underneath they'd certainly check the watchtower.

A rat in a trap.

I looked through the slit again. Challese was strolling round the rampart towards me. He moved two cannons along, then leaned again, keeping the Schmeisser pointed in the general direction of the other end of the quadrangle. It looked as if he was moving around the rampart so as to stay opposite Alberto as he went through the rooms. After a minute or two he moved again, this time going out of the vision line of my slit.

The next time he moved should bring him in range of even a shot like me. I crawled over to the wall of the watchtower that was nearest him and listened carefully. When I heard him move again I was going to stand up, take careful aim through the nearest slit, and shoot him.

252

The only thing was that that shot, whether it got him or not, was going to bring Alberto and all the rest of them on to me like a ton of bricks.

Challese moved.

I hesitated—and suddenly realized there was a way out.

Challese was on my left, and the stairs into the watchtower opened on to the rampart on the right. So if I nipped down them now, before he crossed over in front of the tower, I might be able to make the inside stairway going from the ramparts into the entrance archway without being seen. I'd certainly be out of Challese's view behind the tower; the worst chance of being spotted lay in Alberto coming out of a room and looking up as I was crossing the 6 feet of rampart between one stairway and the other. If it came off and I was lucky I might just be able to slip out of the fort and down to the cars. I didn't hold too many high hopes of that, but it was certainly a better bet than staying bottled up in the watchtower.

Moving as silently as I could, I crept down the narrow steps and out of the entrance to the tower. I automatically looked down into the quadrangle for Alberto. He was nowhere to be seen.

I turned ahead for the dash to the rampart stairway—and looked straight into Larry's eyes.

He was standing about 20 feet away on my side of the rampart. He must have come quietly up the inside steps while I was watching Challese. His eyes bulged with fright and he jumped backwards. He tried to shout, but all he managed was a high-pitched gasp.

Then he remembered he had a gun in his hand. He brought it up. It was another of those bloody Schmeissers.

The roar of it was stunning after the aching silence. Bullets smashed into the stonework and whined away into the distance. I leaped for the stairway, firing wildly as I went. I saw a white smear appear on a cannon beside him.

The Schmeisser stopped just as I reached the entrance. I skidded to a halt. Larry was standing quite still. His gun hand dropped slowly to his side. He was looking down, aghast, at his stomach. Blood suddenly welled out right across his middle, instantly soaking his white shirt and running off the hem. Ricochet, I thought, staring at him stupidly. He made a horrified croaking sound and slowly brought his left hand up to the fearful wound. Hand and forearm immediately glistened red.

He staggered forward a few paces, dropping the gun with a clatter. His mouth worked. He mumbled, "Scip . . . ," instinctively appealing to his stronger brother the way he'd probably done all his life. He turned to Challese, on the opposite rampart, and lurched towards him.

He didn't make a sound as he went over the edge.

His body flailed like a rag doll for an instant as he stepped into space; then he was gone. There was a sickening *thump* from the stone floor of the quadrangle below.

For perhaps two seconds everything was completely still. Then a Schmeisser blared again, echoing thunderously round the Citadel. I came to life and dropped down the stairwell like a rabbit going into its hole. I didn't know who was firing and I wasn't staying to find out. I went down the stairs in reckless giant strides and shot out into the entrance chamber.

And slithered to a stop against the far wall.

He was standing in the entrance archway, silhouetted against the free sky outside. The man from the blue MGB. He had a big automatic in his hand, pointing steadily at my chest.

My gun hand was by my side. Very carefully and deliberately I opened my fingers and the Smith & Wesson clattered to the ground.

The man nodded.

"Very sensible," he said. He had a Tennessee accent. "Now put your hands on your head and walk real slow into that there courtyard."

The muzzle of the pistol yawned like a railway tunnel. I put my hands on my head and walked real slow into that there courtyard.

CHAPTER 30

They made me sit there in the quadrangle with my back against one of the walls and my legs straight out in front of me. It's difficult to make sudden movements from that position. They had me facing into the glare of the sun, which was beginning its evening dive into the sea. The shadow of the opposite wall moved almost perceptibly towards me across the stone floor of the quadrangle. But it still had a long way to go before it got to me. So I sat and sweated and felt the blood running down my face. My throat was parched and my mouth tasted terrible. The man from Tennessee stood stark and still, silhouetted against the brilliant sunlight.

His gun never wavered, even when he got out a Lucky Strike and lit it one-handed.

In the opposite corner of the quadrangle Challese and Alberto were kneeling beside Larry. The fat man wasn't quite dead yet, but it was obviously only a matter of minutes. Every now and then he groaned softly. I could see the blood from here. When I'd walked past him into the quadrangle I'd seen him more closely. The wound in his stomach was appalling: my bullet must have ricocheted off that cannon and been tumbling end over end when it hit him. No ordinary bullet, not even a soft-nosed dumdum, could have made such a ghastly mess of a man. His midriff was laid open right across the front, ugly-looking lumps of flesh spattered on his trousers and chest. His guts were literally spewing out.

I'd expected to be shot through the head immediately.

Instead, Challese had looked straight past me and told the man behind me to sit me over by the wall. Then he'd gone straight to Larry. Alberto had taken the time to stop and press the muzzle of his gun into my temple for a moment. I closed my eyes and expected to be dead without knowing another thing. Then the pressure was gone. I opened my eyes again. He looked at me totally without expression, then drew the automatic back a few inches and lashed forward so that the barrel thumped into my head just above my left eye—right on the old cut. Hot blood immediately welled out and ran down my face, dripping off my chin. Alberto showed no emotion at all—just turned away and followed his father.

So now I sat there in the dust waiting for Larry to die and knowing it would be my turn next.

They say that while there's life there's hope. It's not true. I had no hope now. The man from Tennessee, standing tall in the sun, would shoot me with that big black pistol if I even began to make a move. And when Challese and Alberto came over they were going to kill me as surely as the sun would set in the next hour.

I wasn't even frightened anymore. Fear is for the living.

Finally the blazing disk of the sun rested on the battlements beside the watchtower. Slowly it sank deeper, the gap-toothed wall black against the brilliant yellow orb.

The shadow of the far wall reached my feet and crept up my legs, bringing a tiny relief from the heat. The first tree frog of the evening began a lonely *chirrup*ing somewhere outside the Citadel.

Larry coughed—a choking, bubbling sound in the quiet.

Then he died.

Challese and Alberto stood up beside him. For a minute they stayed there, heads bowed over the body. Then whatever communion they had with their God was over.

Together, they turned and walked towards me.

Challese knelt beside me.

I'd half-expected him to push his Schmeisser in my face and blow my brains out then and there. But instead he handed the gun and the walkie-talkie to Alberto and just knelt down beside me. The man from Tennessee stayed where he was in the fading light, and Alberto moved round to my other side. Between them they had three guns on me. I sat there, unmoving, and looked steadily at Challese.

He said nothing. He reached out a hand, unbuttoned the pockets of my shirt, and took out the stamps and my passport. Shifting slightly so that his hands were hidden from Tennessee by his body, he opened the envelopes one by one and looked the stamps over slowly. Then he put both them and the passport in his own shirt pockets.

Perhaps that was why he hadn't shot me yet. He didn't want to get blood over the stamps.

Finally he spoke. His voice was harsh and grating in the still evening.

"Holland, you know I'm going to kill you?"

I nodded. The words didn't have any impact.

"I'm going to kill you at seven o'clock tonight," he went on. "It's now about half past five. You've killed my brother and several men of mine. I want you to know about your death beforehand.

"I'm going to throw you out of my plane between here and Antigua."

I just looked at him.

I ought to have felt a fresh belt of terror. As with most airmen, the natural, primeval fear of falling is something that reared up in me when I started learning to fly but sank back, considered and subdued, as my air time mounted. The beast should have stirred and reawakened now, but it didn't. I had no terror left. I was already dead.

Maybe I'd feel differently by seven o'clock.

Challese eyed me for a moment, then suddenly drew back his right

257

forearm and smashed me in the face with the back of his fist. My head whipped back and hit the wall. I heard the distant meaty *thump* of the blow, and the world rocked on its hinges. For a few seconds I was stunned; then I came back to life with the taste of blood in my mouth and my eyes watering furiously. I blinked to clear them. My eyelids seemed to move slowly and uncertainly, as if the connections between muscles and brain were shorting out somewhere. I felt my lips starting to swell up where they'd been smashed against my teeth. My nose felt big and blocked-up and numb. My bottom front teeth started to ache.

Challese was standing up now, and he had his gun back from Alberto. The three of them looked down at me.

"You have an alternative, of course," he said harshly. "You can disobey a command between now and then, in which case you'll be shot immediately and you'll be dead or dying when you're thrown out of the plane. That's up to you."

I nodded slowly. Somewhere deep down the will to live stirred itself and kicked a couple of brain cells back to life. The sadistic bastard knew what he was doing, all right: I'd do what he said so that I'd stay alive between now and seven o'clock, even though staying alive contained only the prospect of imminent death. *While there's life*—even when there's no hope.

Challese turned to the man from Tennessee. "Go and bring the Chrysler up to the grass car park," he instructed. "I've already told Johnny to go back to Christian at the cars. Tell him to ride that motorcycle into town and leave it in the Circus. Christian can follow him and pick him up in the Buick; then they're to go back to the casino. Tell Christian not to follow close behind the cycle—I want Johnny picked up a few streets away so there's no connection, see? Don't tell them about Larry; I don't want anyone else to know about that. Bring the MG's soft top back with you— we're going to need something to wrap him in or he'll leave blood all over the car. Got all that?"

Tennessee nodded.

"Okay, then," said Challese. "Here, take this with you." He handed him the walkie-talkie. The tall man nodded again and walked away into the gathering gloom.

The light was almost gone now, the fast, tropical twilight fading into warm darkness. The trilling of crickets and tree frogs wound up to its steady nighttime pitch. As Tennessee's footsteps echoed through the stone archway, Challese turned to Alberto.

"When we've got Holland and Larry into the Chrysler I want you to take the MG to the casino and pick up my passport. I'll stay in Antigua tonight and get a plane to New York in the morning. I want to get rid of these stamps. I'll go with Ed in the Chrysler to look after Holland, and see you at the airport. Okay? Then we can book out to Antigua and pick Holland and Larry up afterwards at the end of the runway. Nobody'll see us if we're quick. We'll have to dump Larry at the same time as Holland—I'm sorry about that, but I can't have him buried properly in that state."

He didn't sound sorry about it. He thought for a moment, then added: "While you're at the casino, pick up that spare list of the stamps from the desk drawer. Second one down on the left. I don't want anyone here finding that if I'm going to produce the fuckin' things in the States. And bring overnight bags for both of us. You can come back here in the morning. Got that?"

"Yeah, I got it." Alberto sounded as if his mind was on something else.

There was silence for a while.

Then he said: "Poor old Larry. I never liked him much, but it don't seem right to chuck him out of the goddam airplane. Couldn't we—"

"No." Challese stopped him with his harsh voice. "We can't afford to bury him with his guts hanging out like that. We've got to get rid of him. He'd understand." Challese didn't sound as if he cared too much whether Larry understood or not. "We don't have any choice."

Alberto subsided.

I didn't think it was right to chuck Larry out of an aeroplane either.

I didn't think it was right to chuck *anybody* out of an aeroplane.

259

A few minutes later we heard the Norton growl into life below the Citadel. The noise tailed off as Johnny, whoever he was, rode it slowly down the hillside. A little while after that, the man from Tennessee, the one Challese had referred to as Ed, strode back through the archway. It was now full dark. His footsteps stopped on the other side of the quadrangle and there was a rustle of heavy fabric as he dropped the MG's soft top near Larry's body. Then the footsteps sounded again, and the Tennessee voice came from somewhere close.

"I've brought a flashlight from the car."

"Good," growled Challese. "Give it to me. Now you and Alberto go and wrap Larry up and carry him down to the car. Put him in the trunk. Don't spill blood in there. Come back here when you've done it."

They went off. Challese switched the torch on and shone it into my face. I screwed up my eyes in the sudden light.

"If you move I'll shoot you," he said simply.

I nodded. I believed him.

There was a rustling in the darkness and then the noises that men make when they're lifting something heavy and awkward. The sound receded. I didn't envy them the job of carrying Larry's fifteen stone or more down the long flight of steps leading to the car park. Then I thought about it for a moment and decided I *did* envy them. I'd have carried Larry down myself one-handed if it had meant I didn't have Challese looking at me over that Schmeisser. I sat in the torch beam and thought about being dead.

After what seemed a long time, the two of them came back. Challese told me to stand up and keep my back to the wall. I did what he said. The movement, after sitting so still, produced a bubble of pain in my hip and reminded my head that it ought to be aching. Challese stepped back so that the yellow torchlight covered me. His harsh voice floated out of the blackness behind the torch.

"Alberto, give me your gun and go and hold his right hand. His fingers, not his wrist. You get his left hand, Ed."

The two of them arrived on either side of me without crossing the torchlight, and did as they were told. Alberto crunched my fingers viciously in his powerful fist. The way he was holding me, fingers entwined, I could have crunched back, but I didn't want to aggravate him. Ed wasn't quite so brutal getting hold of my left hand, but then he didn't have to be. I nearly passed out with the pain as he gripped my broken fingers.

"Okay," said Challese. "Now walk slowly to the car. I'll be right behind you, Holland, so don't try anything."

I nodded again. I couldn't think of anything worth trying anyway.

We started walking and Challese fell in behind us. It was a bit of a squeeze through the archway three abreast, but we made it. We made it right down to the car without incident. I took particular care not to trip on the stone steps. I could feel sweat trickling down my back where Challese's Schmeisser was focused on it.

We stopped by the white car.

"Get in, Holland," said Challese.

The drive was uneventful. Ed took the wheel and Challese spent the whole journey skewed round in his seat, the Schmeisser pointing at me unwaveringly. With the child locks set on the doors I had no chance of pitching myself out into the night, and any other move wouldn't have got halfway started before Challese blew me to bits. So I sat very still, trying to look stunned.

We went through the outskirts of Basseterre, out on the road towards the airport, then turned off left just before we reached the airport turning. We went down this road for about a mile; then the car slowed down, Ed turned off the lights, and we bumped slowly on to a fresh track that showed up on our right in the wan light of the new moon.

After a couple of hundred yards the track opened out on to a big light-colored stuff would probably be stabilized tarrace. At the far end of moment; then, as the car rolled on to the smooth surface, the penny dropped. This was the end of the new runway under construction. The light-colored stuff would probably be stabilized tarrace. At the far end of the workings, over a mile and a half away, I could see the floodlights of a night shift. The growl of heavy machinery drifted down to us on the gentle trade wind. I remembered what they were doing: hacking away a small hill at the end of the new runway. For a moment the noise was a friendly link with the rest of humanity.

Then the car swung round and reversed off the side of the runway into a small track, and the lights vanished behind the long grass that rose up on both sides of us. I twisted round in the seat—carefully, so as not to give Challese any wrong impressions—and saw the beginning of two rows of yellow lights at the other end of the track. After a moment's disorientation I realized I was looking at the lights of the existing runway, which was parallel to the new construction. The small track, probably used by the contractors, linked up the two.

Ed, being the perfect chauffeur, got out first and walked round to open a door for me. The chauffeur image was slightly dented by the big automatic in his fist, but he swung the door wide in the best Harrods flunky manner. If you open a door as far as it will go, the party of the second part can't kick it the rest of the way and catch you in the face with it.

I moved slowly. I was halfway through the doorway when I caught a movement out of the corner of my eye. Ed's arm swinging up. I started to duck instinctively; then the pistol barrel crashed down above my right ear.

I fell back into the car, the world reeling and my head ringing with a thousand bells.

I wasn't quite unconscious, but I closed my eyes and breathed shallowly and evenly and did my best to look thoroughly out. It wasn't hard. Maybe neither of them had seen me start to duck before the gun barrel connected. I'd soon know if they had—they'd probably haul me out and give me another tap for good measure.

They hadn't.

Ed grabbed my legs, thrust them roughly inside the car, and slammed the door again. I remembered to relax so that my body flopped along the seat in what I hoped was a natural-looking manner for an unconscious person. It must have been good enough, because a few seconds later I heard a front door open and felt the car rise slightly on its suspension as Challese got out.

262

"Watch him," I heard him say. "I don't want him comin' round and goin' for a walk or anything."

Ed chuckled. Very funny.

There was a small rustle of footsteps going away from the car. Challese leaving to meet Alberto, I supposed.

The front passenger door opened, the seat sighed, and the suspension dipped as Ed sat in. I was lying bundled up more or less on my side in the rear seat, so I very slowly opened my lower eye a slit to see what he was doing. He was sitting sideways in the seat, staring at me, with the big automatic resting on the seat back and pointing at my chest. Definitely the careful type. I closed the eye and decided not to try looking any more unless I heard him move from where he was. It wasn't a difficult decision.

I tried desperately to think of something to do—but there was nothing. So long as Ed took his job of watching me this seriously, I was better off continuing to be unconscious: I had no chance of moving fast enough to overcome him, and if I tried it the best I'd get would be another slosh on the head. And this time there wouldn't be any mistakes: I'd probably still be unconscious when Challese heaved me out of the aircraft.

Time dragged on. I began to wonder if something had gone wrong at the airport. It couldn't possibly take this long to clear Customs and Immigration, file a flight plan to Coolidge, and get a Twin Bonanza cranked up. My nerves screamed at the delay.

Then I heard it. The unmistakable husking rustle of a pair of flat six Lycomings. The noise got louder as the aircraft backtracked the runway to the end, where we were waiting. Then the machine was very near, and one engine snorted impatiently as the pilot swung round into the direction of takeoff.

Then the noise settled down to the distinctive clanking tick-over of engines with geared-down props, and above the beat of the exhausts I heard the sound of a door dropping open and running feet on the tarmac.

Ed had never moved.

CHAPTER 31

"Okay?" It was Challese's harsh voice, questioning in the darkness.

"Okay. He didn't go for no walks."

"Right. Stay there and watch him. We'll take Larry first."

Sound of the car boot being opened. Grunting, thumping, and rustling as they hauled Larry's body out and bore it off into the dark. Within a short time they were back, their footsteps hurrying.

"Give me your gun," Challese ordered. There was a sound of movement from the front seat and the car rose on its suspension as Ed got out. I stayed unconscious. My chances of coming to life, sizing everything up, and making a break under the noses of the three of them didn't exist. Better to keep my one hole card, my consciousness, for a better opportunity. I hoped.

"Now you two haul him out and over to the plane. I'll follow you in case he tries anything. Hurry it up—the control people are going to be getting impatient."

The rear door at my feet opened, and someone grabbed my ankles and hauled. I remembered to stay limp as I shot out of the car and hit the ground. My aching head collected another nasty crack on the door sill; then rough hands grabbed me under the armpits and the world reeled as they hoisted me up and started carrying me towards the idling aircraft.

The engine noises got louder; then I felt the cool wind of the slipstream rippling my clothes as they carried me round the tail. With my head bumping against the stomach of whoever had hold of the top end of me, I didn't dare open my eyes. The beat of one exhaust got louder still, the slipstream increased, then I was being lifted to near the vertical as they hauled me into the aircraft. My left hand, hanging limp, got banged against the doorjamb, then dragged across Larry's makeshift shroud. Then the hands let go of my ankles and I was dragged round a seat and dropped unceremoniously on the floor. For a few seconds there were sounds of movement from all round.

Then the engine noise faded suddenly as someone shut the door. I nearly tensed as a foot came down on my chest, but caught myself in time. Whoever it was stepped on over me and plumped into a seat nearby. There was the rattle of a safety-belt clip.

A radio loudspeaker blared querulously somewhere in the roof of the cabin.

"Three-two Romeo from Golden Rock, d'you read?"

"Golden Rock, three-two Romeo reading you strength five. We're ready for takeoff now." Alberto's voice. I could hear him panting between the sentences.

"Roger. Three-two Romeo. You got your trouble fixed?"

"Affirmative. One of the door latches wouldn't fasten properly, but we got it shut now. We cleared for takeoff?"

"Roger, three-two Romeo, you're cleared."

The engine noise surged into the roar of full power, and I felt the press of acceleration as we started the takeoff roll. The cabin swayed slightly from side to side from tiny overcorrections on the rudder. Alberto wasn't a top-notch pilot. I suddenly realized I was wasting an opportunity, and opened my eyes. No one was going to be watching me during the takeoff: the natural thing is to look out of the window at what's going on.

The first thing I saw was Challese, sitting above me on a seat on the right-hand side of the fuselage. I was right. His head was turned towards the window. The floor of the cabin tilted upwards as Alberto rotated the aircraft off the ground, and I slid back an inch or two. Something ground painfully into my right side. I glanced down, saw in the dim reflected light of the instruments that it was a large lump of concrete, then looked up again just in time to see Challese's head start to move.

I closed my eyes.

There was a gentle whining shudder through the airframe, followed by a low double *thump* as the wheels came up. They were followed by the flaps; then the urgent thunder of takeoff power diminished as Alberto throttled back to normal climb. He did it clumsily, fiddling about with the pitch of the props for a long time, and even when he'd finished, the engines weren't properly synchronized. Instead of the even rumble of properly matched power units, they were going *rerr-a-rerr-a-rerr* as one ran fractionally faster than the other. The aircraft vibrated gently in time with the undulations. Any competent pilot would have picked it up in seconds and made a small adjustment to one prop to get them together. Alberto seemed to ignore it. Maybe he didn't have much time in twins. I made a mental note of that: if he was having to devote a lot of attention to flying, it might give me a few extra seconds when the time came to try and thump his old man.

The radio crackled and came to life.

"Three-two Romeo was off Golden Rock at four one; say your estimate for Coolidge?"

Alberto cleared his throat, thought for a moment, then replied. I didn't hear what he said over the noise of the engines.

Four one. That meant forty-one minutes past six. If Challese stuck to his schedule, I had nineteen minutes left to live.

I tried to plan what I was going to do.

After climbing for about ten minutes, Alberto leveled off. This time he made a better job of syncing the engines, but they still weren't dead right. Challese waited until he'd finished fiddling with the power, then

266

got up and went forward. At least, I supposed he'd gone forward. I'd heard him leave his seat and he hadn't trodden on me afterwards, so there weren't many other places he could have gone.

I opened one eye just a fraction,

From where I lay I could just see his back as he bent over Alberto. The red glow of the instruments lit up his silhouette. Alberto nodded at something he said; then Challese straightened up as far as the cabin roof permitted and started to turn round. I closed the eye again. A few moments later his foot came down on the right side of my chest and slithered off on to my arm. He stumbled and cursed, regained his balance, and trod on my ankle as he went on down the fuselage.

I felt the aircraft make a small pitch change. Alberto compensating for the shift of weight. Good—that meant there was probably no autopilot. Alberto would have to stay up in the sharp end while Challese did the heaving.

From the back of the aircraft I heard a scratchy rustle and a few mild thumps, as if Challese was shifting something heavy. That was what I'd expected—he'd have to get rid of Larry first, since he was the furthest back. I tensed again, waiting for the roar of the slipstream as he opened the door.

Nothing happened.

The rustling and thumping went on. Suddenly I realized what he was doing—and at the same time what the lump of stone digging into my side was for. Of course! He was tying Larry to his shroud and fastening something heavy to him to make sure he sank. He wouldn't want our bodies floating around on the surface and possibly being washed ashore somewhere.

And when he'd finished with Larry, he'd be along to tie another chunk of masonry on to me.

He'd certainly get the weights on us both before he started heaving anyone overboard—there was no point in opening and closing the heavy cabin door twice.

The realization hit me like a club. I'd been planning to wait until he had the door open and then try to get a shoulder behind him. A pretty

267

forlorn chance at best—but if I had a ruddy great lump of concrete tied on to me it was going to be completely hopeless.

Panic rose in my throat. Any minute now he'd finish with Larry and come forward.

Without stopping to think, I reached up and gripped the seat nearest me with my right hand and hauled myself up. Out of the corner of my eye I saw Challese look round at me—and then I'd grabbed the heavy concrete block on the floor and was lurching forward with it.

Challese shouted something behind me. Alberto looked round and saw me coming—but he was a lifetime too late. I smashed the block down on his head. It hit his skull with a sickening *thump* and I leaped out of the way as it dropped behind his seat.

He slumped forward on to the controls without a sound—and the floor immediately fell away from under me as the Bonanza dropped its nose into a steep dive.

I grabbed wildly at the back of his seat, caught it with my left hand, and reached desperately round his body for the control yoke. He slipped over to the left while I was groping under his chest for it and the left wing dropped sharply, nearly throwing me off balance again. I finally had an attack of sense and hooked my right elbow round his neck and hauled him back off the stick.

Relieved of the weight on the elevators, the Bonanza's natural stability yanked it sharply out of the dive, and I nearly lost my grip on him under the sudden G load of the pullout.

The bright pinpoints of the stars rushed down the screen as the aircraft clawed upwards into a steep climbing turn. I caught a glimpse of the airspeed dropping back through 280 knots and wondered when the wings were going to come off. The Velocity Never Exceed in a Twin Bonanza is 250 — and we were well over that and pulling three or four G. The engines screamed as the props overran the constant-speed units and the revs soared.

Getting myself firmly pinioned against Alberto, I reached out a heavy left hand, grabbed the yoke, leveled the wings, and started easing forward as the speed dropped off. The stars stopped and reversed, marching up the screen at a reasonable rate now. The engines slowed to somewhere near their normal cruise.

With the immediate panic over, I looked back down the fuselage.

Challese was hauling himself forward along the gangway, grabbing seat backs with one hand and waving the Schmeisser in the other. As I watched he stopped and brought the gun up.

"Don't shoot!" I howled over the engines. "You can't fly this thing!"

He hesitated, infinitely menacing, crouched over the gun in the dim red light.

For a moment I thought he was going to shoot anyway and tensed my muscles to push forward on the stick—and then the gun wavered and lowered.

Without taking his eyes off me, Challese pulled himself up to the front seats. The muzzle of the gun came up slowly and ground into my head just below my right ear. I strained back. Challese's face was a mask of hatred. His eyes glittered redly.

"Don't make a single move," he said slowly. His voice was low and hoarse with rage. I nodded—the tiniest of movements. He was right on the edge. One wrong move and he'd blow my head off and to hell with the consequences.

The engines rumbled unevenly. Out of sync again.

For a long, tense moment neither of us moved while he teetered on the brink. I made little twitches with my left wrist to keep us straight and level. Sweat popped out under my ear where the gun barrel was pushing. An involuntary shiver ran up my spine and finished in the short hairs on the back of my neck.

After an age the pressure on the gun muzzle slowly relaxed. I breathed out. Challese backed off to the other side of the cockpit. The gun still pointed at my head.

"Get Alberto out of the seat," he commanded harshly.

I said: "All right, but I'll have to retrim it first or it'll dive again. It's trimmed for your weight in the back at the moment."

"Okay. Do it slowly."

269

I did it slowly. Leaning over Alberto and holding him back with my left elbow, I reached out my right hand carefully to the big white plastic trim wheel. The forward pull on the stick eased as I wound it back.

"She's trimmed. I'll shift him now."

Challese nodded.

I let go of the stick. The Bonanza droned on in the smooth Caribbean night. I unclipped Alberto's seat belt, got both hands under his armpits, and pulled him sideways out of the seat. It was a difficult maneuver, because he was very heavy. His head lolled against my chest and left blood on my shirt as I hauled him over the hump of the mainspar between the two pilots' seats. I finally got him laid down in the gangway between the passenger seats.

"Is he dead?" The eyes and the gun stayed unwavering on me.

"I don't know." Actually, I did: unless Alberto had found a way of continuing to live with a crushed skull and without breathing, he was very dead. But I didn't want to be the one to break the news.

The engines started to labor. I looked out and saw the nose was pitched upwards—the result of Alberto's and my weight being shifted back. The airspeed was dropping through 100 knots.

"I'd better come forward and fly this thing," I said. "She's going to stall any moment now."

Challese just looked at me as if he hadn't understood what I'd said. I stayed where I was. The speed dropped off to 80, then 75 . . .

The stall-warning horn blared.

I'd been expecting it, but Challese flinched and the gun jerked. For a moment I thought he was going to fire; then he caught himself again. The Bonanza started to buffet on the edge of the stall, the horn screeching solidly. I braced myself for the breakaway—the next thing would be the nose dropping sharply, and when it happened I was going for the gun.

"Okay," he said suddenly. "Get in that seat."

I stepped over Alberto's body, leaned over, and pushed the control column forward and held it there while I climbed into the seat. The airspeed picked up and the horn stopped. I got myself settled in, fastened my seat belt, and retrimmed. Quite automatically I reached for the throttle and pitch levers to get the engines synced up.

"Stop!" Challese's voice was a low, vicious snarl.

My hand stopped in midair.

"What are you doing?"

"I'm going to synchronize the engines. They're not running together."

Challese, perched on the edge of the right-hand copilot's seat, leaned across so that his face was inches from mine. The Schmeisser stayed on his lap, nestling in his right hand and pointing at my stomach.

"Okay," he said softly. "You synchronize 'em. But if you make one wrong move I'm gonna shoot you. I reckon I can land this myself if I have to. Got that quite clear?"

I nodded, pushed up the right throttle a touch to bring the manifold-pressure needles together, then made a tiny adjustment to the pitch on the same engine. The *rerr-a-rerr-a-rerr* smoothed out to an even snoring.

"You couldn't land this," I said quietly. "You wouldn't even know where to start." I waved a hand—gently, so as not to excite him—over the knobs and dials. "It's a complicated aeroplane"—it wasn't, but to a layman the cockpit of anything with two engines looks complicated—"and you don't even know how to put the wheels down. Come to that, I doubt if you could even *find* an airfield, let alone land on it."

As I said that I was acutely aware of the needle of the Automatic Direction Finder pointing straight at the Coolidge beacon. Challese, as I'd hoped, wasn't. He glanced out of the windscreen at the tropical night. The only lights in the blackness were the crescent of the moon, the pinpricks of the stars, and a faint sheen on the water 5,000 feet below. He seemed to get the point.

There was a long silence. I noticed for the first time that my left hand was throbbing agonizingly. Well, it was entitled to, the way I'd been banging it and heaving blocks of concrete around with it.

Challese seemed to be thinking.

Eventually he said, "Okay, Holland, I'm gonna let you land it. Back at St. Kitts. You can tell 'em we've got engine trouble or something an' we're coming back. An' no tricks, see?'' His voice was a low snarl again. ''If you do something I don't like I'm going to shoot you an' take my chances. Got that?''

I nodded. I'd got it—and a bit more besides. By going back to Golden Rock, his point of origin, Challese wouldn't have to have customs snooping round the aeroplane. He might not know how to fly, but a man like him would be pretty clued up on the laws of entering a country by aircraft. If we took off from Golden Rock and then went back there without landing anywhere else it would be a ''local'' flight. No customs, no immigration. He could lock the machine up, wait until the airport had closed, then whistle up a car to quietly come and collect the bodies.

And one of those bodies would be mine.

It would have to be. He had no reason for leaving me on the loose. As soon as I'd taxied in he could put a shot through my head with the Schmeisser. One shot wouldn't be heard above the engines—and even if it was it would only sound like a backfire. Since we were supposed to be returning with engine trouble, no one would think twice about that.

I started sweating again.

CHAPTER 32

Challese seemed to be waiting for something.

I said, "All right, turning now," and started a gentle turn. A *very* gentle turn. Real BOAC stuff—twenty degrees of bank and nary a quiver rolling in. The nose ambled slowly across the stars. I leaned forward, frowned at the gyrocompass, and pressed and twisted the Reset button.

"What are you doing there?"

He didn't seem to trust me.

"Resetting the direction indicator. They precess a lot if you dive the aeroplane like we did back there. It was way off. I'm rolling out on three hundred thirty degrees to go back to St. Kitts, see?"

I pointed my finger at the DI as the wings came level. It did indeed say 330 degrees. Part of what I'd said about DIs was true. I'd reset it, all right—but way off the correct heading. I hoped he wouldn't notice the magnetic compasses perched up on top of the windscreen out of the way of the worst of the magnetic disturbance of the radios.

He didn't. He just glanced at the DI and nodded.

273

The Bonanza droned on. North-north-easterly. No land that way until you hit Iceland. I wanted time to think without St. Kitts looming up and spoiling my concentration.

After a moment I reached my right hand forward to the throttles.

"Just going to reduce power a little and come down a bit," I told him. "Now we're going the other way we ought to be at a different height; this is the cruising level for traffic going west."

"Okay. Just do it gently."

I did it gently. The snoring of the engines slid back to a low drone. He glanced at the rev counters—the usual lay reaction when you say you're going to reduce power. They moved very slightly, dropping from 2700 to 2500 when I got the throttles nearly closed.

The airspeed started settling back towards 88 knots. On a Twin Bonanza, that's VMC speed—Velocity Minimum Control. The speed below which you don't have enough rudder control to keep the aeroplane straight on full power if one engine fails.

I leaned over to the right-hand side of the panel, opened a small hatch under the radios, studied the row of circuit breakers for a moment, then ran my fingers down them, popping out the one marked STALL-GEAR HORN as I did so.

"Checking the gear-warning light system," I said. "I haven't flown one of these things before and I like to know where that is."

He looked a bit suspicious, but nodded again. He obviously didn't know what I was talking about. That was fair enough—neither did I. But I did know I'd just cut out the stall-warning circuit, which meant that the horn wouldn't sound the way it had when we got near the stall before. I didn't want that horn sounding—Challese had an idea what it meant now.

The airspeed dropped to about 85.

I pushed the pitch levers to fully fine, then opened the throttles. The engines made a satisfying growl and the revs went back to 2700. The low-speed high-power setting didn't sound much like cruise flight to me, but it ought to take a minute or two for Challese to notice anything.

274

The Bonanza sagged along just above the stall. I retrimmed, let go of the control yoke, and leaned forward to fiddle with the altimeter adjustment.

My left hand, under cover of my body, scrabbled around the fuel panel on the side of the cockpit and finally got the tap to the right engine shut off.

I leaned back again.

"That's set the altimeter on the QFE," I hold him. "I'll call St. Kitts in a minute, when we're in range."

He nodded again. The gun was still on my stomach, but he wasn't going to shoot me provided the aircraft was flying normally and I wasn't doing anything sudden.

Without warning, the right engine stopped.

At proper cruise speed he might not have realized we'd lost one—it's not so obvious as you might think in most twins once they're going fast. But at below VMC airspeed you'd have to be dead not to know what had happened; the engine noise dropped as if it had been cut by an axe, and the Bonanza skidded and rolled sickeningly to the right.

The stars twisted crazily in the screen—and Challese whipped round to look out of his window at the dead engine: he'd have been inhuman if he hadn't.

I slammed the yoke back into my stomach, booted on full right rudder, and grabbed for the Schmeisser with my right hand.

The Bonanza tried to rear up, whip-stalled violently, flick-rolled on to its back, and plummeted into a vicious spin. The giant twisting hand of G force slammed me into the seat as the rotation built up at an incredible rate. With the outside engine blaring and the other one shut down I knew she'd go round fast — but I hadn't expected anything quite like this.

I had a G-laden hand on the barrel of the gun. Challese screamed something and pulled the trigger. Even in the mounting shriek of the slipstream the *boom* was stunning—but at least he hadn't got it on Automatic, thank Christ. I don't know where the bullet went.

275

Then he twisted his wrist and broke the gun free of my grip—and grabbed my right hand with his left. The gun wavered as he tried to bring it up against the force of the plummeting spin.

I looked out of the windscreen and howled, "I've got her!"

He looked out too—and stared petrified at the whirling disk of the moonlit water in front of the nose.

The gun dropped down again and he let go of my hand. He was still going to shoot me—but I was going to get him out of the spin first.

I glanced at the altimeter as I slammed both throttles shut. The needle was unwinding like a mad stopwatch, passing 3000. Plenty of room— if she was ever going to come out at all, that was.

I kicked on full left rudder, paused, then shoved the control yoke forward with both hands.

The spin stopped almost instantly, leaving us pointing straight down with the airspeed winding up furiously. With no noise from the shutdown engines, the slipstream was a rising, eerie howl.

I hauled back on the stick and felt my cheeks sag and my rump press into the seat again as the G force mounted. Slowly, the nose came up. I pushed a heavy left hand across to the fuel panel and twisted the starboard tap to Main. Then I looked across at Challese. He had both hands on the Schmeisser, ready for the moment we were back in level flight.

Well, we weren't going back into level flight. I'd heard the Twin Bonanza was a very tough aeroplane. Now it was going to prove it.

As the nose swung up through level, I thumped the throttles wide open. The engines, way overspeeded, screamed in an agonized explosion of power. I yanked the yoke hard back into my stomach with all the strength in both arms.

The stars zipped down the screen like a handful of falling diamonds, then faded as I started to black out under the tremendous pressure of the pull-up. I wasn't worried—I'd done this hundreds of times before, though never in a twin. It was different for Challese—he'd probably blacked out long before me, and even if he hadn't he'd be unable to move under the pressure. All I was concerned about was how much the Bonanza would take before the wings folded.

And this was nothing, yet.

I held the invisible black force until the engines labored and I guessed we were somewhere near the top of a loop. Then I pushed a heavy hand up to the throttles, snatched the left one shut, jammed on full left rudder . . .

And shoved the yoke forward as far as it would go.

The black curtain lifted instantly from my eyes as the Bonanza dropped sickeningly away upwards. The seat belt gripped me round the stomach like a giant vise and my head tried to lift off my shoulders.

The stars below pirouetted for an instant as we hung upside down and rotated from the rudder and the asymmetric power. Then the right engine died, because the fuel system was never designed to run inverted —and the nose whipped over and down with enormous force and we spun like a top. A wall of red rose across my eyes: the familiar red-out of a high-negative-G maneuver.

We'd spun before—but not like this. The last one had been a positive spin: violent, terrifying if you didn't know what was happening— but relatively safe.

Now we were upside down, in an inverted spin.

I was strapped in and expecting it.

Challese wasn't.

There was a heavy *thump* from my right as the Bonanza slammed through the first turn of autorotation. I didn't see what happened—but whatever it was, it would have to do. I wasn't hanging about.

I hadn't been sure the Bonanza would go into an inverted spin at all: as far as I knew, nobody had ever tried it before in a twin.

Well, it had.

Now to see if it would come out again.

I jammed on full right rudder, counted up to a ragged three, and hauled back on the stick.

Nothing happened. *Jesus!*

The slipstream howled. The negative G and the sickening sense of twisting increased. Blood roared in my ears, and the red veil over my eyes got darker. I remembered the starting altitude of 3,000, made the only honest prayer of my life, and moved the yoke slowly and determinedly full forward and then full back again.

The aeroplane shuddered, a giant hand pushed me to the left . . .

And the spin stopped.

I centralized the rudder and kept pulling back. I was slammed hard into my seat as the stress reversed itself. The red veil slid down, and suddenly I could see. We were pointing straight down. The right engine caught with a ragged blast as fuel started flowing into it again, then died instantly as I yanked the throttle back.

The glinting black sea was a few hundred feet below.

The swell and the wavelets, lit by the moon path, filled the screen. I hauled back as hard as I could and the nose swung slowly upwards.

Too slowly.

The G pushed me down with a giant hand. The airspeed whizzed past 200. No time to be worrying about structural damage now.

I reached out and slammed down the flap lever.

The electric flap motor rumbled heavily in the bowels of the aircraft, protesting against being asked to lower flap at 80 knots above the maximum approved speed. They got about halfway down before the motor stalled.

But it was enough.

The nose clawed up to the horizon. The Bonanza mushed heavily, shaking on the verge of an accelerated stall. The water flicked past seemingly by the tips of the props as I shoved both throttles open. The flap motor trundled slowly again as the speed dropped off.

And then we were climbing away, running free up the night sky. I let go of a long, quivering breath and sagged back in the seat. I couldn't believe I'd got away with it. The aircraft should have broken up a dozen times.

It was half a minute before I even remembered Challese.

He was still in the copilot's seat—only now he was hunched forward awkwardly with his face resting against the radio panel. Whether he'd been knocked out or whether he'd broken his neck when he hit the roof I neither knew nor cared.

I groped around on the floor with my right foot, found the Schmeisser and hooked it over to me, picked it up, and reversed it so I was holding it by the barrel.

Then I smashed it down on his left temple. I felt the bone give way under the butt.

That made sure.

CHAPTER 33

For a while I just flew on, shaking violently with reaction and too dazed to think. I controlled the aircraft by pure reflexes, not knowing where I was heading. The engines pounded away out of sync at full takeoff power, and the flaps were still down.

It was the voice of the man in the tower at Golden Rock that brought me back to life.

"Three-two Romeo from Golden Rock, switch over now to Coolidge on one one niner decimal one. Good night, sir."

I reached dreamily for the microphone, then found I was sitting there staring at it in my hand as if I didn't know what it was for.

"Three-two Romeo Golden Rock, d'you read?"

I snapped out of it.

"Golden Rock from three-two Romeo," I said, trying to imitate Alberto's hard American accent. "Reading you fives, and switching to Coolidge. Good night."

I got a disgruntled double click from the man at Golden Rock. I hung the mike up and looked round. Time enough to call Coolidge later. First

I had to clean up this aeroplane—and get it going in the right direction. I found I was passing 3,000 feet. That was enough. I lowered the nose, trundled the flaps up, throttled back to 26 inches, and brought the pitch levers back to 2,600 rpm. Then I synced the engines as the speed settled; trimmed; reset the gyrocompass to the magnetic compass; and turned towards the ADF needle and Coolidge Airport.

I looked at the clock on the panel. It said 0001. One minute past midnight, Greenwich Mean Time.

One minute past seven, local time. I was still alive.

I called Coolidge in my best Alberto voice, lied like a trooper about my position—since I didn't have a clue *where* I was—and told them I was going to do a bit of sight-seeing at the south end of their island before coming in. They said okay, they didn't have any other traffic at the moment, and I said, Thanks, I'll call when I'm ready to come in.

Then I trimmed the Bonanza slightly nose-heavy, heaved myself out of the seat, and dragged Alberto back to join Larry. I practically fell the last half of the way because the nose pitched up steeply in spite of my nose-down trim. I had to haul my way uphill to get back to the cockpit before she stalled. That was enough of that—I was quite airsick and battered enough already without having the Bonanza stall on me while I was down the back. Live and learn: I'd shift Challese in easy stages. So I trimmed nose-down a bit more this time—and of course, by the time I'd tugged and hauled him out of the seat, we were in quite a hefty dive. I pulled her out, let the speed drop off, left the controls, and dragged the body down the back—and then had to struggle uphill again to the cockpit to push the nose down. This was getting tiring.

My head was pounding, the taste of bile was in my mouth, and my left hand was throbbing fit to fall off. I rested in the pilot's seat for a few minutes, saw the flare light of the Antigua Refinery grow into a yellow pinpoint in the distance, and turned the Bonanza away. No point in getting too close to land for the next bit.

I trimmed nose-heavy for the third time, stumbled round the seat, and found the concrete block I'd dropped on Alberto. It was about 18 inches by a foot by 6 inches deep, and it seemed to weigh about three tons. I couldn't lift it at all. Christ knows how I'd raised it high enough to drop it: panic, probably. After scrabbling around with it for a few moments I found an iron ring embedded in it, with a length of rope spliced to the ring. Of course—it was an aircraft tie-down block. I got hold of the rope and heaved it aft.

Then back to the cockpit, pull the aircraft out, and trim nose-heavy again.

Down in the blunt end once more I stole Alberto's shirt—since he'd bled over me more than he had over himself—then searched the bodies, and finally got the rope on the block tied to Challese's ankle and Alberto's wrist. Then I lugged Larry about until I'd got his clumsy shroud leaning partly against the door.

Now came the difficult bit.

I sat back in the driver's seat, reduced power, lowered the undercarriage in the vague hope that it might provide a stabilizing influence at low speed, and trimmed slightly nose-heavy for a slow gentle descent. Then I wound the rudder trim to the left a bit and the aileron trim to the right a bit less, so that she took up a gentle skidding turn to the left when I took my hands and feet off. That should equalize the drag of the Airstair door when I opened it. I hoped. As an afterthought I leaned down and popped the stall-warning-horn circuit breaker back—I could do with a bit of audible warning if she was going to stall on me while I was standing around the open door.

Then I had a final look round, and went back again.

As I reached the rear the nose pitched up slightly, then steadied. That was all right—no horns blowing yet. I took a firm grip with my right hand on the rearmost seat belt, leaned over Larry, and twisted the door handle.

The door dropped open, the night howled in—and Larry disappeared instantly. The nose pitched down as his weight left the aircraft.

General Declaration papers and maps flew about in the gale that shrieked into the cabin—and in spite of my precautions the right wing dropped and the Bonanza started to turn into the asymmetric drag created by the door. I almost ran downhill to the cockpit, got us back on an even keel and played with throttles and trims for a moment to find a compromise which kept us that way.

Then, moving very carefully, I made my way down the wind tunnel of the fuselage for the last time. It took a minute or so's cautious pushing with my foot to get Alberto over the edge—and then I got lucky, because his weight dragged Challese through the door without getting him caught up in anything.

For a while I thought I wasn't going to get the door shut again. But a last despairing tug on one of the restraining cables that ran from the doorway to the top of the door finally got it under way, and half a minute later I had it home and fastened. In spite of the inevitable dive, the cabin was suddenly quiet after the gale.

I hauled myself wearily into the left-hand seat—and found the Schmeisser on top of the instrument panel. After a moment's debating with myself, I throttled back the left engine and heaved it out of the pilot's little storm window. Too bad if it hit the tail—I wasn't going back down that fuselage again. There was no *clang,* so I suppose it missed anyway.

Then I swung back towards the lights of Antigua, sat looking at the little red-lit faces of the instruments and listening to the rumble of the engines for ten minutes, and finally called Coolidge Approach and told them I wanted to join their circuit on left base leg. They said that was fine, and I failed to acknowledge.

They said it again, and I picked up the mike and said "Ah . . . some . . . slight . . . ah . . . radio . . .here," clicking the mike button between the words and hoping it sounded like someone having a spot of transmitter trouble.

"Three-two Romeo, Coolidge, be advised your transmissions are breaking up, I say again, your transmissions are breaking up. You are cleared to land. You are cleared to land. Over."

I clicked the mike twice, the universal signal of acknowledgment, and a few moments later rumbled the Bonanza in over the threshold. We touched down with a *thump*—not my best landing.

I opened the storm window again as we rolled down the runway, and stuck a cupped hand out to scoop some cool breeze on to my face.

The controller bleated something about three-two Romeo having to stop at Customs and Immigration before going to overnight parking. I taxied smartly—and in radio silence—past a shiny private Beech King Air parked outside customs, and went directly into the darkest, furthest point of the parking area. He was still going on about it when I came to a stop and set the brakes.

I switched him off: he'd tell customs about me, but since he'd mention the supposed radio failure as well they wouldn't get uptight enough to come looking unless nobody showed up from the aircraft after ten minutes or so.

Nobody *was* going to show up—but then, I didn't need any ten minutes, either.

I was over the perimeter fence and walking down a track through the scrub alongside the airport in half that. Walking was a painful business, but I only had a mile or so to go to the Sugar Mill Hotel.

I checked my back pockets carefully as I stumped along. Everything was still there. Passport and envelopes of stamps in the left, wallet with the check in it in the right. I'd been surprised to find the check in Challese's billfold when I searched him for the stamps: maybe he hadn't wanted to leave it lying around.

Careful type.

From the airport, the distinctive whining howl of a pair of small turboprops announced the departure of the King Air. Rich man's aeroplane.

Well, now *I* could buy a King Air, if I wanted one. *And* a Jungmeister. *And* some First War replicas. *And* a D-type Jag and a GT40 and a big house on the Thames. . . .

I tried to tell myself that the thought made me happy. It didn't. I just felt . . . lonely.

The night insects zinged and chirruped, and the familiar ache started up in my left hip as I walked along the moonlit track.